D1367200

SWEET SURPRISES

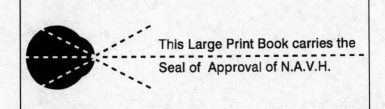

This Large Print Book carries the
Seal of Approval of N.A.V.H.

SWEET SURPRISES

SHIRLEE MCCOY

THORNDIKE PRESS
A part of Gale, Cengage Learning

GALE
CENGAGE Learning®

Farmington Hills, Mich • San Francisco • New York • Waterville, Maine
Meriden, Conn • Mason, Ohio • Chicago

LIBRARY OF CONGRESS CATALOGING-IN-PUBLICATION DATA

Names: McCoy, Shirlee, author.
Title: Sweet surprises / Shirlee McCoy.
Description: Large print edition. | Waterville, Maine : Thorndike Press, 2016. |
  Series: A home sweet home novel ; 2 | Series: Thorndike press large print clean
  reads
Identifiers: LCCN 2016026724| ISBN 9781410491985 (hardback) | ISBN 1410491986
  (hardcover)
Subjects: LCSH: Large type books. | BISAC: FICTION / General.
Classification: LCC PS3613.C38574 S943 2016 | DDC 813/.6—dc23
LC record available at https://lccn.loc.gov/2016026724

Published in 2016 by arrangement with Zebra Books, an imprint of
Kensington Publishing Corp.

Printed in the United States of America
1 2 3 4 5 6 7 20 19 18 17 16

SWEET SURPRISES

CHAPTER ONE

There it was. Just the way Brenna Lamont had left it: Benevolence, Washington, in all its small-town glory. Porch lights glittering in the darkness. Pristine yards and beautiful old trees lining quiet streets. The post office at the north edge of town. The library tucked neatly into a large lot on Main Street. From her vantage point in the parking lot of Benevolence Baptist Church, Brenna couldn't make out the details of the buildings, the yards, or even the row of brownstones that housed her family's chocolate shop. She didn't need to see the details to know what they were. She'd spent seventeen years in Benevolence. Not long by some people's standards. By Brenna's, it had seemed like an eternity.

And now it was going to be an eternity more.

Granddad needed her help at Chocolate Haven. Just for a few weeks. That's what he'd said. She knew how these things worked, though. A few weeks would turn into a month which would turn into more months. One day, she'd blink and realize she'd been working in her family chocolate shop for a lifetime. She'd be an old woman puttering around in sturdy white sneakers, a cat T-shirt, and elastic-waist polyester pants. Probably red. Or, maybe, blue.

Blue was more her style.

Yep. She'd be an old lady in white shoes, blue pants, and a cat shirt, nibbling chocolate and getting chubbier by the minute. The best part? She wouldn't give a crap that her hips were as wide as a houseboat or that her tummy threatened to break her waistband. There'd be no one to impress. No one to please. Just hundreds of customers who only cared about getting another taste of the famous Lamont family fudge.

The thought almost made her smile.

Almost.

The thing was, she'd needed to return to Benevolence as much as her grandfather had needed her to return. Probably more. Sure, she'd hemmed and hawed and put on a good show — she couldn't make chocolate, she had a busy schedule, she didn't want to leave home for very long. She'd told at least a dozen lies to her family, and she

8

felt bad about it. She really did, but she hadn't wanted them to know how desperate she was.

And, she *was* desperate.

Her family knew that she and her ex-fiancé had parted ways. They knew she wasn't sorry about it. What they didn't know was that Brenna had nothing left. Not the upscale clothing boutique in Manhattan that she'd worked so hard to establish. Not the fancy penthouse she'd shared with Dan. Not the beautiful furniture and expensive art work that had decorated it. Not the sporty Corvette. Not the money, either, and that's all she really needed.

The rest of the stuff? They were Dan's style, his choices, his preferences. The money? It would have been nice to have a couple of nickels to rub together. Brenna did not. Dan had cleaned out their bank accounts. He'd also embezzled funds from his business partner. Then he'd skipped town with his girlfriend and left Brenna to clean up the mess he'd made.

"Bastard," she muttered.

A magpie answered, his warning trill filling the silence.

She ignored it and the hollow ache of disappointment in her stomach. Disappointment in herself as much as in Dan, because

9

she wasn't sure if she'd ever loved the guy. He'd been there at a time when she'd needed someone. She'd liked him. He'd been fun and exciting and complimentary.

Love should be so much more than that.

Shouldn't it?

She had no idea, and she had no plan to find out. One attempt at happily-ever-after was enough. Now, she just wanted to get herself back on track. Returning to Benevolence would give her an opportunity to do that.

If it didn't drive her absolutely insane first.

If her *family* didn't.

She loved them.

God knew she did, but her mother was hell-bent on making sure her three daughters were all happily married. Her grandfather wanted them to live in Benevolence and work at the family chocolate shop. Her sisters . . .

They just wanted the best for Brenna.

And, Brenna wanted the best for them.

That's why she hadn't told them everything. They'd both found happiness, and she didn't want to ruin it by telling them how much her life sucked.

The night after Brenna had found out Dan was cheating on her, she and Adeline and Willow had opened a bottle of wine and

10

planned exactly how she was going to kick him out of her life. They'd gotten just tipsy enough to do a bonding ritual, lighting a white candle and swearing that they would stand beside each other. No matter what.

Of course, none of them had known just how deep Dan's betrayal had gone. By the time Brenna had realized it, Willow had gone back to Seattle and her law practice. Adeline was busy planning a wedding. Brenna hadn't had the heart to tell them the truth.

Or, maybe, she hadn't had the courage.

Maybe she hadn't wanted to be the Lamont family failure, the one everyone had to worry about, the one most desperately in need of rescue.

She frowned, a cool breeze ruffling her hair. There was a hint of fall in the air, a tinge of burning firewood. Someone in town had a wood-burning stove going. Late August and already people were preparing for winter. Not too many weeks from now and there'd be ice hockey and skiing, snowman building contests and ice skating on the frozen pond in the Andersons' field. Hot chocolate after a day spent outdoors. As a kid, Brenna had enjoyed those things. Now — at twenty-seven — all she wanted was quiet, peace, a chance to think about where she wanted to go next, what she wanted to do with her life.

Her cell phone buzzed and she snagged it from her purse, eyeing the number that flashed across the screen. Her mother. Calling for the fiftieth time. Janelle had probably readied Brenna's old room, smoothed the flowery sheets and bright green blanket, swept dust bunnies out from under the ancient twin bed in some vain hope that Brenna would change her mind and decide to stay there.

That wasn't going to happen.

Secrets were easy to keep when you lived thousands of miles from the people who cared about you. They weren't as easy to keep when you lived in the same town. Living in the same house would make keeping them nearly impossible.

And, Brenna *was* going to keep her secrets.

She didn't want her family's pity, and she didn't want them pooling their funds trying to help her out. She just wanted time to get her life back together. Whatever that meant.

Brenna pressed the phone to her ear and leaned her hip against the hood of the 1977 Chrysler New Yorker she'd bought from a former neighbor. Two-hundred dollars. A steal considering it had only had ten-

12

thousand miles on it. "Hello?"

"You finally decided to answer," her mother replied.

"I was driving."

"Where are you now?"

"Stopping to stretch my legs." The truth, because she'd told one too many lies in the past few months, and they weren't sitting well on her conscience.

"You should find a hotel. Spend the night. It's not safe for a young woman to —"

"Don't worry, Mom," Brenna cut her off. "I have everything planned for the night."

"What hotel are you staying at? It's not one of those seedy motels is it? The kind that have roaches and bed bugs and —"

"It's clean." Brenna cut in again.

"You don't have to be short with me, Brenna. I'm your mother. I have a right to be concerned."

"I wasn't being short. I was just making a statement."

"I wish you would have let me fly out and drive across country with you," Janelle continued, ignoring Brenna's comment. "Twenty-five-hundred miles is a long way for a young woman to travel alone."

"I've traveled alone dozens of times, Mom. Besides, I'm almost there, and everything has been fine. *I've* been fine." There she went. Another lie. She wasn't fine. Not really. She hadn't been since she'd realized that Dan had cleaned out their mutual bank accounts, taken all of their stuff, and skipped town. Skipped the country, actually. The best that the police could figure, he was somewhere in Thailand, living the high-life off of other people's money.

"You're always fine, dear," Janelle said, an edge to her voice. "I don't suppose you've changed your mind about staying at the house?"

"The apartment will be more convenient." Short. Simple. To the point.

"Right, and you're all about convenience. Which is why you drove here instead of doing the rational thing and buying a plane ticket. Call me when you arrive. I made chicken potpie. It's in the fridge at the apartment." She hung up before Brenna could thank her.

"Great. Perfect," Brenna muttered. "You pissed her off before you even laid eyes on her."

She tossed the purse and the phone into the car and shut the door. No way did she want to answer another phone call from well-meaning family. Her neck was stiff, her shoulders tense. She'd been driving for hours and she was ready for a break.

14

She'd been ready for a break before the drive.

Two jobs waitressing so she could pay the rent on an efficiency apartment? Countless meetings with Dan's former business partner, lawyers, police? A twenty-five-hundred-mile drive across country to help her family, because she'd been too damn proud to admit she didn't have the money for a plane ticket? Those things made a person tired, and Brenna was not just that. She was to-the-bone weary.

She also wanted a cigarette the way other women might want chocolate or a slice of cake.

You've got an addictive personality, babe, she could almost hear her imbecile ex-fiancé's voice, see his smarmy, irritating grin. *And I thank God every day that I'm what you're addicted to.*

"Bullsh—" She stopped herself just short of saying it.

She was standing in the parking lot of Benevolence Baptist Church, for God's sake!

And she had a niece or nephew on the way.

She didn't want to fill little ears with words she'd rather not hear a tiny kid say.

Yeah, she'd given up swearing the day her sister Adeline had called and told her she

15

was pregnant. She'd given up cigarettes the same day. That had been five weeks and six days after she'd found out exactly what kind of ass Dan was. Not that she'd been counting the days. Much.

"Water under the bridge," she said, as if there were anyone around to hear.

Leaves rustled, the sound following her across the parking lot and around the side of the church.

The cemetery was there, tombstones dotting a gentle knoll that looked out over the town. A pretty little place to be buried. Her father had said that to her once. She'd never forgotten it.

Weird how things stuck with a person. Even after all these years, she could see her father's craggy face, his bright blue eyes, hear him telling her how lucky they were to live in a town like Benevolence.

She'd never felt lucky.

She'd felt different. A square peg in a round hole.

While her sisters were outside playing with friends, she'd been inside, her head in a book, her imagination carrying her deep into the stories. She'd loved reading the way Adeline loved numbers, the way Willow loved the chocolate shop.

Her father had understood that about her.

16

He'd been the one to sneak books into her room late at night. *A new one I saw at the library, Bren,* he'd whisper, and then he'd tuck a little flashlight under her pillow, kiss her head, and leave the room. He'd always made sure to close the door so Janelle wouldn't see the glow of the light held under Brenna's thick blanket, wouldn't hear the soft rustle of pages turning late into the night.

He'd loved his wife. There was no doubt about that, but he'd loved his girls, too, and they'd all loved him. Somehow, when he'd been alive, it had all worked — the diverse personalities, the differing interests, the three girls who were growing into young women.

Things had changed when he'd died.

The before and after? They were as memorable as anything else.

If he'd lived long enough, he might have given Brenna some sage piece of advice that would have kept her from running off at seventeen and taking a job she'd hated just so she could be free of Janelle's expectations. He hadn't, and Brenna had been hellbent on getting out of town and away from her mother.

Not Janelle's fault. Not really. Brenna had been the daughter most like her, and she'd wanted desperately to mold her into something great. She'd nagged about posture, about skin, about hair and nails. She'd complained about Brenna's lack of friends, about how many books she had stashed under her bed.

You could be so popular if you'd put a little effort into it.

Brenna hadn't wanted to be popular. She hadn't wanted to disappoint Janelle either, so she'd done the only thing she could. She'd left town.

And now she was back.

She didn't mind nearly as much as she thought she would.

She'd traveled the world as a fashion model. She'd been a lot of places, experienced a lot of things, but nothing could compare to the solitude of this place, the beauty of the old cemetery in the moonlight. She might not know anything else — like what she was going to do with the rest of her life, how she was going to be something other than a New York fashion icon, a store owner, a doctor's fiancé — but she did know that there was no place in the world like this quiet little bluff behind the church.

Brenna reached the cemetery gate and strode through it, ignoring the sadness that nudged at the back of her mind. She'd been here many times, visiting the graves of her father and grandmother, listening to the wind rustle in the evergreen trees, hearing whispers of the past in the soft summer breezes and cold winter winds.

Shaded by mature pines and a giant willow, the Lamont family plot sat apart from the rest of the graveyard, a huge marble angel standing in the middle of it. Brenna walked past it, heading to the newest graves. Her grandmother's, sheltered under the willow, a bench just beside it. Her father's a few yards away. Someone had placed flowers on both.

A pretty little place to be buried.

Yeah. It was, but she didn't think her father had planned to be interred there quite so soon. He'd had big plans for his life and for his family. He'd sit at the dinner table every night, talking about trips that he wanted to take, new recipes he wanted to develop, books he'd wanted to read. He'd been full of life, a bookworm and a chocolatier, a guy who'd loved tradition as much as he'd loved adventure. He'd been a little bit of each one of his daughters. Maybe that's why he'd understood them all so well.

Brenna settled onto the bench, the coolness of the stone seeping through her jeans. Eventually, she'd have to go to the apartment, drag in her suitcase, let herself get used to the idea that she was home for a while.

Home?

Was it really that? After all this time?

She didn't know, but she guessed she'd find out, because she was here, and she had nowhere else to go. She'd given up the lease on the efficiency, said good-bye to the few friends she had left in New York, and left without a backward glance.

She ran a hand over her short-cropped hair, imagining Janelle's reaction when she saw it. She'd be horrified. Or slightly disapproving. Or outspokenly and overly supportive.

Things could go any of the three ways, because Janelle really tried to be the kind of mother her daughters needed. She just missed the boat. A lot.

"Things don't always work out the way we've planned. Right?" she said to the angel statue.

"They sure don't," someone responded, the masculine voice so surprising, she nearly tumbled sideways off the bench.

Leaves crackled, a twig snapped, and a dark shadow appeared in front of her. Tall. Broad shouldered. A man, moonlight gleaming in his dark hair.

She screamed so loudly she almost expected the angel to take flight.

It didn't, but *she* sure did, her head slamming into willow branches, leaves falling all around her as she darted behind the tree and raced back through the cemetery.

She was pretty damn certain her feet never touched the ground.

Scaring the hell out of a woman wasn't cool. Chasing her through a cemetery to apologize? Even worse.

Both beat getting tossed in jail.

Which could happen if River Maynard didn't convince the lady he'd scared that he was harmless. Tough to do when he was wandering around a cemetery in the middle of the night.

Of course, she'd been wandering around in the cemetery too.

He'd say they were even, but he figured she was a local, and the police would be a lot more likely to listen to her side of things. He also figured that she had a better track record in town than he did. Not a farfetched assumption since River had been one of the worst things to happen to Benevolence in its hundred-and-twenty-year history.

Not his words.

Those were the words of the sheriff who'd

21

been working in Benevolence when River was a teen. River couldn't blame the guy for feeling that way. Breaking and entering. Petty theft. Arson. River had even taken the radio from a police car that had been left unlocked in the church parking lot. He'd been fifteen at the time. Just young enough that the sheriff had taken pity on him. Otherwise, he'd have been tossed right back into the juvenile detention center his foster parents had pulled him out of.

Dillard and Belinda Keech had been taking in troubled teens for nearly a decade when they'd come for River. They'd heard about him through friends who worked with child protective services. A week later, they'd signed him out of juvenile detention and brought him to Freedom Ranch, a sprawling property right on the edge of a little town called Benevolence. A place for at-risk kids. That's what River's case worker had said.

It had turned out to be way more than that.

The Keeches had changed his life.

He owed them. Big time.

It was too late to repay Dillard, but as long as Belinda was around, River would keep trying to repay her.

That would be difficult to do from a jail cell.

"Hold up!" he called as the woman reached the cemetery gate and sprinted through it. She moved fast, long legs eating up the ground, arms pumping like she'd spent the past few years training to run the hundred-meter dash.

"Ma'am?" he tried again, because if Belinda got wind of the fact that he'd scared the crap out of some woman in the cemetery, she'd be stressed, and that wasn't going to help with her recovery from the stroke she'd suffered a month ago.

"I'm calling the police!" the woman yelled back.

The police? That was just what he didn't need. Not only would Belinda be hearing about him chasing some woman through the cemetery, she'd be hitching a ride to come bail him out of jail.

Again.

Only this time, he wasn't an angry young teen. He was a successful adult with two restaurants in Portland, Oregon, and no time to waste in a locked cell.

"No need for that," he called, his tone calm and easy. No sense fanning the flames by being loud and demanding. "I just wanted to apologize for scaring you."

23

"You didn't scare me," she panted, yanking open the door of an ancient Chrysler and hopping in, "you terrified me."

She slammed the door, and he thought she'd speed off to wherever she'd come from, tell whoever she lived with all about the guy who'd chased her through the cemetery. If she happened to know who he was, he'd be screwed. Benevolence was a typical small-town with a typical small-town rumor mill. Everyone in town knew he was back. Everyone in town knew he'd been taking care of Belinda since her stroke.

Everyone in town also knew his past, knew his teenage mistakes, his foolishness. They had good reason to eye him with suspicion, but he didn't have time to play up to them, mend fences, prove that he'd grown up, and become someone. There was too much going on at Freedom Ranch. Too much that he hadn't expected and wasn't all that prepared to deal with.

He was doing it. For Belinda.

Otherwise, he'd have washed his hands of the motley crew he'd found living there a month ago.

He reached the car, leaned down so he could look in the driver's side window.

The woman was sitting still as a statue, her forehead resting against the steering wheel, her shoulders slumped.

He tapped on the glass.

She didn't move.

God! He hoped he hadn't scared her into heart failure.

"Ma'am? Are you okay?"

"I've been better," he thought she said, but the window was closed, her voice muffled.

"I can give you a ride home if you're not up to driving," he offered.

She lifted her head, looked him right in the eye.

"I just ran for my life because of you," she said, and this time her words were clear as day. "Do you really think I'm going to let you drive me somewhere?"

"Maybe not, but I hope you'll give me a minute to explain."

"No need for an explanation. You go your way. I'll go mine." She shoved keys into the ignition, started the car, and probably would have pulled away if he hadn't tapped on the glass again.

"What?" she snapped, watching him dispassionately. She looked . . . familiar. Something about her face — the angle of the jaw, the shape of the nose. He couldn't quite place it, but he was certain they'd met before.

"Do you live around here?" he asked.

"Do you always wander around cemeteries in the middle of the night asking women questions about where they live?" she replied, and he laughed.

"It's an unusual night. For both of us, I'd say."

"You're right about that." She grabbed a phone from the seat next to her. Maybe to show him that she had one. Maybe just to check for messages. For a moment, her face was illuminated by its light. Pale freckled skin. Bright red hair.

He had a flash of a memory: a young girl with long red hair and freckles, trudging down the road, a red wagon filled with books rattling along behind her.

One of the Lamont girls. Little Brenna.

That's what Belinda had told him. He wasn't sure why he'd been curious enough to ask. Maybe because the little girl was so much the opposite of every kid he'd ever known. She'd been clean, her clothes pressed, her shoes shiny and new. And, she'd looked . . . content, as if the wagonload of books had filled her up to overflowing.

That had changed after her father died.

He knew that part of her story, too.

Just like he knew that she could be the

answer to one of his most pressing problems. He needed access to her family's chocolate shop. Scratch that. All he really needed was a piece of the Lamont family fudge. That damn kid Huckleberry had eaten the last of Belinda's supply.

Huckleberry . . .

Just thinking about the eighteen-year-old made River's blood boil. If he'd known Belinda had a houseful of people living with her, he'd have been back for a visit a long time ago. Instead, he'd believed every word she'd told him over the phone. Probably because he'd wanted to believe them. He'd had a restaurant to run. Another one to open. He'd been back for Dillard's funeral two years ago. Once more after that a few months later. He'd promised a visit at Christmas but had had to cancel because one of his chefs had quit. He hadn't worried, because Belinda had assured him that things were great. *Everything is wonderful. The house is so peaceful. I miss Dillard, but I've got my friends, and my women's clubs.*

She might have thought things were wonderful, but there was no way in hell she'd thought the house was peaceful. Not with the scraggly group of people she'd collected living there.

He shut down the thought, forced himself

27

to let go of the anger, focus on the red-haired woman in the old car.

"You're Brenna Lamont," he said. Not a question. He already knew who she was.

"And?"

"Your family owns Chocolate Haven."

"Is there a point to this, because it's after midnight, Mr . . . ?"

"River Maynard." He didn't add anything else. He knew he didn't need to. She might not remember his face, but she'd remember the name.

Her eyes widened, and she rolled down the window, studying him for a few long moments.

Finally, she smiled, an ear-to-ear grin that made her look about ten-years-old. "Holy sh— crap! You're the kid who sheared all of old man Morris's sheep."

"And his dogs," he added.

"That's right. Three Old English Sheepdogs, shaved down to their skin."

"It was summer. They were hot." And he'd been young and stupid and itching for a fight.

"Is that why you let Henderson Baily's bull out of the pasture?"

"I did that because Henderson was an asshole."

She laughed, a light, easy sound that rang

through the quiet parking lot. "So, River, what brings you back to Benevolence?"

"Belinda had a stroke a month ago."

Her smile slid away. "I'm so sorry. Is she okay?"

"No, but she will be. With enough therapy and enough time." And a little more peace than what she'd been getting. River was working on that, but Belinda's "guests" were a touchy subject with her, and kicking them all to the curb was out of the question.

"I wish I would have known. I'd have sent her some flowers, come for a visit." She brushed the thick bangs from her forehead, shook her head. "We've had a lot going on in the family this past year. I guess the news of Belinda's stroke got lost in the chaos of everything else. If there's anything I can do-"

"There is," he said, cutting her off, because he saw an opportunity, and he wasn't going to miss out on it. "I need to buy some of your family fudge."

"We open at ten. Stop in then, and I'll hook you up with some." She started to roll up the window, but he put his hand on the edge of the glass.

"I told Belinda I'd do everything I could to bring some home tonight. It's the one thing she looks forward to after a long day at physical and occupational therapy. When she found out some punk had eaten the last piece, she started crying."

"Were you the punk?" she asked, that smile hovering on her lips and in her eyes again.

"For once, I'm innocent. Belinda has houseguests. If they can be called that. They're more like squatters, making messes and eating her out of house and home. Huckleberry is one of them. He ate the fudge."

"If they're squatters, you could tell them to leave."

"It seems like it, right? But, the night I arrived back in town, I went to the hospital to see Belinda. The right side of her body was paralyzed. Her words were slurred, and she could barely speak, but she managed to tell me that she had people staying with her. She begged me not to make them leave. I promised I wouldn't."

Never make a promise before you've thought it through, son. A man is only as good as his word. You utter that promise, and you're obligated to fulfill it. No matter what it costs you or how much it hurts.

How many times had Dillard said that? How many times had River rolled his eyes?

All that eye-rolling was coming back to

30

bite him in the butt. If Dillard's spirit happened to be hanging around nearby, the old guy was probably nodding his head and smirking that smirk he'd always worn when something he'd warned would happen did, because River? He'd thought about tossing every one of Belinda's guests out, but he'd made that damn promise, and he couldn't.

"Well, that sucks," Brenna said. "But, I have some good news for you, River. I have the key to the shop, and I'm happy to give you some fudge. Belinda was a long-term sub in my class the year my dad died. I've never forgotten how kind she was to me."

River wanted to tell her that he was sorry about her father's death. It was old news, an old wound, but he didn't think a person ever really got over losing someone she loved.

"I'm —" *sorry you lost your father at such a young age. That had to be tough,* was what he was going to say, but she cut him off.

"I'll meet you over at the shop." She rolled up the window and drove away, the Chrysler coughing up clouds of exhaust.

He jogged across the parking lot, jumped into his truck and followed. Maybe he *should* have just let Brenna go back to whatever she'd been doing when he'd heard her walking through the cemetery, but the thought of returning to Freedom Ranch empty-handed appealed to him about as much as getting a root canal. Actually, the thought of returning to Freedom Ranch *with* the fudge in hand didn't appeal to him, either.

He'd go back, though, and he'd play nice with the people who were living there.

He'd promised Belinda.

He planned to keep his promise.

Unless that little pipsqueak Huckleberry made Belinda cry again. Then the promise would be out the window and Huckleberry would be out on his scrawny behind.

CHAPTER TWO

River Maynard was nothing like Brenna remembered.

And she *did* remember him.

How could she not?

He'd been the talk of the town from the time he'd arrived until the day he'd left when he was eighteen. Every parent worried about him, every girl secretly crushed on him, every guy was jealous. At least, that's the way it had seemed to Brenna, but she'd been three years behind him in school, and she'd been too busy worrying about other things to pay all that much attention to the long-haired demon who'd descended on their quiet town.

His hair wasn't long now.

He'd cropped it short. He probably also went to the gym, because his lanky teenage body? It had filled out. A lot. Shoulders. Thighs. Biceps.

She'd noticed.

God help her.

She had.

She might be off the market forever, but she knew a good-looking guy when she saw one. She knew trouble when she saw it, too. River might have changed, but she was certain he was still that. The curve of his lips when he smiled — just a little sardonic and a little wicked — the gleam in his eyes; they were all the clues she needed. That was fine. She'd keep her distance from him the same way she planned to keep her distance from everyone else in Benevolence.

It wasn't that she didn't like the people there. It was more that she didn't want to be a fraud, and she couldn't see a way to be authentic. Not around all the people she'd grown up with who thought she'd made it big. Janelle liked to talk, and she talked about Brenna. A lot. At least, that's what Adeline said.

Adeline, who'd never left Benevolence, who'd built a nice accounting business that served almost everyone in town, who'd jumped in and taken over Chocolate Haven when Granddad broke his hip and femur. Who'd gotten married to a guy who adored her, given a home to a couple of kids who needed one. Who'd never disappointed anyone. Ever.

Brenna loved her sister, but she'd never be like her.

She was too much herself in a town where being like everyone else was important.

And now she was going to be running Chocolate Haven.

Her birthright.

That's what Granddad had said when he'd been trying to convince her to return to Benevolence.

If she was going to claim a birthright, why couldn't it be crown jewels or a cabin in the mountains? Better yet, why couldn't it be a huge pile of books in a little house in some faraway corner of the world? Why did it have to be a chocolate shop where everyone in town could traipse in and ask questions about Brenna's life, her ex, her modeling career, and her business?

She drove into the heart of town, the old buildings, the wide storefront windows, the soft exterior lights as familiar as breathing. She *knew* this place. Every house. Every alley. Every street.

And, she loved it.

She could admit that now. Just like she could admit that she'd only left because she'd been drowning in the weight of other people's expectations. She'd wanted to be herself, and everyone else had wanted her

35

to be bigger, brighter, better. When she'd been discovered by a talent scout while she was on her senior trip to Washington, D.C., she'd jumped at the opportunity to sign with his modeling agency.

It had seemed like destiny, like finally coming into her own.

It had taken her a long time to realize that she'd simply jumped from one set of expectations to another.

She sighed, turning onto Main Street.

Years ago, the town council had voted to hang flower baskets from the curved streetlights. Every year since then, Brenna's mother had spearheaded the project. She'd solicit donations and volunteers, organize an entire community effort to get those baskets up. Usually there was a vote on the flowers' colors and a few heated arguments about what they should choose and why. Blue and pink because Louise Rockingham had twins. Orange because it was different. Yellow because Lila Samson's husband needed a little cheering up. Pink because Matilda Reed had breast cancer. The list of colors and reasons spanned the ten years Brenna had been away.

This year, though, Janelle had been silent.

No calls in the middle of the day to complain about the bickering council members. No early morning texts asking if fuchsia was too bright for a town like Benevolence. Not even a hint at what color had been chosen. Brenna had wondered if the tradition had stopped, but she hadn't asked. She'd been too distracted by her circumstances, too busy worrying about how she was going to pay the next bill to worry much about flower baskets or, even, her mother's silence.

Now that she was back, she could see that the baskets were hanging. It was too dark to see the colors, but they were glimmering in the streetlights. White maybe. Or pale pink.

She'd have to ask her mother how the process had gone, whether or not the vote had been unanimous, what pressing Benevolence issue had led to the color choice. That would make Janelle happy, and asking questions was a whole hell of a lot better than having to answer them.

She pulled up in front of Chocolate Haven, the bright glow of the exterior lights splashing across the sidewalk. The place looked like it always had: a pretty little brownstone butting up against what had once been May Reynolds's fabric store. She'd closed the store after she'd found true love. Her wedding had been the beginning of the end of Brenna's very short engagement to Dan. While Brenna had been sitting in a pew watching two seventy-something-year-olds exchange vows, Dan had been in New York cleaning out their bank accounts.

She shoved the thought aside.

The police were searching for Dan.

There was nothing more she could do but move forward.

And she would.

She *had.*

She turned into the narrow alley that led to the back parking lot. It was darker there, the exterior light off. She'd been here a thousand times before, though, and she knew which key opened the door, knew just how much pressure it took to get the old key into the lock.

The door creaked open and she stepped inside, the cool darkness filled with the scent of chocolate and a million memories. She'd spent hours in the shop kitchen, sweeping the floor and washing pots and pans. When she hadn't been helping, she'd been sitting in her grandfather's office, a plate of chocolate on her lap, a book in her hand. She'd listened to her grandparents chat about business and customers. She'd bickered with her sisters over the last piece of fudge. She'd heard her parents giggling in the kitchen after the shop closed.

Janelle giggling?

Brenna frowned. She'd forgotten about that, forgotten just how happy and content her mother had been before her father's diagnosis.

Things had been different then, and she could remember just enough about how happy they'd all been to know how much things had changed after Brett Lamont was told he had brain cancer. It hadn't been his death that had changed them. It had been that long decline, the year and a half of watching him fade. It had been the silence, the pretending, the constant fear all covered with a layer of cheer. They were the Lamonts, after all. They couldn't do grief the way other people did.

At least, that's the way Brenna had felt. She'd been young, though. She might have misread things.

She flicked on the light and walked into the pristine kitchen. Not a pot or pan out of place. Not a smudge of chocolate on the counter. If she walked into the pantry, she'd find milk chocolate, dark chocolate, white chocolate, and pecans, all of it in old mason jars. She'd see the old 1920s canister set, filled with sugar and coffee, cinnamon and salt. There'd be large bottles of vanilla on the shelves. Dried figs, raisins, apricots displayed in large glass jars. Local ingredients if possible, and always only the finest quality.

That was the way Granddad did things.

It was the way generations of Lamonts had done them before him, and it was the way Brenna would be expected to do them.

That was fine. She liked neat and tidy and orderly.

She just wasn't sure how good she'd be at making chocolate. It was an art, and she didn't think she had the talent for it. She could barely toast bread without burning it.

Cross the bridge when you come to it.

One of Grandma Alice's favorite sayings. The problem was, Brenna wasn't sure there was a bridge. She wasn't even sure she was on a road. Right now, it felt like she was running on a treadmill and getting nowhere fast.

"Just look for the fudge and go to bed," she muttered, hurrying through a narrow hall and into the shop's service area. The display cases nudged up against one another, each one filled with chocolates. She opened the first one, lifting a layer of waxed paper and eyeing dozens of candies. Chocolate hazelnut. Chocolate bark. Caramel rolls with dustings of nuts over the top. Chocolate filled with raspberries and topped with tiny flecks of candied fruit. Mint bars. Praline bars. No fudge, but she pulled out a couple of caramel rolls, their paper wrappers crinkling as she set them on top of the display case. They were Belinda's second favorite candy. She could remember Dillard Keech buying a half pound of fudge and a half dozen caramel rolls for her birthday and their anniversary every year. Granddad had always thrown in a few mint bars and a piece of dark chocolate bark for good measure.

She did the same, placing the candy in a pink box embossed with lighter pink flowers. That was new. Adeline's idea maybe? Brenna couldn't imagine Granddad choosing anything as fancy. He was more apt to use sturdy white boxes and plain gold ribbon.

She opened the second display case, lifting the waxed paper and eyeing row after row of glossy bonbons and squares of silky fudge. Chocolate. Chocolate peanut butter. Marshmallow. Rocky road. That was the newest addition to the family fudge recipes. Her father's contribution. Since he'd died, there hadn't been anything new added to the shop's menu. At least nothing Brenna knew about

She took several pieces of chocolate fudge, a piece of peanut butter and one of marshmallow, added two cocoa-dusted bonbons, and closed the box. She'd have to replace the inventory before the morning rush, but she'd deal with that in the morning.

Five o'clock in the morning.

That's when Granddad began his day. Apparently, it was also when Adeline started hers. Which meant it was when Brenna would have to be in the kitchen, re-creating all the gorgeous chocolates her family had spent generations perfecting.

Early mornings weren't a problem.

She liked getting up before the sun.

It was the chocolate that was going to be an issue.

That and pretending.

She'd worn her façade of happiness just fine when she'd been talking on the phone. Texting was even easier.

How are you doing? Adeline or Willow would type.

Fantastic, Brenna would reply. Glad to be done with the jerk.

Janelle would always get a variation of the theme: I'm doing well, Mom. How about you?

Yeah. Texting a response was easy.

She wasn't sure how she'd do face-to-face. She didn't know if she could look in

Adeline's eyes and tell her things were hunky-dory or if she could smile at Grand-dad and tell him how happy she was. As for Janelle . . .

Another bridge she'd have to cross when she got to it.

She carried the box across the room, unlocked the front door, and stepped out-side.

A truck had pulled up in front of the shop and was idling near the curb, its engine humming happily. She'd figured River to be more the kind of guy who would have got-ten out of the truck and banged on the shop door, but he was sitting in the cab as she approached, a phone pressed to his ear.

He unrolled the window, held up a finger, and mouthed, "One minute," then nodded in acknowledgement to something the person he was speaking to must have said.

"Right. Call a repairman, clean up the mess, and wash the dishes by hand if you can't get the damn thing working before the morning rush. You'll all survive it. I can guarantee you that." He listened for a mo-ment, then chuckled. "Yeah. We'll talk about overtime when I get back. Keep me posted."

He ended the call, smoothed his hair, his gaze suddenly focused on Brenna. "Sorry about that. I had some business to deal with."

"Dish-washing business?"

"Today it's broken dishwasher business." His gaze dropped to the box of chocolates, and he smiled. "That's a pretty big box for one piece of fudge."

"No one can eat just one piece of Lamont fudge," she said, handing it to him. "I packed some of Belinda's other favorites, too. And a few goodies for Huckleberry and the rest of your houseguests."

"Now, why would you go and do a thing like that, Brenna?" he asked, setting the box on the passenger seat and climbing out of the truck. He was taller than her by a good three inches. Quite a feat considering that she was five-foot-eleven.

"Because it will make Belinda happy."

"You've got a point. Otherwise, I'd eat every one of those chocolates myself before I let any of that group get their hands on them." He fished a wallet out of his pocket, peeled a few bills out of the fold.

"There's no need to pay. Take the chocolates as a gift. Granddad would want Belinda to have them." Byron was like that — always giving away chocolates and candies to people he felt needed a little cheering up.

"Your grandfather runs a business. He

won't make a profit if he gives away his product."

"My grandfather has never cared all that much about making a profit. If he did, he'd have moved the shop to some big city decades ago."

"I'm going to tell you something, Brenna. I'm not much for taking charity. I hope that's not what those chocolates are." He smoothed the bills and eyed her as if she'd offered him a box of poison and told him to swallow it down with a bucketful of horse pee.

No smile. No friendly twinkle in his eye. Not a hint of the guy who'd laughed in the church parking lot.

This dude?

He looked like an older version of the demon kid who'd taken Benevolence by storm a decade ago — angry and belligerent.

It didn't bother her.

He could be as pissy and ornery as he wanted, and she was still going to give him the damn chocolate. It was the one thing she could do for Belinda, the one thing she could offer, because — God help her — she couldn't afford flowers or hair ribbons or body lotion or any of the other things she might want to give as a cheer-up gift.

"How about you tell me something else, River?" she responded, her hands settling on her hips. And, she knew, without even having a mirror in front of her, that she looked exactly like her mother did when she got on one of her rants.

God!

Not only was she back in Benevolence, she was turning into Janelle!

"What?" River asked.

"Is the chip on your shoulders as heavy as you're making it seem?"

The question surprised a laugh out of River, and he shook his head, sliding the money back into his wallet. "Probably heavier. I spent a lot of years having to accept a lot of charity. I prefer not to do it now."

"I bet you're more than willing to give it, though. Aren't you?"

"When I can." Every Sunday when he was in Portland, as soon as the restaurants closed, River and his executive chefs would head to the local shelter and make meals for the homeless. They provided the ingredients. No leftovers. No overstocked product. Everything River brought was fresh and high-end, because he refused to offer anything less.

"Which is probably a lot." Brenna had her

hands on her hips, her shoulders back. She looked ready to do battle, but there were circles under her eyes and a gauntness to her face that made him wonder what she'd been doing with herself for the past decade. Last he'd heard, she'd gone off to be a fashion model. She had the look of it — the racehorse lean build, the long gangly body.

Somehow, though, the idea of her strutting down runways wearing killer heels and fancy clothes didn't mesh with his memory of that little girl tugging a wagon full of books.

"Maybe," he conceded. "When I was a kid, I promised myself that if I ever stopped needing to take other people's old crap, if I ever had the money to give someone something better, I would. Dillard taught me to always keep my promises. So, I have."

That seemed to mollify her. Her hands slipped from her hips, and she sighed. "Dillard was a great guy. Belinda is a great lady. They did a lot for my family after my father died. The chocolate is just a gesture that says I remember and that I appreciated it."

"I'll accept it as such," he said, adding a formal edge to his voice that he knew she caught.

She smiled, a tired little lift of her mouth.

"That's very gallant of you."

"And, *that's* a very old fashioned word."

"I know, and it's a shame that it is. We need a little more gallantry in the world. Then, shi — crap like stolen fudge wouldn't happen nearly as often."

"You're a funny lady, Brenna Lamont."

"I'm a *tired* lady. I just finished a twenty-five-hundred-mile drive from New York City."

"In that old Chrysler?"

"I sure as heck didn't drive a brand new Jeep and then trade it in for a 1977 Chrysler New Yorker when I arrived."

"I'll take that as a yes."

She didn't laugh, but her smile widened. "To be fair, the car might be old, but it only had ten-thousand miles on it when I left the city. Midge bought it with insurance money after her husband passed. She lived in the city and had never learned to drive, so it was only used when one of her kids or grandkids borrowed it."

"Midge?"

"A former neighbor. She's 94, but she acts like she's nineteen. She liked to skinny dip in the community pool. When the police were called, she refused to get out of the water and made them come in after her. I bailed her out of jail twice last year."

"You're kidding."

"Not a bit. Midge is a hoot, but her family finally convinced her to move to a senior center. Apparently, skinny dipping is legal there."

He laughed. Again. How many times was that now? Two? Three?

"You laugh, but Midge made that a criteria for the move. Once her family found a place, she sold me the car. Probably to spite her son who seems a lot more interested in what he can get from her than in what he can give."

"Sounds like a nice guy."

"He sure as heck isn't a gallant one." She smoothed her hair, glanced at the shop. "I'd better go lock things up. It's been a long few days, and tomorrow I start working."

"At Chocolate Haven?"

"You sound surprised."

"I'd heard you were working as a model."

"I was. It got old. I had a shop in New York City for a while, but I decided to change directions. Now, I'm back in Benevolence until my grandfather doesn't need me anymore." She said it so blithely that he knew there was more to the story.

It wasn't his business, and he didn't ask. "I'll walk you to the door."

"The door," she responded, "is a hundred

feet away. I can walk myself."

"I'm sure you can, but until tonight, I hadn't laughed in a month. I figure I owe you one for that."

"Things are tough at the ranch, huh?" she asked, not arguing as he walked beside her.

"That depends on who you ask."

"I'm asking you."

"They're not great. I think Belinda must have been at loose ends after Dillard died. To fill the time, she's taken to offering homes to adults who don't have anywhere else to go."

"Adults? I thought Huckleberry was a kid."

"He's eighteen." At least, that's what he told Belinda. River had yet to see proof of that, and he suspected the kid was a couple of years younger, a runaway who'd found a nice comfortable place to live.

"And freeloading off Belinda?"

"He wouldn't call it that. Neither would Belinda. He's got a job working as a janitor at the church. He also does odd jobs for people in the community. Belinda says he's bought groceries a few times and cooked dinner a lot. All I've seen him do is eat and make messes. If he were the only one staying there, it might not be so bad, but there are three other *guests,* and Belinda's fi-

50

nances can't support them all. She's used up all her savings, and she didn't pay property taxes last year. If something isn't done, she's going to lose the ranch."

"Does she know how bad things are?" she asked, getting straight to the heart of the issue.

"She knows she's behind. She doesn't know how far. I don't want her to. Not while she's still recovering."

"How about her guests? Do they know?" They'd reached the door, and she stopped, turning to face him. A breeze ruffled her hair, sending short strands of it across her cheeks. It was fiery red against her pale skin, and for about three seconds, he thought about brushing it away, seeing if it was as silky as it looked.

"The better question is: *do they care?*"

"You won't know unless you ask."

"I'm too busy dealing with dozens of maintenance issues and driving Belinda back and forth to therapy to take the time to ask anyone anything." He sounded pissed. He felt pissed.

"They say that communication is the key to successful relationships."

"I don't want damn successful relationships with those people," he growled. "I want them gone."

She laughed. "Sorry, River. I can't help you with that. I can tell you one thing, though," She opened the shop door, and he got a whiff of something chocolatey and sweet. "Belinda is lucky to have you in her corner."

She closed the door, waved at him from behind the glass, and walked away, her slender hips swinging, her hair bouncing.

He was half-tempted to follow her.

Because it was a lot more fun to be around her than it was to be at Freedom Ranch.

He turned back to the truck, to the fudge he'd left on the seat, to the next thing on his agenda — returning to whatever new chaos he was going to find at the house.

And, there *would* be chaos.

There hadn't been one day without it since he'd arrived.

River didn't mind devoting his life to Belinda. She'd sure as hell have done it for him. She *had* done it for him. He didn't mind the time spent away from his restaurants, his coworkers, his friends. What he minded was cleaning up shit that other people left all over the house, breaking up arguments between immature kids, putting out fires before they began.

He hoped to God everyone was asleep when he got home, but the way the past few weeks had gone, he was pretty damn sure that wasn't going to be the case. Unless he missed his guess, Huckleberry would be in the kitchen rummaging for food. Angel was probably lying on the sofa, her seven-month-pregnant belly peeking out from under a threadbare T-shirt. Mack . . .

Yeah.

Mack.

No last name. Not that River had been given. Maybe forty, with burn scars on the side of his neck and a permanent frown. Mack didn't sleep in the house. Near as River could tell, he slept in one of the outbuildings. He worked, though. He'd fixed the fence in the old cow pasture, planted a garden that had filled the fridge with produce, and seemed to be working on getting Dillard's old tractor running.

River climbed into the truck and drove through town, then out onto the country road that meandered through farmland and wound its way through golden bluffs. Two miles in, and he turned onto what had once been a gravel drive. Now it was covered with grass and dirt, the sign that welcomed people to Freedom Ranch hanging listlessly from two wooden beams Dillard had planted in the ground himself.

He'd had a vision and he'd followed

through on it. According to Dillard, there could never be any regret when a person did that.

He'd been the one who'd encouraged River to attend culinary school. He'd shelled out the money for River's business degree, too, and when his first restaurant had opened, Dillard had cheered louder than anyone else.

Funny how much more present Dillard's memory was on the ranch he'd loved.

River pulled up in front of the house he'd spent five years living in, all those memories washed away by the reality of what was. One of the *guests* — as Belinda insisted on calling them — had turned every downstairs light on. The living room curtains were open, and he could see Angel lying on the sofa, a can of pop on the end table nearby.

She seemed like a nice enough kid, but that's what she was: a kid about to give birth to another kid. No mention of the father. No mention of her parents. Except that they'd kicked her to the curb when they'd found out she was pregnant.

She worked. River would give her that. She had a full-time waitressing job at Carla's Diner and a part-time job cleaning houses for a few of the wealthier residents. But when she was at the ranch, she spent her time lying on the couch, sipping pop, and scrolling through TV channels.

He grabbed the box of fudge, got out of the truck, and locked the door. Not because he was worried about a stranger taking off with the vehicle. No, he was worried about Huckleberry deciding to go for a joyride. The kid didn't have a vehicle. He hitched rides into town with Angel or bummed rides with Mack. The guy had a nice looking Chevy truck, and Belinda said he paid rent.

How much? A dollar? Two?

That's what River had wanted to ask.

Not his business. He knew it wasn't, but he'd seen the bills piled up on Belinda's desk. He knew how close she was to losing the ranch. She and Dillard had owned the place flat out, but there were property taxes to pay. She owed money for water and electricity, and she'd taken out a loan to pay for a car when her old Chevy died. She was three months behind on paying that. Or had been. River had paid off the loan, and he was working to have the tax penalties waived. If that happened, the ranch would be safe. For a while. But if Belinda was going to keep Freedom Ranch, she was going to need more than the measly Social Security checks she received monthly. Especially if she insisted on supporting other people.

He strode into the large foyer, bypassing the coatrack that still held one of Dillard's old bowler hats. A couple of dust-coated umbrellas leaned against the wall, a pair of flip-flops beside them. Probably Angel's.

The scent of fried onions hung in the air, mixing with the smell of furniture polish and floor wax. Someone had cleaned. Surprising because River hadn't seen anyone but Mack lift a finger since he'd arrived.

"Hot date?" Angel called.

"Yes," he responded as he walked into the living room. "With the chocolate shop."

"You got the fudge?!" Angel jumped up from the couch. Or tried to jump. She was the skinniest pregnant woman he'd ever seen, her arms and legs tiny, her hips non-existent. Compared to that, her pregnant belly was oversized, her balance completely thrown off by it. Instead of leaping up, she lumbered, her skinny arms hugging her belly.

"Yes, and it's for Belinda."

"I know who it's for, nimrod," she snapped, her black hair falling lank around her face. "You're not the only one who cares about Belinda, you know!"

There were a few things he could have said. Most of them regarding the fact that none of the people who said they cared did anything to show it.

"Did Belinda go to bed?"

"Hours ago. She was worn out from all that crying she did."

"Today was a tough day," he said. "Tomorrow will be better."

Angel cocked her head to the side, offered a hesitant smile. The first she'd ever given him. "Belinda says that all the time."

"Yeah. I know. She raised me. I guess a lot of what she taught me stuck," he responded, grabbing an empty pop can from the floor. There was a chip bag right next to it, and he picked that up, too.

He didn't say a word about the crap Angel had been feeding her kid. Pop. Chips. Burgers from the diner where she worked. What she needed was milk, homemade yogurt, salads filled with vegetables and topped with lean protein.

"What?" she snapped, and he realized he was staring, thinking about that kid she was percolating and wondering how healthy it would be when all she'd fed it was junk food.

"You hungry?"

She blinked, her face suddenly so child-like, he wondered if she was younger than the nineteen years she claimed to be. "Nah.

57

Huckleberry cooked."

"And you're all still living?"

She laughed. "Yeah. He's a good cook. We had meat loaf, little red potatoes, and green beans." She patted her belly, the T-shirt riding up just enough to reveal the edges of a tattoo. "The baby is happy."

"He might be happier if you didn't drink this crap all the time." He held up the pop can, and she shrugged.

"I gave up the cigarettes, the alcohol, and the weed. I think the kid will survive a little caffeine. But *she* probably needs more sleep, so I'm going to bed. 'Night." She waddled from the room, her narrow shoulders stiff with anger.

Obviously, she'd felt judged.

And, just as obviously, he should have kept his big mouth shut.

He flicked off the light, walked into the dining room and did the same. Then went into the kitchen. Huckleberry sat at the table there, a laptop opened in front of him, earbuds on. His foot tapped against the black-and-white tile floor, his eyes closed as he bobbed to whatever music he was listening to.

River tossed the can into the recycling bin, threw away the empty chip bag, all while

Huckleberry still tapped along with the music.

More than likely, he knew River was there.

More than likely, he was ignoring him.

The kid had a chip on his shoulders almost as big as the one River used to carry.

Is the chip on your shoulders as heavy as you're making it seem?

Brenna's words echoed through his head. He *did* still have a chip on his shoulders. He just hid it a lot better than Huckleberry.

"Food in the oven for you, bro," Huckleberry suddenly said, pulling out the earbuds and opening his eyes.

It was probably the freckles that made him look so young.

Or the copper-colored hair.

Whatever the case, Huckleberry looked about fifteen.

"And I'm really sorry about the fudge," the kid continued, his gaze dropping to the box River held. "I told Ms. Belinda that, and she said it was just fine, but it wasn't cool. I should have thought before I ate." He stood, grabbed the battered laptop and a cup that had been sitting beside it.

"I'd appreciate it if you keep your paws out of the new stuff." River set the box on the counter.

"And me and the rest of the group would

appreciate it if you'd stop walking around the house like you got a stick up your butt," Huckleberry replied. He washed the cup and set it in the drainer, the laptop under his scrawny arm. "Everything was fine around here until you showed up."

"Everything was a free ride until I showed up. Belinda did everything, and the rest of you sat on your asses and let her serve you."

"A lot you know," Huckleberry spat. "We all worked together and made sure Ms. Belinda was okay. Then you drove into town thinking you were some kind of superhero and tried to take over."

"I wasn't interested in taking over anything. I was interested in making sure Belinda was okay."

"She was fine. We all were fine. You're just too much of a butt wipe to admit it, and too much of a control freak to go back to whatever rock you crawled out from under and leave us alone." Huckleberry yanked open the door that led to the backstairs, walked into the narrow stairwell, and slammed the door shut with enough strength to shake the door frame.

"Damn kid," River muttered, hoping to God that Huckleberry hadn't woken Belinda.

Damn kid who put a plate of food in the oven

for you, Dillard would have said.

He'd have been right, but that had been Dillard, always seeing the big picture, always looking for the good in the people around him.

River was more of a cynic, and at thirty, he had no intention of changing. Huckleberry had cooked dinner, and he'd cleaned the kitchen. It was spotless: every dish put away, the table cleaned off for the first time since River had returned. No spots of food on the floor. No overflowing trash can. Even the window above the sink had been polished. The place looked like it had when River had lived there.

Kind of made him wonder why it hadn't looked like that in the weeks since he'd been back.

He opened the oven. He wasn't sure what he expected, but it wasn't moist meat loaf topped with brown gravy, fingerling potatoes tossed with butter and parsley, and glossy beans mixed with garlic and onion. Looking at the food — plated neatly and begging to be eaten — made River feel exactly like the butt wipe Huckleberry had said he was.

A perfect end to the perfect day.

He hoped to God that tomorrow would be better, but seeing as how he was meeting with Adeline Lamont to discuss Belinda's tax problems, he wasn't holding out much hope.

People in town said Adeline was a miracle worker when it came to taxes. Based on what he'd seen when he'd looked through Belinda's books, River thought she might need to be even more than that.

CHAPTER THREE

By eight thirty in the morning, Brenna had broken every vow she'd made about keeping her language PG. She'd cursed the chocolate bark that had broken into seven thousand pieces when she'd tried to take it out of the pan. She'd cursed the caramel that she'd let burn on the stove. She'd even cursed her clumsy fingers when she'd dropped the only decent batch of bonbons she'd managed to make.

And now?

Now, she wanted a cigarette, and she wanted one bad.

She'd settle for some eggs or toast or a salad or soup or anything other than chocolate, fudge, nuts, or coffee. Of which she'd had one or two (or ten) cups too many.

Her stomach growled.

"Hungry?" her grandfather asked as he pressed a cutter into glossy peanut butter bars.

"I'm fine."

"So you are. Take a break anyway. Go to the diner and get yourself something to eat. Or go to the store and get some groceries. I didn't think to fill up your fridge before you got here."

"Mom left me potpie. It was enough for three people." She'd devoured it in one sitting, because she'd been hungry enough to eat that and the remainder of a sleeve of crackers she'd found in the Chrysler.

"You ate that for breakfast?"

"No."

"Then, go get yourself something. You're skinny as a rail. I've got to fatten you up if we're going to find you a new man."

"First, I don't want a new man. Second, we're already behind on production." She filled a pan of congealed and separated chocolate with hot water, squirted a few drops of soap into it. "I can eat after we get caught up."

"Caught up? I decide how much product we need, and I've decided we're right on track. Besides, your sister hasn't been eating enough to nourish a bird, much less a grown woman carrying a child. The only thing we can get down her gullet are those pecan rolls Laura Beth makes."

"Laura Beth?"

"She took over managing the diner a couple of months ago. Used to wait tables there? Tall. Pretty. You go on in and ask for her. She has a dozen pecan rolls she sets aside for me every day." He fished two twenties out of his pocket. "Get yourself something to eat while you're at it. My treat, because I've missed you terribly, kid."

"I've missed you, too. But, I don't need your money," she lied, thrusting the cash back.

"No more arguing. I'm old. I get my way." He waved snatched the money from her hand and shoved it into her apron pocket, and she saw a hint of something in his eyes. A little bit of darkness and doubt and concern, and she knew all those things weren't for Adeline. They were for her.

Did he know she'd lost everything?

Could he?

She almost asked, probably would have asked, but someone knocked on the back door.

"Pops!" whoever it was called through the closed door. "It's Chase."

"You forget your damn key again, son?" Byron unlocked the door and flung it open, a faux scowl on his craggy face. The sun had risen hours ago, the musty scent of moist earth and damp pavement drifting in as a young, gangly kid walked through the doorway. Chase Lyons looked just about the same as the last time Brenna had seen him: lean as a flagpole, his face too somber and serious for a kid his age.

He met Brenna's eyes. "Ms. Brenna, it's nice to see you again."

To his credit, he didn't even glance at the mess in the sink or the drips of chocolate on the floor.

"You too, Chase. How's your sister?"

"Lark is great. She's anxious for school to start, though. She's the only person I know who loves school more than I do." He grabbed a white apron from a hook beside the door and tied it around his waist.

"Maybe you've forgotten," Byron said. "That you've got classes this morning."

"My first class was canceled. I don't have to be there until noon, so I thought I'd help you open." He stepped into place beside Byron, taking a second pan of peanut butter bars and flipping them out onto waxed paper, his movements smooth and practiced. He'd only been working at Chocolate Haven for a few months and he already looked like a pro, pushing the cutter into the smooth bars, pulling it out without even one of the bars crumbling.

"What classes are you taking?" Brenna asked.

"Just a couple of summer courses. Calculus and accounting, ma'am."

"A numbers guy, huh?"

He nodded, his cheeks going three shades of red.

That made her smile. She liked Chase. He was a good kid with a good heart. There weren't many people like that in the world. "That's cool. I'm more into literature."

"You went to college?" He grabbed flowered wrappers from a shelf, spread them out onto a tray, and set a peanut butter bar into each one.

"No, but if I had, I'd have gotten a degree in literature and library science."

"You could still do that," Chase said, lifting the tray and heading for the front of the shop. "It's not like you're old, and even if you were, a person should never stop learning."

"Out of the mouth of babes," Byron murmured as Chase carried the tray down the hall.

"Life is a lot less complicated when you're that age," Brenna said, taking a pan of s'more fudge from the fridge and flipping it onto waxed paper. Not as smooth as Chase, but the fudge slipped out easily.

"It's only as complicated as we decide to make it, baby doll."

"What's that supposed to mean?" She grabbed a cutter, slid it into the cool fudge. She lost two pieces, but overall, it wasn't a bad effort.

"Sometimes the easiest path really is the best one to take."

"Granddad." She turned to face him. "If you have something you want to say to me, just say it. I'm too tired for word games."

"When have I ever played those? Your grandmother? Now, she was good at that kind of thing. Alice always had a way with words. Me? I'm more likely to just say whatever it is on my mind. Screw the consequences." He shifted a tray of caramel creams onto a rack. "Things are under control here, so how about you run and get those pecan rolls for Adeline? Stay and chat with her a while. It'll do her good."

He didn't add, *It'll do you good, too,* but Brenna was sure he wanted to. She knew what she looked like: tired, worn down, discouraged. She even felt like all those things, but she wasn't going to let Byron know it.

"Want me to bring you something back from the diner?" she asked, her voice as bright and cheery as colored lights on

Christmas morning.

"Nah, but tell Laura Beth I said hello." He glanced away as he said it, and that made her wonder just who Laura Beth was and just why Granddad looked almost embarrassed when he mentioned her.

A girlfriend?

She didn't ask because she didn't want the subject of *her* love life to come up. Better to keep her nose out of everyone's business and have them keep their noses out of hers.

As if that were even possible in her family. Prying was just part of who her mother was. Byron was just as good at digging for information. Adeline, in her own sweet way, had been known to ask pointed questions.

Only Willow kept her focus on her own life. Maybe because she had her own secrets that she wanted to keep hidden. There had been a lot of times lately when Brenna had wanted to ask what they were. Unlike Adeline, who'd always been an open book. Willow was difficult to read. She'd called a couple of weeks ago and told Brenna about her plans for a spring wedding. Small. Intimate. Janelle wasn't to know about it until a few weeks before the event because Willow didn't want things to get out of hand. She'd said it all like she was talking about a dinner party rather than a lifetime commitment, and Brenna had wanted to ask why. Why was Willow settling for a guy who spent his Saturdays watching sports and his Sundays drinking Scotch and watching more sports? Why was she working as a prosecuting attorney in a city when what she'd always loved was hiking through the woods and spending hours riding horses through the meadows and fields outside of Benevolence? Why didn't she have a dozen kids already when all she'd talked about when she was ten and eleven and twelve was how she wanted to be a mom?

When had that changed?

After their father died? Before?

Brenna frowned as she walked out into the bright August day. She needed to call her sister to make sure that the decision she'd made was one she wanted to stick with. Unlike Brenna, Willow tended to go with the flow. She didn't like rocking the boat, and she didn't like to change her mind. Those were good qualities. If they didn't get you stuck in a situation you didn't want to be in.

She walked around the side of the building and headed down Main Street. The diner wasn't far, and Adeline's house was just a little farther than that. The exercise and fresh air would do Brenna good and maybe get her mind off the cigarette she'd been craving all morning. Besides, she didn't have money for gas and her car was on empty.

Actually . . .

She pulled out the twenties Byron had given her, remembered the look in his eyes when he'd told her she had to take it. The last thing she wanted was charity from her family. The last thing she wanted to believe was that they somehow all knew that she needed it.

For some reason, that thought brought an image of River, standing outside Chocolate Haven, scowling. He hadn't wanted charity because he'd had to take it too many times in his life. She'd never had to take charity. Until now.

It wasn't a good feeling.

At all.

She crossed the street and walked into the diner's parking lot. There were only a few vehicles there this time of morning. A couple of SUVs. A few pickup trucks. One or two sedans. In a few hours, the place would be filled with families coming for breakfast before they went fishing or hiking or berry picking. At least that's the way it had been when Brenna was a kid.

She stepped inside the diner, the soft clink of tableware and the quiet murmur of voices oddly comforting. She'd washed dishes there when she was sixteen, saving money for her senior trip to D.C. Back then, she'd had dreams of getting a scholarship to an out-of-state college. She'd imagined herself living on campus, making a bunch of new friends who knew nothing about her childhood, her father's death, her mother's perfectionist nature.

"Brenna Lamont! As I live and breathe! What are you doing here?" A woman hurried across the room. Tall and pretty, her face lined with six decades' worth of living, Laurie Simpson had been the head waitress at the diner when Brenna had worked there.

"I'm back to help Byron with the shop," Brenna said as Laurie pulled her into a bear hug.

"I heard you might be coming, but Byron wasn't a hundred percent sure you'd show up."

"He said that?"

"Nah. He just said you'd come when you were ready. What can I do for you, kid? Breakfast?" She took a pad from her apron, snagged a pen from her shirt pocket, and eyed Brenna expectantly.

"Byron sent me for pecan rolls. He said I

72

should talk to Laura Beth?"

Laurie laughed, the sound filling the quiet dining room. "That would be me, kiddo. Laura Beth. Man! Aside from my mother, your granddad is the only one who's ever called me that." There was something soft in her face as she said it, something sweet and young and a little revealing.

She must have realized it. She shoved the pad back in her pocket, grabbed Brenna's wrist, and dragged her to the Formica counter that had been in the diner for as long as the diner had been around.

"The rolls just came out of the oven. I'll box 'em up and bring 'em out for you. Angel!" She waved at a waitress who was setting plates of food on a table. "Bring Brenna some coffee and some biscuits and gravy. You still like that, right, kid?"

She didn't give Brenna a chance to respond, just hurried into the kitchen.

"Coffee," the waitress said, setting a mug in front of Brenna and pouring coffee into it. She looked young. Maybe seventeen and obviously pregnant, her apron tied below her burgeoning belly. "Sugar or cream?"

"Black is good."

"Yeah. I figured that." The girl's gaze dropped from Brenna's face to her body, and then she smiled and patted her stom-

73

ach. "Me? I'm all about the sugar and cream. Got to keep the kid fed. I'm Angel, by the way." She held out her hand. "And, you must be one of the Lamonts."

"Brenna. What gave it away?"

"The hair. And the fact that Laurie is running back to get those pecan rolls that Byron loves so much. She only used to make them once a month. Now she makes them every single day." She leaned in close, her belly bumping Brenna's arm as she whispered, "She and Byron have got a little thing going on."

"Really?"

"Yep. Neither wants to admit it, though. Laurie was married to a bastard. The guy nearly killed her."

Brenna knew the story. Laurie had been a street kid in Los Angeles, a runaway who'd hooked up with the first guy to offer marriage. On her fifth anniversary, her husband had beat her so badly, she'd been hospitalized for a month. When she'd finally been released, she'd filed for divorce and left town. She'd stopped in Benevolence on her way to somewhere else. She'd never left.

"And Byron," Angel continued. "He's still got the hots for his dead wife, and he feels guilty for finding another woman attractive." She flushed. "What I mean is —"

"You don't need to explain. I know what you're saying."

"Okay. Good. I've got a great job here. I'd hate to lose it because one of Byron's grand-daughters complained about my big mouth. Give me a minute and I'll bring you the biscuits and gravy."

"Can you put them in a carry-out container? I don't have a ton of time." And, she'd want to bring some of them home for later.

"No problem." Angel walked into the kitchen, leaving Brenna with black coffee and a thought that she never would have even considered before.

Laurie and Byron?

She couldn't imagine Byron with anyone other than her grandmother. He and Alice had been a perfect team, but Alice had been gone for five years, and Byron was still young enough and healthy enough to want something more than to be alone.

Why hadn't she thought about that before?

Maybe because she'd been too caught up in the minidrama that her life had become.

"Things change," she muttered, taking a sip of her coffee.

"Except when they don't." River dropped into the seat beside her, his legs encased in faded denim, his white long-sleeved shirt rolled up to the elbow. He hadn't shaved and black stubble shadowed his jaw.

God, he was sexy.

And handsome.

And every single thing Brenna needed to avoid.

"What's that supposed to mean?" she asked, and he gestured to the counter, the pictures on the wall, the old diner tables that had been there for as long as Brenna could remember.

"This place looks exactly the same."

"Things like this should never change," she responded, and he smiled, an easy gentle smile that made a tiny little seed sprout in her stomach.

She felt it there — new and fragile.

It felt like. . . .

Happiness?

Hope?

Excitement?

"You're a romantic, are you?" he asked.

"No, I'm practical. If the diner changed, people would stop coming. They're here for the food, but they're also here for the memories, for the connection to the past that they feel when they sit in a booth they've sat in dozens of times before."

"You *are* a romantic," he confirmed, his eyes looking straight into hers, and she could swear he could see whatever it was she felt, whatever new and fragile thing she was hiding.

"And *you're* out and about early." She changed the subject, and his smile broadened.

"It's nearly nine," he pointed out, and she felt young and foolish. Which only added to the all-around foul mood she'd been in since she'd ruined her first batch of Lamont family fudge at 5:38 that morning.

Not River's fault, so she took a deep breath, tried on a smile that felt more like a scowl. "I guess it is. I was working. I must have lost track of time."

"First day on the chocolate job, right?" He reached over, rubbed a smudge of chocolate from the back of her hand.

She felt that one little touch all the way to her toes.

Her cheeks were hot, and she knew they were red, but she'd be darned if she was going to act like a schoolgirl with a crush. "That's right."

"That explains it then. Kitchen work will make anyone lose track of time."

"You spend a lot of time in the kitchen?" she asked.

"I own a couple of restaurants in Portland."

"I guess that explains the broken dishwasher emergency," she said, and he nodded.

"I've got some good managers, but they like to call me when things like that happen. Which is a little too often for my liking." He lifted her hand, studying a smear of fudge that decorated the side of her wrist. "Looks like you and the chocolate weren't getting along."

"Chocolate. Fudge. Peanut butter. Caramel. You name it, I fought with it this morning."

"And now you're taking a break before going back to the battle?" He still had her hand, and she could feel the warmth of his fingers, the roughness of his skin. It reminded her of things she'd be better off forgetting.

She tugged her hand away, lifted her coffee as if that were the only reason why she'd wanted to free it. "I'm picking something up for my sister."

"Adeline? I've got a meeting with her this morning."

"Is she helping you with the. . . ." She didn't finish. There were people in the diner who knew Belinda, and she didn't want anyone spreading rumors about the financial trouble she was having.

River nodded. "Yes. Hopefully. If you want me to, I can bring the stuff to her."

"It's okay. I haven't seen her in a few months, and I'm looking forward to catching up." She also didn't want to go back to Chocolate Haven.

She'd have to be there before it opened, but for right now . . .

She'd use whatever excuse she had to stay away.

Angel rushed out of the kitchen, a Styrofoam carry-out container in one hand and a white bakery box in the other.

"Laurie is checking on a delivery, so she asked . . ." Her voice trailed off as she caught sight of River. She didn't look pleased to see him. He didn't look all that happy to see her either.

"What are you doing here?" she snapped.

"Belinda said you forgot to take these this morning." He pulled a bottle of prenatal vitamins out of his pocket and set it on the counter. "She was worried, so I brought them."

"Thanks," she said begrudgingly as she set the box and carry-out container in front of Brenna. "Laurie says this is on the house because it's your first day back in town."

"I can't —"

"No sense arguing. Laurie calls the shots

79

here, and if she says you're getting it free, you're getting it free." Angel snatched up the bottle of vitamins and swallowed one without water. "I've got work to do, so see you around."

She flounced off, her hips swinging, her belly bouncing. She looked like a kid, and she acted like one, and something about that made Brenna feel sorry for her.

She took out one of the twenties Byron had given her and set it under her coffee cup.

"Nice tip," River commented, and she shrugged.

"She looks like she could use it."

"She can. Belinda helped her get insurance coverage for the kid, but Angel doesn't want to go on welfare. She's been working hard so she can provide for both of them. She's still not making enough. If Belinda hadn't taken her in, she'd be on the streets."

"She's one of the guests?"

"Unfortunately."

"I don't think it's unfortunate for her."

True.

Very true, and River wasn't so much of an ass that he didn't realize it. He watched as Angel cleared off a table, handed menus to a group of older men, poured coffee for an elderly couple. She did her job well and she worked long hours. He knew she was making decent money, but she wore the same pair of jeans almost every day, the same faded shirt. Every cent she spent was on stuff for the baby.

So maybe he was an ass, because he'd been so caught up in worrying about Belinda that he hadn't spent more than a few minutes worrying about Angel.

He pulled three twenties out of his wallet and set them with the one Brenna had left.

"Nice tip," she murmured, grabbing the box and carry-out container and standing. She looked just as thin as she had the night before, her eyes just as hollow and tired. She had a smear of chocolate on her neck and one just under her jaw.

"She looks like she could use it."

She smiled. "You're a quick learner, River. I'd better get this over to my sister's. Chocolate Haven opens at ten and I need to be back by then."

"Want a ride?"

"To Adeline's?" She looked surprised and maybe a little appalled.

"That *is* where we're both going, right?" He held the diner door open for Brenna and then followed her out into the warming day.

"Yes, I just didn't think . . ."

"That we'd be there at the same time?"

"I didn't think we'd be going there together, but I'm tired, and a ride would be good, so I guess I'll accept your offer."

"No need to sound so excited about it," he said lightly as he led the way to his truck

She climbed into the cab, all long arms and legs and skinny frame. "Sorry. The only thing I'm excited about right now is the thought of making it to the end of the day and tucking myself back into bed."

"How long did your drive from New York take?"

"Four days."

"You made good time."

"I had good motivation." She snapped her belt into place, the box and carry-out container on her lap.

"What kind of motivation?"

She met his eyes, and he realized hers were blue with specks of violet and green in them. Pretty eyes in a stunning face. "The kind that makes a woman drive 2,500 miles in four days."

Obviously, she didn't want to share any more than that, and it was just as obvious he didn't need to add anyone else's trouble to his plate.

He was curious, though.

He'd admit that.

"I can think of a lot of things that might

make a woman do that. None of them are very pleasant."

"*Not very pleasant* sums up the last past months of my life beautifully. Now," she said, "how about we head to my sister's house. I really do have to get back to the shop this morning. My family is counting on me to help out until Adeline gets over her morning sickness and can stand the smell of chocolate again."

"She's expecting?"

"You hadn't heard?"

"I've been a little too caught up in my own family dramas to worry about anyone else's."

Brenna's foot tapped against the floor of the truck, her fingers playing a rhythm on the carry-out box. "I wouldn't call Adeline's pregnancy a drama. It's more like . . . a distraction."

"From the things that sent you running from New York?"

"I wasn't running. I was coming here to help. I was just doing it very very quickly."

"Why?" He was back to that again, and he knew she wasn't going to answer, but he wanted to know. Maybe just because thinking about her problems was a whole hell of a lot easier than thinking about his own.

"Why not?"

"Do you always answer questions with questions?"

"Do you?"

He laughed. "Yeah. Actually. When I don't want to answer. So, I guess I'll take your question as a subtle hint that I should mind my own business."

"It wasn't subtle and it wasn't a hint, but I'll say thank you and we'll leave it at that," she responded. "Perfect timing for it, because there's my sister's place."

She pointed to a small house sitting in the middle of a well-manicured lot. Flower baskets hung from the eaves of a narrow porch. More flowers decorated mulch beds near the corners of the house. An old Cadillac was parked in the driveway, and he pulled up behind it.

The front door flew open before he could put the truck in PARK and Adeline Lamont stepped out onto the porch. No, not Lamont. Jefferson. She'd gotten married a few months back and, according to Belinda, was happier than she'd ever been. He might not have heard about her pregnancy, but he'd heard plenty about her marriage.

"She looks fantastic," Brenna murmured, flinging open her door and hopping out of the truck.

Adeline squealed and raced down the

porch steps, straight into her sister's arms, the box and carry-out container smashed between them. Neither seemed to notice; they were too busy talking over each other, exclaiming about hair and makeup and happiness.

Finally, Brenna pulled back and held the crumpled box out to her sister. "Grandad asked me to bring these over. I don't think he expected them to be smashed."

"They're not . . ." Adeline glanced toward the house and whispered, "pecan rolls, are they?"

"Of course. Grandad said they're your favorite."

"Favorite? I crave these things like other people crave alcohol." She was still whispering, her gaze darting back to her sister.

"So?" Brenna replied. "They're not alcohol, and there's nothing wrong with feeding the kid some sweets." She patted her sister's belly. There wasn't much of it. Just a slight swelling beneath her gray T-shirt. "Besides, Granddad says you're not eating enough. He says you're fading away to nothing."

"Yeah? Well, Mom says if I keep eating junk food, the baby will be born addicted to sugar."

Brenna snorted. "You're nearly thirty, Addie. I don't think you need to worry about what Mom thinks."

"I don't," Adeline said. "Unless she's sitting in my kitchen when I carry in a box full of pecan rolls."

"Is she here? Now?"

"Yes."

"Shi . . ." Brenna's gaze dropped to Adeline's belly. "Shoot. I knew I should have hidden in the apartment for the rest of the day."

"She would have hunted you down eventually."

"Well, she can go ahead and do that then, because I'm not in the mood to answer a dozen questions." She turned on her heel and probably would have walked away, but Adeline grabbed her arm.

"She won't ask anything. Not with a guest in the house." Adeline smiled at River. "Sorry for keeping you waiting, River. Did you bring the documents?"

"I've got copies of everything Belinda has." He reached into the truck, grabbed the manila envelope filled with letters from the state demanding payment of back property taxes.

"Great. Come on in and we'll go over everything." She hooked her arm through Brenna's and dragged her to the house.

River followed, walking through a small

foyer and into a living room. It was empty for about three seconds and then a petite brunette hurried in. Janelle Lamont hadn't changed much since River was a kid. She was still thin, pretty, and well dressed, her dark slacks and white shirt perfectly pressed. She had a few fine lines around her eyes and bracketing her mouth, but other than that, it didn't look like she'd aged.

"River, it's so good to see you. How is Belinda? I've been meaning to sto . . ." Her voice trailed off as she caught sight of Brenna. "Brenna! When did you get into town?"

"I got in really early this morning."

"I thought you were staying in a hotel for the night? Did you change your mind?"

"Yes." Brenna's answer was straightforward and simple, her tone just a little abrupt.

River was pretty sure Janelle noticed.

She frowned. "You should have called. What if your car had broken down or —"

"You'd been kidnapped by some good looking guy who wanted to ravish you," Adeline cut in. "Mom could have stopped him before he had his way with you."

"Adeline!" Janelle snapped. "You have a guest."

"That's never stopped me before."

87

"It should have! Anyway, it doesn't matter that you didn't call, Brenna. I'm just glad you're here." She pulled Brenna into a quick hug, reached up to pat her daughter's pale cheeks. "You look exhausted. Why don't we go back to the house? You can take a nap."

"Actually," Brenna said, "Grandad is expecting me back at Chocolate Haven."

"I'll call Byron and —"

"Mom," Brenna cut her off, "I'm here to help out at the shop. It doesn't make sense for Grandad to run the place by himself after I drove all the way from New York."

"One more day isn't going to hurt. I'm sure Byron would want you to get some rest before you start working. Don't you agree, Adeline?"

Adeline glanced at her sister, then met her mother's eyes. "What I think," she said, her hand settling on her tiny baby bump. "is that the baby is hungry and wants one of these delicious pecan rolls you brought me, Brenna." She lifted the box, waving it in front of her mother's face.

"Pecan rolls?" Janelle gasped. "Where did you get those, Brenna?"

"The diner."

"And, she brought enough to share," Adeline gushed. "Want one, River?"

Not really, but he could see where this

was going. One sister distracting Janelle for the other one. Not only could he see it, but he could appreciate it. Sibling camaraderie? Not something he'd ever experienced, but he could sure value what it could add to a person's life.

That being the case, he played along. "I'd love one."

"You're a chef!" Janelle said, her eyes wide with horror. "You went to culinary school. Belinda told me all about the elegant meals you make."

"I am a chef, but that doesn't mean I can't enjoy pecan rolls."

"Thank goodness," Adeline said happily, "I'd hate to have to eat all of them myself. Give Granddad kisses for me, Brenna." She blew her sister a kiss, winked at River, and walked out of the room.

Janelle followed, tripping over her words as she tried to convince her daughter to have a green smoothie instead.

"God, that never gets old," Brenna said with a smile that mirrored her sister's. Happy. Content. Just a little smug.

"You do that to your mother often?"

"Do what?"

"Get her riled up."

"Oh, she's not riled up. She's distracted. Which means I am free to go another round at Chocolate Haven." She sighed and opened the crushed carry-out container. "No fork. Looks like my biscuits and gravy will have to wait until later."

"Most houses have kitchens," he pointed out. "And most kitchens are supplied with forks."

"Most kitchens do not have my mother standing in them. This one does. Which reminds me . . ." She reached over and patted him on the shoulder. "Good luck."

"With?"

"You're part of the distraction, remember? Now make like a hero and go rescue my sister." She winked, just like her sister had, and then sauntered out the door.

CHAPTER FOUR

She'd meant to save some of the biscuits and gravy for later. She really did, but Brenna ate everything on her walk back to Main Street. *With her fingers.* And she enjoyed every last bite. She'd have licked the last few crumbs out of the container if she hadn't seen Millicent Montgomery marching toward her down the street. She tried to duck behind a light pole, but Millicent had already spotted her.

"Brenna Lamont!" she called in a high-pitched, nasally voice that reminded Brenna of fingernails on a chalkboard. "How are you, dear?"

"Fantastic," she lied as she stepped back onto the sidewalk.

"Are you really? I heard from your mother that you and your darling fiancé broke up."

"You met Dan once, Millicent. What would make you say he's darling?"

"No need to be rude, dear. I understand

it's tough to be an unattached woman at your age, but you shouldn't take it out on others."

"I was just asking a question, Millicent." And avoiding an answer, because Millicent loved gossiping as much as she loved spending money. Maybe more. Which was saying a lot, because Millicent had more clothes, shoes, jewelry, and cars than ten people needed.

"As was I, Brenna," Millicent huffed. "Really, just because you've traveled the world doesn't mean you have the right to look down at those who have not." She tugged at the princess neckline of her tight-fitting pink sundress, pulling it up a micro-inch. That wasn't nearly enough to cover the burgeoning white flesh that spilled out. The woman needed to invest in a good bra. Better yet, breast reduction surgery. Or, maybe, just larger clothes.

"I'm not looking down my nose at anyone. Just heading into work." She started walking toward Chocolate Haven, hoping and praying that Millicent wouldn't follow her.

Of course Millicent did, because that seemed to be the way Brenna's life was going lately.

"At Chocolate Haven?" Millicent asked as if she didn't already know the answer. "I'm sure you could find better work than that."

"I'm sure I could, but my goal isn't to find better work. It's to help out my grand-father."

"I'd think he has plenty of help. Your sister and that boy she's got living with her." She glanced around, lowered her voice. "I'm very certain none of my husbands would have approved of me having a young man living in the house with us."

"Weren't all your husbands" — *Don't say it, Brenna. Do. Not.* — "ancient?"

She'd said it, and poor Millicent looked like she was about to blow a fuse. Her face went from spray-on tan orange to fire-engine red. "None of my husbands were ancient. I'll have you know that Jeremiah — may he rest in peace — was only seventy when he passed."

"And you're how old? Forty-five?"

"Forty." Millicent scowled, tugging at the top of her dress again. "And most people say I don't look a day over twenty-five."

Most people lied, but that was a thought Brenna was definitely not going to share. Millicent loved to cause trouble and stir pots, and that was the last thing Brenna wanted. She was in town to help Byron and to get her crappy life together. She was not there to make the local snob angry.

"I'm sure they do," she said sweetly. "And I wasn't trying to offend you when I mentioned your husbands' ages. I just thought that men of their . . . maturity . . . might have been a little more intimidated by a nineteen-year-old kid. Sinclair is young, fit, and absolutely not worried about having a boy and his sister living with him and his wife."

"If you say so. Personally, I think most men would frown on it, but that's just me. I'm old-fashioned." She patted her overly processed blond hair. "You and your sisters just have modern ideas about things. If I were you —"

"You're not," Brenna pointed out, hoping to forestall whatever advice the older woman wanted to give.

She should have known it wouldn't work.

Millicent was on a roll, walking beside Brenna, her heels clicking against the sidewalk. "I'd have stuck it out with Dan. After all, no one is perfect. I know that better than most because I have been married and widowed more than once. A woman like you . . . you want everything: youth, charm, looks, money. But most of those things don't come tied up in the same package. You've got to keep that in mind when you're looking for a husband."

"I'm not looking for a husband," Brenna said, but Millicent just kept talking.

"Of course you are, dear. *All* women are. With your height, it's going to be challenging. I think that if you put on something pretty and do something with your makeup and hair, you could go back to New York and ask Dan to give you a second chance"

"Give *me* a second chance?"

"You certainly didn't break up with him. He's a doctor."

"He's also a bastard, Millicent," Brenna said.

Millicent's mouth opened. Closed. Opened again. "No wonder he broke up with you. No man wants to be disrespected by the woman he loves."

"No man wants to look at yellow hair, orange skin, and a size twelve body squeezed into a size ten dress, but you've still managed to find yourself four husbands." The words just kind of flew out of her mouth.

Flew out and hit Millicent right straight in the heart. She slapped a hand to her chest as if she wanted to make sure it was still beating. "Are you implying that I squeeze myself into too small clothes?" she demanded, her eyes blazing.

"That didn't come out the way I meant it."

"Then, how, exactly did you mean it to come out?"

They'd reached Chocolate Haven. Thank God. The OPEN sign hung in the front window, a few people lingered near the door, holding white bags or gold boxes.

"I'd like to explain," she said as she opened the door. "But, I have to work."

She walked inside, skirting past customers who were peering into display cases. Byron was behind the counter, his craggy face set in the smile she remembered from her childhood. He was in his element at Chocolate Haven, happy and content and always a little excited by the people who came for his chocolates.

"Sorry I'm late, Grandad," she said.

"Late? I opened ten minutes early. We're getting close to the end of summer vacation. People are anxious to have their last few treats before the kids are back in school. I had extra help this morning and was ready to open, so I didn't see any reason why I shouldn't." He smiled at a young mother who was holding a baby and the hand of a toddler. "What can I get for you this morning?"

"My sanity?" the woman said with a sigh as the toddler pressed his face against the glass case. "Matthew, no. You'll smear the glass."

"How about some chocolate drops for you, young man?" Byron put several into a small white bag and handed it to the boy. "And a pound of s'more fudge for you this morning, Annie?" he asked the young woman, and she smiled tiredly.

"You know me well, Byron."

"Also know that husband of yours. He'll probably eat half of it, so I'll just give you a little extra. A woman needs to keep nourished when she's got little ones." He motioned for Brenna to step behind the counter. "You want to fill the order for me, doll?"

"Sure."

"You remember how to use the scale?"

"Yes."

"Ring up the order?"

"Sure." It had been years since she'd helped at Chocolate Haven, but she'd worked retail in New York City. How much more difficult could this be?

"We've got those fancy new boxes." He nodded toward the boxes that lined a shelf. "And stick one of those gold stickers your sister likes on it to keep it closed."

"Okay."

"Good. Now, I'm going to walk on over to the diner. I decided I had a hankering for one of the pecan rolls."

"You're kidding, right?"

"I never kid about pecan rolls."

"Sh—" She pressed her lips together, eyeing the cute little kid and the tiny baby. "Okay. Fine. I can hold down the fort."

"I never doubted it."

Brenna lifted three pieces of s'more fudge and set them on a waxed-paper-covered scale. She wasn't paying all that much attention to the weight, though. She was too busy watching Byron looking at his reflection in the display window, smoothing down the flyaway remnants of his silver hair.

Good God in heaven!

He really did have a thing for Laurie.

"You look great, Grandad."

He scowled. "And I care why?"

"Don't ask me. You're the one looking at your reflection in the window."

"Hello!" Millicent called from the back of the line that had formed. "Are people actually going to be served this morning? I have other things I could be doing."

"Better get that order, doll," Byron said as he pulled off his apron and set it next to the cash register. "I'll be back in two shakes of a stick."

"Take your time," Brenna called as he walked out the door. She could see him as he passed the shop windows, his stride still hitched from the accident that had broken his hip and femur. He was recovering well, but he'd never be 100 percent. He'd always have the limp, and he'd probably never regain the strength he had before the accident. If he found comfort in a relationship with a sweet woman, she couldn't fault him for it.

It felt weird, though, thinking about him dating someone other than her grandmother.

Then again, everything felt strange lately. She'd been part of a couple for a long time. Now she wasn't. That wasn't bad. It was just odd and a little ill-fitting. She was so used to making plans based on someone else's schedule, hanging out with someone else's friends, making decisions as part of a team.

"Are you okay?" the young woman asked, and Brenna realized she was just standing there staring out the window while more and more people lined up in the queue waiting for Lamont chocolates.

"Fine." She finished the order quickly, filled the next and the next. Two hours later, the last customer walked out of the shop carrying the very last piece of Lamont fudge and the shop was finally quiet again.

Brenna wiped down the exterior of the display case and eyed the empty spots inside it. She knew what she was supposed to do: go into the kitchen and whip up a few batches of fudge. In theory, that should be a piece of cake. She'd just go into Byron's office, open his safe, take out the top-secret recipe, and follow it.

Yeah. In theory, it should be easy.

She wasn't sure how it was going to work out in actuality. She couldn't remember the last time she'd cooked a meal or baked any kind of treat. For the past few months, she'd been living off microwaved meals and cold cereal.

"Might as well give it a go," she muttered as she walked into her grandfather's office. It was tiny, with just enough space for a desk, a chair, and a file cabinet. He had an ancient desktop and a corkboard filled with business cards and Post-it notes. He'd put his wedding picture there: he and Alice smiling into each other's eyes.

Brenna's eyes burned as she looked at it. She missed her grandmother. She missed the way things used to be: uncomplicated, filled with opportunity. She hadn't even hit thirty yet and she felt like life had passed her by.

Which was stupid, because it hadn't.

She had plenty of time to get back on track. Once she finished helping Byron, she'd figure out what she was going to do with her life. Not modeling again. Been there, done that. Not a man either.

Maybe she'd go to college. Once she saved enough money to do it.

Okay, so getting a better job was priority number one.

Priority number two was figuring out what she wanted to do with her life.

She opened the safe, scrolled through an index file filled with recipes. The fudge recipe was right where it had always been, sandwiched between a note Alice had written about adding marshmallow and nuts to the recipe and Byron's response: *I love you for always, my darling.*

Brenna didn't know how the notes had ended up there, but they'd been there for as long as she'd been allowed to open the safe.

Her eyes were burning again.

Fatigue making her weepy.

She'd blame it on that, because she'd always been known as the practical sister, the one never prone to being overly emotional. She liked to think of herself as pragmatic. When she had a problem, she came up with a solution. Until lately. Lately, there'd been way more problems than she'd been able to find solutions for.

"So, make the fudge," she muttered, carrying the recipe into the kitchen, the glossy laminated card yellowed with age and stained with chocolatey fingerprints. Adeline's? She could almost guarantee her sister was the one who'd left prints there. Addie was nothing like the rest of the Lamont women. She was easygoing and uncomplicated and just plain fun to be around.

And that little baby belly of hers?

Adorable.

If Brenna didn't love her sister so much, she might be jealous of her happiness, but she did, and Adeline deserved every bit of joy she could get out of life.

Brenna's cell phone rang as she scooped sugar into a double boiler. She measured out some milk as she answered, the phone pressed to her ear. "Hello?"

"Brenna? Jeff Winthrop."

Dan's former business partner. One of the best plastic surgeons in the country, Jeff was smart, driven, and mad as hell that he'd been tricked by a guy he'd known since medical school. Brenna couldn't blame him for that, but she couldn't help him either. She'd told him that so many times, she should have just recorded the message and played it for him every time he called.

"What's up, Jeff?" She turned the heat up under the double broiler, stirring chocolate nibs into the goopy mix she'd created.

It looked like crap.

She was pretty sure it was going to taste like it.

"Just wondering if . . . ?"

"I haven't heard from Dan. If I had, I would have called the police first and you second."

"You were together for a long time. Your loyalty —"

"Why would I be loyal to a lying, cheating scumbag?"

"For the same reason the receptionist I hired helped him steal six million right out from under my nose."

"Simone wants him for the money and he wants her because she has no moral values and no compunction about following the law," she responded as the fudge mixture began to boil, bits of chocolate goop splattering across the kitchen.

She turned off the heat, tried to stir the fudge.

It had thickened so much, she could barely move the spoon through it.

She slammed the entire mess into the sink and stalked to the front of the house.

"Simone was a very sweet young woman,

Brenna. Until your fiancé —"

"Look, Jeff, I know you're pissed and I know you want your money back." She walked into the service area, smiling at two girls who were standing at the counter, their fists full of dollar bills. "But Dan has not contacted me. He will not be contacting me, so calling me every couple of days asking about him isn't going to do you any good."

"You're wrong. You're the best thing that ever happened to him and he knew it. He used to tell me that all the time. He got caught up in his addiction and he made a boatload of stupid decisions because of it, but he loved you and he *will* be contacting you. When he does, I want you to call me." He hung up. Just like he always did. She'd never much liked the guy, but she couldn't blame him for his anger or, even, his rudeness. He'd almost lost his medical practice because of what Dan had done.

Dan caught up in his addiction? Brenna didn't think so. She thought he'd been caught up in the adrenaline rush that came from gambling, cheating, lying. He'd been arrogant enough to think he could keep on doing what he was doing and never be caught, but Jeff wasn't stupid.

Neither was Brenna.

She'd been blind for a while, but she

wasn't stupid. Dan had always lived beyond his means and he'd always wanted more. She'd noticed that. She'd even talked to him about it. She'd been socking money away, making sure they had something for their future while he'd been planning their next big trip, his next big purchase, the nicer car he was going to buy. That had been a huge red flag. One she'd ignored because she'd been desperate to have all the things she'd secretly been dreaming of since she was a kid.

The house with the white picket fence. The doting husband. The cute and obnoxious children. The dog and cat and minivan.

"What can I get for you ladies?" she asked, her voice taking on the faux cheerful quality she'd been practicing for months. It was the one she used with her mother and sometimes with her sisters and always with Byron because she didn't want him to worry.

"Fudge," the shorter of the girls said, leaning in close to the glass, her long ponytail falling over her shoulder.

"We sold out. How about some chocolate bark? Or peanut butter bars? Those are really good."

"We wanted fudge," the other girl piped up, leaning in to whisper something in her friend's ear.

"Yeah." Ponytail girl nodded. "We'll come back when you have some. Thanks."

They both flounced out, and Brenna felt like a failure because she couldn't make the sale and hadn't made the fudge and because she was standing in Chocolate Haven pretending she was there because Byron needed help when, in reality, she was the one who needed it.

She might have gone into the kitchen and battled with the fudge again, but the door opened and more customers streamed in. They all wanted fudge. Of course. She managed to talk them into bonbons and chocolate bark, pecan bars and peanut butter balls. She was ringing up the last sale when Byron finally returned, a box in his hand and a huge grin on his face.

"Had fun, did you?" she asked as she handed a tall, skinny kid a dozen chocolate-covered pretzels. Fourteen, actually. He looked like he needed to eat and she didn't think Byron would miss two of his product.

"I've always had a fondness for sweets, doll. That's why I ended up taking over this chocolate shop." He grabbed his apron and put it on, whistling a little as he headed straight for the kitchen and the mess she'd left.

"Grandad!" she called, and he turned, the

happiness still all over his wrinkled face.

"Yeah?"

"There are more customers coming." She could see them approaching the door. Thank God. "Why don't you serve them and I'll . . . start a new batch of fudge."

"You sure you want to do that? You didn't seem all that keen on making candy this morning."

"I have to learn sometime. It might as well be now." *Before you get a look at the pot of crap I left back there.*

She hurried into the back, grabbed the pot of hardened chocolate, and tried to dump the contents into the trash. It stuck fast. She could hear Byron talking to someone, his voice cheery and loud. Typical Byron. He never let anyone walk away without giving them a piece of advice. He loved people and they loved him. Right now, that was going to benefit Brenna.

She dropped the pot into the sink again, ran hot water into it, and tried to loosen the chocolate that way. It stayed cement hard, the brown-gray goo mocking her from the bottom of Byron's favorite chocolate pot.

Someone knocked on the back door. She ignored it.

She had more important things to do than deal with whoever was out there.

She grabbed a butcher knife from a drawer and started cutting the fudge, the hot water still running, chocolaty drops of it flying into her face and across her shirt.

Whoever was at the door knocked again. And again.

She marched to the door and yanked it open.

"What do you . . . ?" The words fell away as she saw Belinda, her once-full cheeks hollowed out, her bright blue eyes dimmed by illness. The wheelchair she sat in seemed to be swallowing her whole, the black leather making her look even paler in comparison. Someone had scraped her hair away from her face, holding the short white strands with huge brown barrettes.

Belinda must have noticed Brenna looking at them. She reached up and touched the strands with her left hand, her right hand lying lax in her lap, a brace pressing against translucent skin. She looked old and frail, but when she smiled all the years fell away, and she was just the kind teacher who'd helped Brenna through some tough times.

"Belinda!" Brenna said, moving toward her.

The next thing she knew, she was on the ground, some guy with burn scars on his neck and fire in his eyes, holding her arm and growling, "You breathe too hard and you're dead."

"Mack!" Belinda called, her voice weak, the name just a little slurred. "Stop!"

Someone barreled into the kitchen, but Brenna was too busy trying not to breathe too hard to look to see who it was.

"What the hell is going on in here?" Byron demanded, and the guy with the scar looked into Brenna's eyes, blinked. All the anger left his face. All the color, too.

He released her arm, scrambled up.

"I'm sorry," he said, and she could see that he was. "I'm so sorry. The knife . . . I . . ." He shook his head, his shaggy hair falling over his forehead. "Sorry, Belinda," he said, and then he took off running.

Police sirens screaming through a small town weren't good.

Three police cars parked in front of Chocolate Haven? Even worse.

River pulled up behind a sheriff deputy's vehicle and jumped out of the truck. A small group of people were blocking the entrance to the store. He barged through them, muttering "Excuse me" as he went. Byron Lamont had sounded mad as a hornet when he'd called. Something about Mack, a knife,

109

an attack, and Belinda. That could have meant just about anything, but the guy hadn't seemed willing to explain. He'd shouted for River to get his ass to Chocolate Haven and then he'd hung up.

River had driven like a bat out of hell and it still hadn't felt like he was going fast enough. All he could think about was Belinda, somehow injured or worse, by a guy she'd taken in.

A deputy stood in front of the door to the shop, his arms crossed over his chest, his eyes shaded by sunglasses. River had seen him around town before. Usually in uniform. He had a thick white scar that ran the length of his face, touching the corner of his eye and the edge of his jaw.

"You're going to have to come back later," the deputy said.

"I'm here for Belinda."

"River Maynard?"

"That's right."

"Deputy Sheriff Jax Gordon." He offered a hand, his grip firm. "Belinda is in the kitchen. We offered to call her doctor, but she's insisting that she's fine."

Call her doctor why?

What the hell happened?

Why in God's name are there police cars everywhere?

River didn't have time to ask questions.

The deputy opened the door, gesturing for him to walk through. The shop was packed with people. A deputy sheriff. The sheriff. Byron and Janelle. Belinda and Brenna. They were the only two people in the room who weren't talking. Brenna had a tissue in her hand and was dabbing at tears that spilled down Belinda's cheeks.

"Belinda?" He crouched next to her, lifting her good hand. Her palm was cool and dry, her skin paper thin. He remembered when she'd kneaded bread and rolled out pie crust. When she'd hung bedsheets from the line in the back of the house on warm spring days just because she liked the way the fresh air made them smell.

Now she couldn't even do her own hair.

Someone had done it for her, though. Ugly brown barrettes pulled her hair away from her face, but they probably didn't do a whole lot to make her feel pretty. He needed to buy some nice headbands. Those would be easy enough for Belinda to use herself. "Are you okay?"

"It's Mack," she said, the words a little garbled.

"Mack?" He glanced around. No sign of the guy. "Where is he? What happened?"

"He knocked Brenna down and then he ran."

"He didn't just knock her down, Belinda," Byron cut in, his voice tinged with anger. "He attacked her."

"Don't exaggerate, Granddad," Brenna said, pressing the tissue into Belinda's hand and straightening. "Belinda is upset enough without you adding to things."

"She's got no need to be upset," Janelle Lamont retorted. "Mack did this. Rest assured, my family harbors no ill will toward *you*, Belinda."

At her words, tears began pouring down Belinda's face again.

"Mother, seriously," Brenna hissed, grabbing a fresh tissue from a box on the counter and wiping at the tears.

"It's okay, Belinda," River said, barely managing to keep the irritation out of his voice. He was sitting there in a shop with half a dozen people and he still didn't know exactly what had happened. Except that Mack had knocked Brenna down.

Attacked her?

He found that hard to believe. Mack had issues, but River didn't think violence was one of them.

"It is not okay," Belinda insisted. "Mack wouldn't hurt a fly. You know that, River."

"I know that you're upset and it's not good for you." He touched her cheek the way she'd done to him when he was young and brash and too stupid to know how fortunate he was to be in the Keeches' home.

"Mack —" she started to say, and he cut her off. Kindly, because Belinda had always been kind to him.

"I'll find him and I'll make sure he's okay. I promise."

She nodded, the tears still sliding down her cheeks, the tissue crumpled in her good hand. River would call her doctor once he got her home. Henry Monroe still made house calls, and River knew the guy would be happy to do a quick check of Belinda's vitals.

He patted Belinda's shoulder, turned his attention to Brenna. She looked fine. No visible bruises. No tears. She had a smudge of something on her cheek. Chocolate, maybe. A dot of it near her hairline and more spattered across her apron and shirt. If she'd been in a fight with anything, he thought it might have been a vat of fudge.

"Are you okay?" he asked.

"Sure, but I'd be a whole lot better if people weren't making such a big deal out of nothing."

"Nothing?" Janelle nearly shrieked. "You could have a concussion. An internal brain bleed. A ruptured organ."

"I don't," she said simply.

"That man attacked you!"

"Knocked me down. It was not an attack, and I already told you, I had a butcher knife in my hand when I opened the door. He probably thought I was going after Belinda."

"Whatever his motivation, he was wrong," the sheriff finally spoke up. He wasn't a young guy. Not old either. From what River had heard from old Benevolence friends, Kane Rainier was fair-minded and good at his job. "I'll need to speak with him. To make sure he knows it. You said Mack drove you here, Belinda?"

"Yes. My therapy finished early and I wanted to come see Brenna. I should never have asked Mack to drive me; then none of this would have happened."

"How about you don't play the blame game, Belinda?" River said gently. "There's nothing you could have or should have done any differently. Did Mack drive your car or his truck?"

"My car."

"Is it still here?"

"I . . . don't know."

"What color and make?" the sheriff's

deputy asked.

"Dark blue Chevy Impala."

"He drove away," Byron offered. "Ran to the car, jumped in, and left."

"Then he's probably back at the ranch," the sheriff said. "How about we head out there to see what he has to say for himself? You can go on ahead. That'll give you a little time to talk to him before I get there."

"Prepare him, you mean?"

"I don't want to cart him off to jail," the sheriff replied. "So, if you getting there ahead of me and smoothing the road will keep him from doing something we're all going to regret, then . . . yes, prepare him."

"Poor Mack," Belinda said quietly, and Janelle patted her arm, all of the anger gone from her face.

"He'll be fine, dear. How about I take you over to my house? It's been months since we've had any time to talk. We women can have tea and sandwiches and catch up while the men go deal with the pro . . . find Mack."

"I should go home," Belinda responded.

"You should spend time with your friend," River countered. "Let me handle this and then I'll come get you, okay?"

"I —"

"I'll go with him," Brenna offered. "I want

to let Mack know there are no hard feelings."

"There damn well are hard feelings," Byron muttered. "And I'm going out there to tell that young man so."

"No. You aren't," Brenna said. "Someone has to stay to run the shop. Don't even spend one more minute worrying about this, Belinda. Your friend is going to be just fine. Come on, River. Let's get this done."

Before he could respond, she grabbed his hand and dragged him out the back door.

CHAPTER FIVE

Time had not been kind to Freedom Ranch. The pretty white farmhouse Brenna had admired when she was a kid was now dingy and neglected, the porch sagging, the shutters listing at odd angles. The once lush lawn had gone dry, the grass brown and brittle. The roof looked like it needed work. So did the windows. One was cracked. The others were covered with a layer of grime.

Poor Belinda. She loved this place. It must be breaking her heart to see it this way. It was breaking *Brenna's* heart and she'd never spent more than a few hours at a time at the ranch.

River pulled up in front of the house and turned off the ignition. Silent. The same way he'd been for the entire ride.

He was angry, and she couldn't blame him. There'd been a lot of drama over nothing, and it had upset Belinda. She expected him to get out of the truck, march to the house to search for Mack without uttering one word. Instead, he speared her with a look that made her breath catch.

For a moment, she was just kind of sitting there, staring into a face that was handsome and interesting — high cheekbones, sharp jawline, dark gray eyes that had specks of silver and blue in them — and she was wondering what in the world she'd been thinking, getting in the truck with River.

"What are you going to tell the sheriff when he gets here?" River asked, the words breaking the tense silence.

"I wasn't planning on telling him anything. I answered his questions before you got to Chocolate Haven."

"So, you weren't withholding information for Belinda's sake?"

"What good would that have accomplished? Belinda may be in a wheelchair and she may have lost some of her physical abilities, but she's a strong woman. She can handle a lot more than people give her credit for." She reached for the door handle, ready to escape the truck and River. He was a little too intense, a little too good-looking, a little too much of everything she needed to avoid.

He touched her shoulder, his fingers skimming down her arm and resting on her knuckles. He wasn't holding her in place, but she didn't open the door.

Probably because she was an idiot when it came to men.

Obviously, because she was.

How many years had she wasted with Dan?

How many years of her life would she never, *ever* get back? All for the sake of a guy who hadn't wasted one moment of his precious time on her?

"The sheriff is going to ask if you want to press charges. You know that, right?" River asked, his voice smooth and deep and just a little cajoling.

She'd heard the tone before. Plenty of times from Dan and other men who'd wanted one thing or another from her. She might be an idiot when it came to men, but she wasn't going to be manipulated. "If you want to ask if I'm going to press charges, just do it. I don't need to be petted and stroked into doing the right thing."

She opened the door and hopped out of the truck, the scent of late-summer sun and dry earth filling her nose. She'd always loved it out here, just a little set apart from town and all the gossip and minidramas. There'd been days when she'd sat in the town library, a musty old book in her hands, her mind wandering to all the things she could do with her life.

It had often wandered here, to this old farm and its pretty little house on its pretty little piece of land.

The perfect place to make dreams come true.

That's what she'd thought then. Looking at it now, she was just reminded of how quickly dreams could turn into nightmares.

"You're angry," River said as he fell into step beside her.

"No." But she sure sounded like she was. Even she could hear the curtness in her voice.

"I wasn't trying to manipulate you, if that's what you think."

"Does it matter what I think?" She stepped onto a wide porch that wrapped around both sides of the house. Someone had replaced several floorboards, but the swing hung from one chain, a corner of it resting on the floor.

"Yes. It matters. I didn't come to town to cause problems. I came to help Belinda. I'm not going to be able to do that if I make enemies everywhere I go."

"Enemy is a strong word, River."

"So is friend. I'd rather be one than the other."

That made her smile, some of the tension she'd been feeling melting away. This wasn't her previous life; he wasn't Dan, always trying to make things work the way he wanted, always trying to convince her to give him what he thought he deserved. This was the beginning of her new start, her fresh beginning, an opportunity just waiting for her to take it.

She couldn't afford to screw that up by carrying baggage under each arm.

"Fine. We'll be friends, and for the record, I had no intention of pressing charges. Mack freaked out when he saw the knife I was holding. As soon as he realized I wasn't any danger to Belinda, he ran off. The guy must have PTSD. He needs help, not jail time."

"For Belinda's sake, I hope you're right. She doesn't need any more trouble than she's already got." He opened the front door, stepping back so she could cross the threshold.

The place smelled like must and age mixed with just a hint of furniture polish. The once shiny floor was scuffed and dingy from too many shoes and too many years of not being tended to. Pictures lined the walls of the large foyer, each one of a different foster child. Most of them were teen boys, the pictures spanning years from middle school through high school graduation. Some went beyond that: to college, families, children.

Brenna touched the closest one, running her finger along the dust-coated frame and wiping a smudge from the glass. It really was a shame, the mess the place had become.

"It needs a good cleaning," River said unapologetically. "I'm working one room at a time, trying to dig out from under it. There was a hole in the roof, and that had to be the first priority. I think one of the kids tried to clean yesterday, but when a place gets this far gone, it takes a lot more than a touch-up to get the job done properly."

"Kids? You mean Angel and Huckleberry?"

"Yeah. They may be adults, but they're kids to me."

She touched a piece of old, peeling wallpaper. Flowers from the eighties, it looked like. Had it been that long since the house had been updated? "There's the two of them, and Mack. You said she had four guests, right?"

"You've got a good memory. Joe stays on the weekends. He's thirty-one. He lives in some kind of group home during the week and stays here Friday and Saturday nights and all day Sunday."

"Doesn't he have family? People who would like him to be with them?"

"Belinda says he doesn't. She met him while she was teaching a painting class at the group home. One thing led to another, and now he spends every weekend here."

"Belinda is probably the best thing that has happened to him in a long time," Brenna said.

"Yeah, but *he's* not the best thing to happen to *her*. She's in her eighties and she deserves time to just chill out and enjoy life."

"Who says she's not doing that? Belinda was always happiest when she had lots of people here. Remember the big parties for Halloween and Christmas? The Easter egg hunts on the front lawn? The corn maze?"

He smiled. "She really did love having this house filled with people."

"Maybe she still does. And maybe having it empty just reminds her of all the things she used to have and doesn't anymore." She followed him into the kitchen. Unlike the rest of the house, this room was spotlessly clean. Not a dish in the sink, the floor scrubbed to a high shine, the counters empty except for one plate. Two pieces of

123

fudge lay in the middle of it, a tiny rose blossom someone must have plucked from overgrown bushes in the backyard lying right next to them.

"Huckleberry?" she asked, touching the soft petals of the rose. Once upon a time Dan had bought her roses. Beautiful, extravagant arrangements he'd have delivered to photo shoots or to the boutique. It hadn't taken her long to realize they were a show meant not for her but for others. This, though? It was lovely and simple and sweet.

"Probably," River said with a sigh. "That kid drives me batty. Leaving messes one day and doing something like this the next. Makes it really hard to dislike him."

"Then maybe you shouldn't," she said.

"Stop being reasonable, red. I'm not in the mood." He winked and stepped outside. "Mack is probably in the barn. Why don't you wait for the sheriff while I go find him?"

"I'll come with you," she said, stepping outside, her cheeks warm from that one wink and that one word: red.

It had been years and years since anyone had called her that. Before modeling and runways and everyone in Benevolence suddenly thinking she was more than what she was, back when she'd just been a weird little kid with her nose stuck in a book, hiding away from all the sadness at home, she'd had friends who'd called her red. She'd felt like one of a group then, like someone who mattered to somebody else, and she'd loved it.

Funny how she'd forgotten that.

"I'm not going to tell you what to do or not, but we can't count on Mack acting reasonably." River stepped through grass that had grown wild, tall blades of it twining together to make walking difficult.

Brenna picked her way through, skirting around beautiful pear and apple trees that lined the edges of the yard. A ladder leaned against one of them, a wicker basket abandoned beside it.

Someone had been picking fruit. For canning? Brenna had always wanted to learn the skill. Then again, she'd always imagined herself in a place like this, living a simple life: no glitter, no makeup, no fancy clothes and too-high shoes. No people pretending to be something they weren't to impress people who really didn't matter.

"River!" someone called, and Brenna nearly bumped into his back as he stopped short, glanced over his shoulder. She looked, too, and saw a kid with coppery hair and freckles, his skinny frame drowning in an oversized T-shirt and too-long jeans.

"Shit," River muttered, no heat in the word or in his eyes. "Huckleberry, go in the house and stay there until I tell you different."

"Who died and made you the boss?" the kid challenged, all arms and legs and petulant expression. "I heard something happened to Belinda. I came home to check on her." His gaze skirted past Brenna, landed full out on River.

Obviously, the two didn't get along.

And, obviously, River was exasperated.

He looked like he wanted to pick Huckleberry up and chuck him back into the house.

"Belinda is with a friend. I need to talk to Mack. You need to give us some space." He said it kindly enough, his words clearly enunciated.

"I will repeat my question," the kid said, something oddly refined about his speech. "Who died —"

"How about you don't repeat the question?" River cut him off. "The sheriff is on the way and I need to make sure Mack isn't going to make an ass of himself when he arrives. The last thing Belinda needs is one of you tossed into jail."

That seemed to seal Huckleberry's lips. He nodded, a curt, tight gesture that didn't go with his young face and gangly body. River might be right. The kid *might* be young, but he'd lived through enough for it to show in his eyes.

"What are you staring at?" Huckleberry asked, his attention suddenly on Brenna, his glare filled with fury and helplessness. Maybe he needed someone to take his frustration out on, but it wasn't going to be her.

"You. I was thinking that if you want to make yourself useful to Belinda," she responded, "you should clean the foyer and the hallway."

She turned away before he could respond, rushing after River. Who seemed hell-bent on getting to the barn and getting the meeting with Mack over with.

She wasn't sure what he thought he'd accomplish, but anything was better than having the guy tossed in jail.

She jogged through a wide gate that had once separated lush lawns from beautiful cornfields and pastures. Nothing remained but wilted cornstalks baked brown from the sun. The barn was just ahead, double-wide doors opening into a cavernous interior. There were horse stalls on one side, farm equipment on the other. Twenty years ago, the ranch had been bustling, every outbuilding humming with life; teenagers helping with the harvest or the planting. Now it seemed lonely, the empty stalls a reminder of the horses Dillard had once owned, the ponies he used to bring to parties and festivals.

They reached the threshold of the door, the scent of hay and dust filling Brenna's nose. River grabbed her hand when she would have walked farther into the building. "Wait here. Just in case."

"In case what?"

"I was wrong."

He walked deeper into the barn, dust motes dancing in the sunlight. "Mack?" he called. "You in here? The sheriff wants to talk to you. Nothing serious. Just a chat."

Something rustled in the loft, bits of hay raining down around River and falling onto his dark hair.

He glanced up. "Do you want me to come up there or are you coming down?"

"Coming down" was the gruff reply.

The wooden beams above Brenna's head groaned as Mack made his way across the loft. Seconds later, he appeared, climbing down a rickety ladder, a duffel bag slung over his shoulder.

He turned as he took the last step, his gaze settling on Brenna. "You okay?"

"Fine."

He nodded, the scars on his neck and cheek deep purple and painful looking. "I'd better get on my way, then."

"On your way where?" River asked, grabbing Brenna's wrist as she tried to walk past. She didn't know what she'd planned to do. Follow Mack? Tell him it was okay, that he didn't have to leave?

"To a place I can't cause any trouble. Tell Belinda —"

"No way," River cut him off, his voice sharp. "You're not getting off that easy. You want to go, you can look her in the eyes and tell her."

"I'd like to see you make me," Mack responded, hiking the duffel higher on his shoulder and heading toward the back of the barn.

There was an open door there, and Brenna expected he'd walk through it, head across the acres of fields to some little road that led to nowhere.

"You need to stop him," she said loudly enough that she knew Mack would hear.

He didn't even hesitate, just kept moving toward the door and whatever place he thought he'd be better off.

"Mack!" she called, trying to pull away from River.

He dragged her in a little closer.

"Don't," he whispered, the word just a breath against her ear. "He'll be happier if he stops himself."

What if he doesn't? she wanted to ask, but she met his eyes, found herself caught in his gaze. Again. Caught in that beautiful face with all its angles and sharpness. She wanted to look and keep looking. She wanted to spend an hour, a day, a week, studying him.

Surprised, she looked away, focused on Mack, who'd stopped at the threshold of the door and was standing there as if some invisible force kept him from walking through.

Finally, he turned, his shoulders slumped, his head down. "Fine. I'll talk to the damn sheriff," he muttered. "But I won't go to jail. I'm not going to jail. And I'm not staying around here causing more trouble than I already have."

He dropped his duffel and walked past them, heading back toward the house. Broad-shouldered, lean to the point of emaciation, he looked exactly like what he was: a soldier tired of the fight.

Brenna tried to dart after him, wanting to offer something — words of reassurance, promises that she wasn't going to press charges, apologies for her part in the fiasco.

"Don't," River said quietly, not holding her back this time. Except for that word and all the meaning she heard in it.

"I just want him to —"

"Know that you pity him?"

"I don't." She swung around, saw that he hadn't moved.

"You do, and he doesn't want it any more than you or I would."

"I just want to make sure everything is okay with him and the sheriff."

"You think he can't handle that himself?" He moved closer, his eyes glowing oddly in the muted light.

"I don't know what he can handle. I've barely spoken to him."

"Then don't presume to fight his battles, okay? You've got your own to worry about."

"What's that supposed to mean?" she demanded as he cupped her elbow, urging her out of the barn.

"Just a statement, red. A woman like you doesn't just end up in her old hometown because she's having a great life."

"I'm here to help my grandfather. I already told you that," she retorted, her cheeks blazing hot. Was she that obvious? Did she look that desperate? God, she hoped not!

"Maybe you're here to help your grandfather," he said, his hand still on her elbow, his fingers warm and callused against her skin. "But maybe you're also here because you need to be. For you."

"Look, River, you know nothing about me or my situation —"

"I know you like books," he replied, a smile hovering at the edges of his mouth and dancing in the depth of his gray eyes. "And that you used to hide in the corner of the library with your book hoard, reading until they kicked you out."

"That was a long time ago."

"Not that long. You're the same person you were then. Except that your hair is shorter." He touched the shorn strands. "Looks like the sheriff is here." He gestured to the house and the sheriff standing on the back porch with Mack. "Let's go see how this all plays out."

The day had gone to hell in a handbasket, but at least Mack hadn't run off. No matter how much River wanted Belinda's house empty and free of trouble, he couldn't stomach the idea of breaking her heart. He walked across the dried-out yard, Brenna beside him.

Chocolate and strawberries; that's what she made him think of. Probably because the scent of both clung to her, drifting through the air every time she moved.

Soft hair. Soft skin. The sweet scent of strawberries and the darker scent of chocolate? Not an easy combination to resist, but he would because he had more than his fair share of trouble to deal with, and Brenna? She looked like more.

Sheriff Rainier nodded as they approached, just a quick acknowledgment, his gaze on Mack. Neither seemed angry or defensive. That was good. What was better was that Huckleberry was still in the house, minding his own business and staying out of the way.

"Everything okay?" River asked as he walked up the porch stairs. Two of them needed to be replaced, the warped boards rotted from rain and exposure.

"We were discussing a meeting I attend twice a week. For vets. We get together, hash things out," the sheriff said, pulling out a business card and pressing it into Mack's hand. "I think it would be good for you, Mack, and good for Belinda. She wants to see you healthy and happy. I'm sure you want the same for her."

Mack shoved the card into his pocket and didn't comment.

If he planned to attend the meetings, he

133

didn't let on.

"Anything else, Sheriff?" he finally said, and Rainier shook his head.

"You're free to go. Hopefully, we won't have another incident like this one, though."

Mack shouldered past River, offered a curt nod in Brenna's direction, and headed back to the barn.

He looked defeated, and that bothered River. He didn't know squat about the man, but he knew the guy deserved better than whatever he'd gotten.

"Mack," he called. "I'm going to start scraping the trim on the windows. You want to grab the tools from the shed?"

Mack didn't slow his stride, but he did offer a thumbs-up.

Progress compared to what he usually gave River.

"I guess we'll see if he shows up at the meeting," Sheriff Rainier said, his gaze following Mack's progress. "For Belinda's sake, I hope he does. She's had her hands full around here the past couple of years. I'd like to see her live the next part of her life in peace."

"Had her hands full how?" Obviously, what River was seeing — the house falling to ruin, the strangers living in a place that had once been filled with family and friends

— was just the tip of the iceberg.

"People in and out all the time. A few of them not the kind of people I'd want living with my mother. Fortunately, Belinda always seems to win the lottery when it comes to the people she helps. Mack has been around for a while and he's chased more than one bad seed off. It's why I don't want to be too hard on him. When you leave, Belinda is going to need someone who has her back."

"Who says I'm leaving?"

"You're not?"

"Until things are settled around here, no." River sounded defensive. He felt defensive. He loved Belinda more than he'd ever been able to love his biological mother. That was the truth. The other truth was . . . it had been easy to pretend Belinda was doing just fine because she'd wanted him to believe it.

And because he'd wanted to be convinced.

He'd had his life, his business, his thriving career, and he'd been so focused on that, he'd happily swallowed every half-truth she'd fed him.

"Belinda says you own a couple of restaurants in Oregon," the sheriff commented.

"That's right."

"She's pretty proud of that. She says you were the hardest headed of all of her kids, but seeing you thrive has been the most rewarding thing she's ever experienced. The way she says it, the sun rises and falls on you." Nice to know, but River was certain there was a hell of a lot more the sheriff wanted to discuss. He was also sure it had nothing to do with what Belinda thought about him or his restaurants.

"Look, Sheriff —"

"Kane. People around here aren't big on formalities."

"Fine. *Kane,* you've got something you want to say. How about you just come out and say it."

The sheriff nodded. "Fair enough. People around here are worried."

"I'll bite," he said, forcing the word out through gritted teeth. "What are they worried about?"

"Angel is saying you're planning to move Belinda to Oregon when you go back."

"We've discussed it." Briefly, just a few days after Belinda had finally been released from the hospital. He'd been outlining all her options for therapy and recovery. She'd listened silently for a long time before she'd told him that she wasn't moving anywhere.

Obviously Angel had been eavesdropping and hadn't listened to the entire conversation.

"You discussed it with Belinda?"

"Does anyone else's opinion matter?"

"It doesn't, and as long as she's onboard with the plan, I guess I've got nothing to say about it." Kane glanced at his watch, frowned. "I've got a meeting with the mayor. I'll check in with Mack in a couple of days. See if he wants to attend that meeting with me. See you around, River. Brenna." He disappeared around the side of the house, and River was left standing there with Brenna who looked about ready to blow a gasket.

"Are you really moving Belinda to Oregon?" she demanded.

"I said we discussed it. I didn't say we were doing it."

"In other words, you wanted her to move there, and she refused."

"I want what is best for her. This," He jabbed his finger at the nearly rotted porch stairs, then at the yellowed grass and dried out fields, the peeling house paint and sagging eaves "is not what's best."

For a moment, she didn't say anything. Just stood there, her hair lying soft against her nape, her cheeks sprinkled with freckles, her gaze tracking the path his finger had taken, lingering on one mess after another.

"I'm sorry, River," she finally said.

"For what?"

"It sucks to see something you love falling to pieces."

"It sucked the night I got here and realized how far things had gone. Now, it's just a job I have to do to make sure Belinda can stay in the home she loves."

"You're a good guy. That's going to shock a lot of people in town."

"And you're a bookworm disguised as a fashion model. That will probably shock them too."

"How'd you guess? The hoard of books in the library when I was a kid?"

"And, the red wagon that you used to pull down Main Street. It was always filled with books, and you always looked like the most contented person in the world."

She smiled, but her eyes were sad. "I can't believe you remember that. *I'd* almost forgotten."

"It's hard to forget finally seeing what happiness was supposed to look like."

"That was a long time ago," she murmured, her cheeks tinged with pink, her eyes more purple than blue.

"Not so long ago," he said, wrapping his fingers around her wrist, tugging her a few steps closer, because she was there, and he was, and he thought it might not be a bad thing to get a little closer.

"I see, you were back in the battle," he murmured, touching the speck of chocolate on her temple.

"It wasn't a battle. It was an all-out war."

"Should I ask who won?" he said, rubbing the speck away.

"The fudge. But, I plan to win the next round. Which reminds me. I've got to get back to the shop." She tugged away, darted to the back door and into the house. He followed, walking into the kitchen, the scent of furniture polish hitting him in the face. It smelled like someone had sprayed an entire can of the stuff.

"What the hell?" he muttered, stalking into the hallway.

Huckleberry was there, one of the kitchen chairs beside him, piled with pictures and frames. The kid had a dust rag in one hand and a spray bottle in the other, and for the first time since River had been back, the wood banister wasn't coated with dust.

"What are you doing?" he asked, the question as redundant as the squirt of polish Huckleberry added to the rag.

The kid lifted a picture, swiped the rag around the frame, and hung it back on the wall. "Cleaning. No sense in Belinda coming home to a mess."

"Good job," Brenna said, sashaying past

Huckleberry and out the front door.

She was keeping her distance.

No doubt about that, and that's what River should be doing too. His life was full to overflowing, and he didn't need or want to add anyone or anything to it.

He needed to bring Brenna back to the shop, get Belinda from Janelle's, call his restaurant managers to make sure all their suppliers had come through. Fresh and local: that was his goal with every dish served. He'd made his fortune and his reputation off that, but maybe it wasn't as important as he'd once thought. Maybe there were other things he should be focusing on.

He left the house, the scent of furniture polish seeming to follow him out into the bright sunshine. He could remember the place the way it used to be. He could make it that way again if he wanted to. He had the money. He could make the time.

But . . . Benevolence?

Not the place he'd ever wanted to return to. Not a place he'd ever wanted to live.

He crossed the porch, trying to ignore the broken swing, the railings that still needed to be whitewashed, the empty flower baskets, but Brenna was waiting at his truck and he could see she was looking, taking in all the little details of a house that had been neglected for way too long.

Her phone rang as he approached and she pulled it out of her apron pocket, glanced at the number.

"Perfect," she muttered, tossing the phone into her pocket again.

"Your mother?" He opened the truck door and she scrambled in, her cheeks red. Embarrassment or anger, he couldn't tell which.

"My mother would be easy compared to him."

"Your ex?"

"I wish it *were* my ex, I'd like to give him a piece of my mind. Actually, I'd like to give him a kick in the . . ." She pressed her lips together. "I've really got to stop."

"What?"

"Thinking about Dan, because I promised myself that I'd clean up my language before Adeline's baby is born, and that's just not going to be possible if I keep dwelling on the jerk."

"If he's a jerk," he said, climbing into the truck and starting the engine, "why are you dwelling on him?"

"He screwed up my life, that's why."

"What did he do? Cheat on you?"

"That question is a little personal, don't you think?"

"Me asking doesn't mean you have to answer."

She didn't say another word as he backed out of the driveway and headed back into town. The way he saw it, no answer was *the* answer.

The guy had cheated. Brenna had dumped him. Life had gone on, but she hadn't.

It seemed to River that she would have. Unless something else had happened. Something to do with the call she hadn't taken.

"Can you drop me off at the shop before you pick Belinda up?" she asked quietly. "I don't want to leave Byron by himself for too long."

"Sure." He didn't point out that Byron seemed perfectly capable of running the shop. He thought she probably already knew it. He also didn't point out the fact that her phone was ringing again.

He thought she already knew that, too.

He pulled up in front of Chocolate Haven and she jumped out of the truck, offering him a quick thank you before she darted inside.

Whatever Brenna's problems, she was home.

That had to feel good.

Or maybe not.

Maybe, like for River, Benevolence had

been the one place she'd never planned on returning to.

An odd thought, considering the fact that she was one of the Lamont girls. If there had ever been Benevolence royalty, they'd been it. The little world they'd grown up in had been theirs for the taking, and he'd had moments of pure jealousy about that. He'd had to work his butt off every moment of every day to prove his worth. All Brenna and her sisters had to do was smile.

That had been a long time ago.

People changed.

He sure as hell must have, because the town he'd always looked down on, the place he'd hated when he was a kid, looked a lot better through adult eyes: the quaint shops that lined Main Street, the mature trees that shaded the sidewalk.

Autumn was just around the corner. There were hints of it in the golden leaves of a willow, the deep yellow of distant hayfields. It made him think of the parties Belinda used to host: harvest festivals for the church kids and Halloween parties for the schools. She and Dillard would open up the house and let dozens of kids run in and out. There'd always been games and food, sometimes a live band, and always the ponies Dillard had loved so much.

When had he gotten rid of those?

Sometime after River had left.

Dillard and Belinda had never mentioned it. They'd never asked for help or begged him to come home. They'd seemed content to fly out to visit every couple of months, to play tourist in Oregon and ooh and aah over the big city.

He'd always known they were doing it for him — staying in a place they didn't really like for the sake of someone they loved.

He couldn't do any less for them.

He wouldn't.

He'd stay in Benevolence as long as he needed to.

And, maybe, while he was there, he'd learn to love it the way Dillard and Belinda had.

CHAPTER SIX

Four days into her job at Chocolate Haven and Brenna realized something: she hated fudge.

Hated it with a passion that rivaled her hatred of Dan the dope. Probably hated it more than Dan because she couldn't really say she hated the guy. Angry? Yes. Disgusted? Of course. But hate? That took a lot of emotion, and she'd realized long before Dan had skipped town that she didn't have a whole lot of that left for him.

Wasn't love supposed to be about passion? About needing to be with someone almost as much as you needed to breathe?

Or was that all just a romantic notion, written in books and songs, but never the reality of what real love was meant to be?

She had no idea because all she'd really ever felt for Dan was attraction and affection. He'd swept her off her feet. She could admit that, but he'd never really had her heart.

She dumped another batch of rock-hard fudge into the trash can, scraping bits of it off the edges of the pan. She needed to wash it, but she'd run out of energy hours ago. All she really wanted to do was go up to the apartment, curl up with a hot cup of tea, and read the book she'd borrowed on the sly from the library.

Candy Making for Dummies.

Because she couldn't keep pretending to be good at this, and Byron really, truly believed she had the knack, the magic touch, the thing that made a simple piece of chocolate into something decadent.

Only she didn't.

She tossed the pan into the sink, water splashing up over the edge and onto the floor.

"Darn it," she muttered, and Byron peeked out of his office.

"Everything okay, doll?" he asked, and she smiled that big fake smile she'd been practicing for the past few days.

Four days of torturous hell, but she'd never let him know it.

"Sure. Just cleaning up."

"I've finished the books, so I'll give you a hand."

"What good is it doing for me to be here if you do all the work?"

"I'm not doing all the work."

"Granddad, you've been here every hour of every day I've been here."

"Helping you get settled into the job so when I leave on Monday —"

"Leave?" She went cold at the thought. With Chase in college every day, she'd be left alone to make the fudge, the bonbons, the candy hearts, and pretty chocolate roses.

"I've got that Alaskan fishing trip planned. I know I told you about it." He took a cigar from his pocket and clamped it between his teeth.

He was lying. She could tell by the gleam in his eyes.

"No. You did not say one word about a fishing trip. Ever. Not before I got here and not after."

"Really?" He tried to look confused, but he wasn't pulling it off.

"You lied to me, Granddad," she accused. "You didn't need my help while Addie was out, you needed me to run the shop while you went fishing!"

"Could be I was thinking about that when I asked you to come." He grinned. "But you can't say it hasn't been working out nicely for you to be here."

"Do you see the mess I've made in your kitchen?" She swung around in a circle, pointing at dirty pans and overflowing bowls. She wanted to cry. She really did, and she wasn't even sure why. "This is not working out."

"What you need," Byron said calmly, "is a little time to yourself, a little space with me not hanging over your shoulder telling you what to do."

"More space to make a bigger mess? Is that what you're saying? That's not going to solve the problem."

"More space to let the magic happen." He winked, and she was tempted to yank the cigar out from between his teeth and stomp it into dust.

"There is no magic here. There is just a bucketload of wasted ingredients."

"How can there be magic when you've got an old man getting in the way of you making it? Once I'm on my trip, and you're on your own —"

"How long are we talking about?" she asked through gritted teeth. She would not let Byron know how much she was panicking.

"Two weeks," he said cheerfully.

"Your business will be a bust by then, Granddad. I'll have run Chocolate Haven out of the chocolate world. You'll come back from your fishing trip —"

"It's not like you to be melodramatic, Brenna." He eyed her thoughtfully. "You've traveled all over the world. On your own. You've lived on your own in New York City, for God's sake. What's so scary about being alone in this shop for two weeks?"

"I —"

"If you're afraid of failing, stop. You can't fail at a family business. If you're worried about the fudge." He poked his finger toward the batch she'd just tossed. "It'll come to you."

"You're putting a whole lot of faith in that, Granddad."

"Why shouldn't I? You're a Lamont. Lamonts know fudge. The candy making business —"

"Runs through their blood." She sighed.

"Well, it does," he said with a quiet huff. "Now, how about we get to cleaning? I've got a hot date tonight, and I don't want to miss it."

"Hot date?" The comment was almost enough to distract her from the fact that she'd be running the shop on her own for two weeks. "With who?"

"Might be it's someone you know. Might be it isn't."

149

"Laura Beth?" she guessed, and his face flushed.

"Now, why would you bring her up? I'm actually taking Belinda to the cakewalk at Benevolence Baptist."

"She's in a wheelchair," she pointed out.

"And I am going to roll her around until we win a damn cake. You got a problem with that?"

"No. I just thought —"

"You remember how close Dillard and I used to be? We used to hunt together and fish together. We were like brothers, and that makes Belinda like my sister-in-law. When I saw her the other day . . ." He shook his head. "It nearly broke my heart that I'd let so much time slip away between visits."

"You did have a pretty serious accident, Granddad. It's not like you've been healthy."

"Excuses are easy to make, kid, but time? That's hard to get back once you lose it. So I called Belinda up and we started chatting. Turns out Elmer Wilkinson has been calling on her off and on for the past couple months, but he's afraid to do it now that River is around."

"Elmer Wilkinson?"

"Owns that farm that butts right up to the ranch? Mary was his wife. She passed about ten years ago."

She didn't remember, but she nodded anyway. "So what does that have to do with you and Belinda going to the cakewalk?"

"Elmer is going to be there. The two of them can have a little time together and I can hang out with Lau . . ."

"Aha! This is about Laurie!"

"It most certainly is not!" he insisted.

They probably would have continued the argument, but someone knocked on the back door.

"That's got to be her," he said, rushing to take off his apron and running his hand over his hair.

"Laura Beth?"

"Belinda. River said he'd drop her off after therapy. Get with the program, girl!" he said, swinging open the back door.

Cold air rushed in, and then Belinda was there, being wheeled in by River, who looked . . .

Great.

Really great.

His dark hair ruffled by the breeze, his dark slacks and white dress shirt crisp. A tie hung around his neck, the ends of it brushing the chair as he leaned over to say something to Belinda.

Whatever he said, it made her smile.

She looked pretty. Her white hair styled in

soft curls that framed her face, a little blush on her gaunt cheeks. Someone had painted her nails pale pink and decorated her black wrist brace with silver glitter.

"You look lovely, my dear," Byron said, gallantly kissing her knuckles. She smiled, brushing her hand over her blue dress.

She even had heels on her feet. Low ones with tiny little bows on the toes. "Thank you for taking me, Byron. I'm sure we will both have a good time."

Her words were clearer than they'd been the day Mack had tackled Brenna. Maybe the stress had made speech more difficult.

"Have a good time?" Byron stepped behind the chair and turned her back toward the door. "We're winning a cake, Belinda Mae. You mark my words on that."

She laughed, the sound smothered by the clatter of leaves blowing across the pavement.

"Do you need help getting the chair —" River began.

"Young man!" Byron interrupted. "Belinda and I can handle this just fine."

With that, he rolled her out the door.

"I hope this isn't a mistake," River said, standing in the threshold, probably watching Byron make his way to his old Cadillac.

"They'll be fine," Brenna said, but she

wasn't so sure.

It was true Byron had been moving around the shop like a guy twenty years his junior, but that didn't mean he could help Belinda into a car or lift a wheelchair into the trunk.

"I'd feel a lot better if I were going with them."

"Who says you can't?" she asked, grabbing a dirty bowl and dunking it under hot water.

"Belinda threatened to disown me if I showed my face at the cakewalk. She says I've been hovering." He edged in beside her, grabbing an apron from the hook near the door and tying it around his waist.

"Have you been?"

"Yeah. I have. Huckleberry and Mack picked six baskets of apples and three baskets of pears. Belinda is bound and determined to can every last one of them."

"I've always wanted to do that." She shifted to the side, gave him room to dry while she washed.

"Can pears and apples?"

"Sure. Why not? Laura Ingalls Wilder wrote about her mother putting up jars of vegetables and fruits, and I always thought it sounded like fun." The words slipped out, the childhood memory something she'd never shared with anyone. Not because she was embarrassed by it, but because it had never come up.

In her other life, she'd talked about fashion and photo shoots and a dozen other things that really didn't matter. Not in any way that mattered to her. In her head, though, she'd always been one of those women who bustled around a hot kitchen, baking pies and cakes and feeding everyone who stopped by.

She thought River might laugh, but he stopped drying the dish she'd handed him and studied her for a moment. "I trained as a chef, and I've spent a lot of time learning the old way of doing things. Modern techniques are great, but tradition brings us back to the roots of who we are. Seems like someone like you would appreciate that." He smiled, and she found herself smiling right along with him.

"First you say I'm a bookworm. Now, you say I'm traditional? What clued you in this time? My old-fashioned hair cut?" She touched the hair Dan had always insisted go with her image: hip and chic, modern and edgy.

"Image isn't always the same as identity," he responded. "Look at me. If you asked around town, people would probably say I rode off into the sunset to rob banks and run drugs. In reality, I graduated from college, went to culinary school. Opened restaurants. I spent more than one summer feeding ranch hands. I learned to bake bread, can vegetables, and make a lot of good food out of a few very good ingredients while I was at it. If you really want to learn, I can teach you."

"I couldn't ask you to do that." She *wouldn't* ask him because there was no way on God's green earth she was going to spend any more time than necessary with River.

There was just something about him . . .

Something she hadn't been able to put out of her mind. She knew, because she'd spent four days trying, four nights tapping her fingers against an empty cigarette box, thinking about the way he'd been with Mack and with Belinda and with her.

Idiot, her mind shouted, but her heart gave a tiny little jump as she looked into his eyes.

"I could teach you a little about chocolate, too," he continued as if she hadn't spoken. "I apprenticed under a master chocolatier in France. It's not my thing, but I did learn a lot. There's an art to tempering. Once you learn that, the rest is pretty easy."

"Like I said, I couldn't put you out."

"You wouldn't be. Besides," he set the

bowl in the cupboard, "I have a favor to ask of you."

"What kind of favor?"

"No need to sound so suspicious, red. It's all on the up-and-up."

She grabbed a pan from the stove, this one filled with the remnants of the marshmallow she'd been trying to make. "What favor?" she repeated.

"I've been thinking about what you said regarding the ranch, about how much Belinda always loved having people around. She needs a way to make money to keep the ranch running. *Local* and *organic* are big terms in the food market. People want to eat clean and they want to be closer to their food sources."

"Okay," she said, her pulse beating a little faster. Not because she was looking in his eyes or because he was staring into hers. No. This time, it was because she heard passion in his voice, determination. He'd been thinking about this a lot, and whatever it was, he planned to make it work.

"Belinda has that huge old farmhouse, and aside from the dust and age, it's in pretty good shape. I'm going to clean it up, furnish it, and advertise it as a bed-and-breakfast where people can come to help with the harvest and learn to make good, wholesome food from ingredients grown right in their own backyards."

"That," she said, trying to wrap her mind around it, trying to envision this big thing happening in Benevolence, "is huge."

"Yeah." He grinned, setting another bowl into the cupboard, his biceps bulging against the cotton fabric of his shirt. "I like huge projects. I love when people tell me something won't work. It gives me the incentive to prove them wrong."

"Have you been talking to people about it?"

"I ran it by one of my restaurant managers and my financial adviser. They think I'm nuts. I also talked to the business council in Benevolence. We had a meeting yesterday."

"And . . . ?"

"That's where the favor comes in." He stopped drying, turned her so they were face-to-face. "They seem . . . interested. The idea of local produce, local products, local business benefiting is never a bad thing for a town this size. Seasonal tourists are moneymakers, and if they can add to them, it's a win-win."

"I still don't see what that has to do with me."

"They want me to prove I can use local people and businesses to get the farmhouse

157

up to snuff. Once I've proven it can be done, they said they'll grant me the permit to add a large demonstration kitchen. I can have classes there, show guests how to use what they harvest at home to create restaurant-quality dishes."

"And the favor?" she prodded, because she still had no idea where she fit into this thing.

"I was talking to Adeline about finances this morning and she mentioned you had a shop in New York City."

"A *clothing* shop."

"Which you designed. She showed me photos: lots of antiques and vintage wall-paper. Old books on shelves on the walls."

"Those were just small details. No one paid much attention to them." She went back to scrubbing the marshmallow pot because her cheeks had gone hot. She'd added the antiques, the books, the vintage wallpaper, after the interior designer Dan had insisted on had finished his work. The posh modern shop had been exactly what Dan thought would match her reputation as a runway model.

"Details make the dish, red," he replied. "The right cheese, the perfectly ripe tomato, the crisp spinach for the salad. Details are what make the person, too. Like your freckles." He touched a spot on her cheek, and a shiver of excitement raced up her spine. "Your spiky hair. The way your mouth curves downward when you're thinking."

He didn't touch that.

Thank God!

She moved out of reach. Just in case.

She was done with excitement, with men, with complications.

But she was intrigued by what he was saying and the fact that he wasn't talking about making a buck. He was talking about saving a lifestyle, maintaining a tradition that was nearly as old as the town. "What does Belinda think about your idea?"

"I haven't run it by her yet. I don't want her to be disappointed if it doesn't work out. If you agree to help me out, I'm just going to tell her that I've hired some people to update the farmhouse. What I'd like you to do is go to some of the local antique shops, pick up some things that will work in the farmhouse. Choose the paint colors. I know you're busy here during the day, but Adeline said she'd talk to some shop owners to see if they'll let you look around after hours. She does all their taxes so she's got an in with most of them."

"Decorating my own shop is a lot different from helping you with a project like this." But the idea excited her. She couldn't deny that any more than she could deny the little ping of heat that danced up her arm when he grabbed her hand and pulled her to the pantry.

"You see all this?" he asked, gesturing to dozens of ingredients that lined the shelves. "This I know about. Decorating? Not so much. You have an eye for it that I lack, and you're the only local person who has any experience. I know. I've been asking around."

"There's a lady in Spokane —"

"*Local,*" he emphasized. "Otherwise I'll lose the bid for the permit."

"River, I really don't have experience. I decorated one shop."

"A highly successful shop," he pointed out.

Until my fiancé emptied out the business account, she almost said, but that was a story for another time. One she had no intention of telling anyone. "I really don't think —"

"I hear Byron is going on a fishing trip next week," he cut in, grabbing a clean dish towel and scrubbing the stove with it. Somehow the chocolate and marshmallow and peanut butter splattered all over it disappeared.

There was the magic Byron had been talking about.

Which sucked, because she needed it way more than River did. "Who told you that?"

"Your sister. She's concerned you might be in over your head."

"Does it look like I'm in over my head?" she muttered, because she knew damn well it did.

"Fair trade, red. I come in three nights a week to help you make candy. You come over to the ranch the other two nights and get the place ready for the business council's visit."

"When is that?"

"Two weeks from today."

"That's not much time."

"You're saying no?" He rinsed the rag in steamy hot water, swiped chocolate from the edge of the sink. Somehow, the kitchen was nearly clean, and all she'd done was wash one marshmallow pot.

"I'm saying yes," she found herself saying, the words tumbling out of her mouth before she could stop them.

River grinned, the kind of I-got-what-I-wanted smirk that should have made her blood boil.

Instead, she was grinning, too, smiling like

some inane schoolgirl who'd pleased her crush.

"I . . . need to take out the trash," she managed to say, grabbing the bag and yanking it out of the can.

She was pretty sure she'd left a trail of chocolate on the shop floor. She didn't bother looking. She'd clean it later. After River left and took his contagious smile and big plans with him.

He'd gotten what he wanted, and that should have been all River cared about. After four fifteen-hour days, long meetings, longer phone conversations, and just about every single thing that could go wrong at the ranch going wrong, he was ready for something to go right.

Yeah. He had what he wanted: an agreement from Brenna to help with the ranch. That would make the business council happy and would smooth the way for the permit he needed.

But he'd lied to get what he wanted, and that didn't sit well with him

Truth? He had an eye for detail and he could have easily chosen antiques from any of the shops on Main Street. He could choose paint. He could choose lighting fixtures, linens, everything a place like he'd envisioned was going to need.

What he couldn't do was all of it himself and still expect a bunch of old-timers who had their heads up their backsides to issue the permit.

They remembered him from his wild days.

That was the problem.

They figured he was shooting for the moon, with no plan for the hard work it would take to get there. They probably also figured he was going to make more of a mess of their town than he would bring in as a profit.

They were wrong on all counts.

He'd showed them facts and figures, charts and financial statements, but River had a reputation. In Benevolence that could be difficult to overcome. Even if the reputation *was* over a decade old.

He grabbed a sponge from the edge of the sink and used it to wipe down cabinets that had somehow been splattered with chocolate and cream and — unless he missed his guess — melted sugar.

Regardless of whether he really needed Brenna's help, she needed his. He doubted she'd admit it, but the evidence was everywhere: the counters, the floor, the trash bag filled with discards she'd just dragged out.

Speaking of which, it was taking her a long

time to return from her trash run.

Not his worry. Benevolence was a small town, and a safe one. If she wanted to wander around after dark, it was nothing to him.

Except he kept remembering that phone call she hadn't answered and the look on her face when he'd asked about it.

There was something going on with her. Something more than the broken engagement everyone in town seemed to be whispering about. He'd heard about it at the diner, at the barber, at the flower shop where he'd bought Belinda a dozen orange daylilies. Everyone, everywhere, seemed to know that Brenna had dumped her two-timing fiancé. But no one seemed to know why she'd gotten rid of her posh, successful clothing boutique.

A broken heart was what most of the women seemed to think.

Not that River paid all that much attention, but it was difficult not to hear the blue-haired ladies at the diner whispering about the lovelorn Lamont sister.

Brenna didn't seem heartbroken to him.

She seemed tired, overwhelmed, and a little sad, but she didn't seem heartbroken.

She also still wasn't back.

He dried his hands on a dish rag and

opened the back door.

Summer was fading quickly, the cold, crisp night air reminding him of all the things that were good about eastern Washington. No humidity in the air, no hot nights at the end of long summer days. Just the sun going down and coolness setting in, the air clean and fresh with the coming fall.

He could hear a woman's voice and he followed the sound around the side of the building and into a narrow alley. A Dumpster stood against one wall and Brenna stood next to it, the trash bag abandoned at her feet.

"Jeff, you really need to stop calling me," she said as River approached. She must have heard him, but she gave no indication of it. The phone was pressed to her ear and she tapped her free hand against her thigh, impatience in every line of her body. "I already told you he didn't. I already told you he wouldn't."

A long pause as River grabbed the trash bag and tossed it into the Dumpster, then a sigh.

"Right. I know what he owes you. He owes me, too, but there's absolutely nothing I can do about either thing. Okay, Jeff. I get it. Like I said the last four times you called, I'll contact you if I hear from him."

She shoved the phone into her apron pocket and raked her hand through her hair. "Sorry about that."

"Who's Jeff?" he asked, and she frowned.

"No one important."

"If he's not important, why has he called you four times?"

"Because he knows my ex and he wants to get in touch with him."

"That explains nothing, red."

"Did I imply I planned to explain?" She tossed the words over her shoulder as she walked out of the alley.

"You didn't imply you weren't going to."

She stopped short and turned, her face a pale oval in the darkness. She'd been thin as a kid, tall and gangly compared to her peers. Now she looked gaunt. Surprising, because she'd been working in a chocolate shop for nearly a week.

"I know that in a town this size, everything is everyone's business," she said quietly, "but that doesn't mean I want everyone knowing I have a guy named Jeff calling me several times a day. I'd appreciate it if you kept that to yourself."

"I'm too busy to spread gossip. Even if I weren't, it's not my style."

"Sorry; that probably sounded rude." She crossed the lot and yanked at the door, breathing a sigh of relief when it opened. "Thank God for small miracles. I forgot to bring the key. We could have both been locked out. Which would have meant finding Granddad and telling him."

"Finding Byron might not be a bad idea." He untied his apron and hung it from a hook near the back door. "He's probably getting Belinda into all kinds of trouble."

"How much trouble can they get into at church?" She pulled ingredients from the pantry, set them on the counter. Unless he missed his guess, she was going to dive into another battle with chocolate.

A useless endeavor unless it was something she really wanted to do. Based on the tension in her shoulders and the expression on her face, he'd say it wasn't.

"Enough that we should probably check on them."

"We?" she asked as he tugged at her apron strings.

"I wouldn't want to face Byron alone," he replied as she batted at his hands and tried to keep the apron in place.

"Seriously, River, I'm not going." She pulled away, the apron sliding off her hips and falling onto the floor in a puddle of white cotton. "I have a million things to do here."

"Like?"

"Chocolate. Fudge. More chocolate. And I might attempt the marshmallows again."

"I'm not sure the stove or the pan can take that," he said, and she offered a tired smile.

"You could be right, but like you said, Byron is leaving Monday. I'll have to run this place mostly on my own, and that means I have to learn how to make all this shi . . . crap."

"Not tonight. Tonight, you need to take a break." He grabbed the apron, took her phone from the pocket, and handed it to her.

"River —"

"There are certain things I know to be true about cooking. One of them is, if your heart isn't in it, you might as well not."

"Who says my heart isn't in it?"

"The look on your face when you took these out of the pantry." He replaced the ingredients, took a last look at the kitchen. Spotless. Just the way a kitchen should be. "We'll have your first lesson tomorrow morning. Six A.M., because it's a therapy day. Just an hour. Tonight, we'll go check on Byron and Belinda, and then we'll go over to my place and you'll give me some ideas for the paint and the décor."

"You're making a lot of plans without asking me if I'm cool with them." She stalked into the hallway, came back a moment later with a jacket in her hands and a backpack over her shoulder.

"I run two restaurants. I'm used to making quick decisions about a lot of things."

She raised a brow, the deep red of it perfectly matching her hair. Her lashes were red, too, a lighter shade, and they made her eyes seem an even deeper blue. "So?" she demanded.

"So, are you cool with them?"

She hesitated for a moment, her gaunt face about three shades paler than he thought it should have been. "I guess I am. I'm sick of the smell of chocolate, and the thought of cleaning out one more marshmallow pan makes me want to puke."

"How do you feel about sirloin burgers with sautéed onions and fresh greens? Maybe some steak fries to go with them?"

"I feel like I could eat a dozen. Of each."

"Good. That's what I was planning to make for Belinda before she announced she had plans."

"You don't mean you're going to cook for me?" She sounded appalled, but he didn't give her time to think about it. He opened the door, hurried her out into the cool, crisp night.

"Why not? I've cooked for hundreds of people in my lifetime. One more isn't going to make a difference. Besides, Angel is home tonight, and she needs meat to keep that kid growing right. You want to take one car or two?"

"Two, but —"

"You know where the church is, right?"

"Yes, but —"

"I'll meet you over there." He climbed into the truck and closed the door, waiting while she walked to her Chrysler and got in. Her headlights went on and she pulled out of the parking lot, driving slowly through the town she must know as well as she knew the back of her hand.

That was the thing about Benevolence: you could leave it for years and come back, and it would still be the same. A few houses might be different colors, the foliage might be more mature, maybe a few of the people would have changed, but the town itself — the easy vibe of it, the slow pace and community sense of it — that didn't ever change.

As a teen, River had been too young to appreciate it. He'd been too brash to think that traditions had meaning, too caught up in his need for success and independence to ever think he'd want to be tied to a place like this.

Now?

He wasn't so sure.

He'd made a lot of plans that were going to take a lot of time to come into fruition. Freedom Ranch, as he envisioned it, would be a tourist attraction *and* a place for locals to gather. It would be that one place people remembered and returned to year after year. He could hire people to fix up the farmhouse, till and plant and harvest the land, raise the chickens, the beef, the sows. Sure, he could do that. He could bring in crews and teams and managers just like he had in his restaurants, but that was a sterile approach to something that had to be deeply meaningful. In a town like this, that was what mattered most: the meaning behind a thing, not the thing itself.

That was something to keep in mind when things got hectic. He knew they would. They always did when shake-ups occurred. In Benevolence, anything different from the status quo was a shake-up, and what he was proposing was more than different. It was an entirely new way of thinking about tradition, an entirely new moneymaking avenue.

People were going to fight it.

River was going to fight back.

He was going to win.

Hopefully, when everything was said and done, the people in town would thank him for it. He had a feeling that was going to be a long, long way down the road.

CHAPTER SEVEN

They spied on Belinda and Byron for ten minutes, standing at a window outside Benevolence Baptist Church's reception hall and watching as an elderly man with a cowboy hat and a long white beard wheeled Belinda around a cake table. She looked happy. The guy looked happier.

Byron looked besotted.

Brenna could see him in the corner of the room, a cup of punch in one hand, his other hand in the pocket of one of his snazziest sports coats, 1920s vintage. She'd bought it for him two Christmases ago. When money hadn't been tight and she'd been able to afford things like clothes, house payments, *food.* Laurie was just a few inches away from him, a pretty blue dress floating around her trim figure. She looked as besotted as Byron seemed to be, her face soft with affection as she leaned down to whisper something in his ear.

From where Brenna was standing, there didn't seem to be one person in the church who didn't have somebody to stand or sit or walk around the cake table with. Interesting, because there also didn't seem to be one person under the age of sixty in the room.

A splash of rain fell on her cheek and she wiped it away, the coldness seeping through her skin and settling deep in to her bones. She'd need to dig a coat out of her suitcase. She'd been living out of her duffel bag, washing clothes every day, happy because she had a small washer and dryer of her own and didn't have to run to the Laundromat, but at some point she was going to have to face the facts: she was in Benevolence for the long haul and she might as well unpack her things and settle in.

"Cold?" River asked, his warm breath fanning her cheek.

"I forgot how chilly it gets at night this time of year." She zipped her jacket — as if that was going to help — and took a step away. They'd seen what they'd come to see: two people they cared about obviously having fun. No one was hurt, crying, or desperate, and the night was playing out the way Byron and Belinda had both wanted it to. A sweet little church and an old-fashioned cakewalk, and there Brenna was, standing on the outside looking in and almost wishing she were part of it.

How sad was that?

Pretty damn sad.

She sniffed back tears and told herself she was tired from all the time in the shop and all the drama of being back home. She had no other reason to cry. Her bank account might still be empty, but she had a nice apartment with a comfortable bed, warm clothes, and enough chocolate to keep her from starving. She was more fortunate than most of the people in the world.

"What's wrong?" River asked, his hands sweeping up and down her arms, providing friction and warmth and a tiny zing of electricity that made her pulse leap.

"Nothing." She tried to smile, knew she had failed. "It's been a long week and tomorrow is going to be another long day. I think we should skip my visit to the ranch. I'll stop by tomorrow after work."

"Funny," he murmured, his eyes black in the light seeping out the church window.

"What?"

"I never would have taken you for a coward."

"Who says I am?"

"Me."

"Because I've had a long week and want to go home?" She didn't feel sad anymore. She felt pissed, and looking into his smugly superior face wasn't helping.

"Because you're not honest about the way you feel." His hands slipped from her arms, and she felt colder than she had before.

"You want honesty? I *am* tired. Being in Chocolate Haven all day every day sucks. Everything I touch turns to glue or mud or cement. Poor Byron is losing money hand over fist while he lets me fiddle around in a place I don't belong."

"Who says you don't belong there?" He put a hand on her waist, and she found herself walking across the churchyard, ducking under the low-hanging branches of a willow tree.

"The pile of trashed candy you tossed in the Dumpster."

He laughed, lifting a willow branch and nudging her out from under the tree. The cemetery was to the left, the gravestones jutting up toward the cloudy sky. To the right, the church lawn meandered down a gently sloping hill. If they walked down it, they'd be back on Main Street. They walked toward the parking lot instead, and the vehicles they'd left at the very edge of the lot. Misty rain fell, adding hazy halos to street and window lights. The town looked quaint and pretty, the kind of place Brenna would have seen illustrated on the front cover of a book and longed to be part of. When she looked — really looked — at the quiet streets and mom-and-pop businesses, the lovely little churches and the Victorian homes, she yearned to have what Benevolence seemed to offer: family and home and a place to belong.

It had been a long time since she'd felt like she had any of those things.

"You do know," River said as they reached the Chrysler, "that you can't expect to walk into a chocolate shop and learn the art of candy making in an afternoon, right?"

"Five afternoons. Five mornings. Five very late nights," she corrected him. "Five thousand lessons from Byron, who really thinks I have *the gift.*"

"He's been making chocolate a long time. He'd be the one who would know."

"He sees what he wants to see, and because he loves me, what he sees is something much more fabulous than what it is."

"Don't limit yourself. There's a hell of a lot to learn about candy making and it can't be done in a limited amount of time."

"Addie did it," she blurted out, and then felt small and jealous, the younger sister who'd never quite lived up to her older sisters' examples.

"That's not what I heard." He took the keys from her hand and opened the Chrysler's door.

"What did you hear?"

"That it was the hardest thing she'd ever had to learn to do. Tougher than college and tougher than dealing with your mother."

"Dang," she breathed. "That's pretty tough."

"Exactly." He nudged her into the car, tossed the keys into her lap. "Come on. Let's get back to the ranch. The council meeting went on way too long and I'm starving."

He closed the door.

She didn't reopen it to tell him she was going home, that she didn't want to eat sirloin burgers or come up with ideas for decorating Belinda's house.

No. She didn't say one damn word.

She just shoved the key in the ignition, started the Chrysler, and followed him out of the church parking lot.

Fat raindrops splattered the windshield and she turned on the wipers, focusing her attention on the dark road and the taillights of River's truck. She'd never really asked Adeline what it had been like to run Chocolate Haven while Byron was in the hospital. Probably because it had never occurred to her that her organized, efficient, hardworking sister would be anything but stellar at it.

She should have asked.

She should have done a lot of things.

Like come home more than twice while Byron was in the hospital. Like ask Adeline if she needed help.

She'd been busy with her own life: the store, Dan, the fancy little parties he'd always wanted to host. She'd let that be her excuse, and Adeline had accepted it.

She'd deserved a lot more.

Brenna really needed to tell her that, because running Chocolate Haven was no joke. It was probably the most difficult thing Brenna had ever done. And she hadn't even really run it yet.

Monday.

That was the day.

She'd be on her own, making all the treats Byron had been coaching her in. The thought filled her with the kind of cold, hard dread she'd had the day she'd returned to New York City and found her condo empty, that stupid note from Dan lying on the counter:

Sorry about this, Brenna, but I'm in a bind and I need some fast cash to get out of town. You've always been a pal, and I know you'll understand. Good luck with the rest of your life. If you ever want that boob job, look me up. I'll be somewhere in Mexico, or maybe Spain. Gotta go where the winds lead! See ya!

"Bastard," she muttered, the Chrysler bouncing onto the long driveway that led to the ranch. The house didn't look any better at night than it had during the day, one lone light shining from the porch, the rest of the house dark and abandoned looking.

She pulled up behind River, parking the Chrysler behind his truck. Before she could get out, he was there, an umbrella in hand, his shirt dusted with raindrops, his hair shimmering with them.

A gentleman.

That's what Janelle would have said.

Just like your father.

Had Brett Lamont been a gentleman?

Brenna couldn't remember. She'd been too young when he'd died, and all her memories were of the sad things. Hospital visits, silent afternoons spent tiptoeing around the house because Brett needed rest. Church services with that empty space at the end of the Lamont pew — the one reserved for a man who was lying in bed, dying of brain cancer.

Brenna remembered those things.

Every once in a while, other memories would pop through: a trip to the pumpkin patch, picking apples at a local orchard, her father's laughter and her mother's contented smile.

It had been a long time since she'd seen that on Janelle's face.

"Angel and Huckleberry must be out. Her car is gone and the lights are off. A miracle, actually, because they usually have every light in the house blazing. Careful on the porch. A couple of the steps still need to be repaired," River said, his arm slipping around her waist, the gesture natural and easy, as if he'd done the same act a million times before.

Maybe he had.

He was three years older than her. He'd have had plenty of opportunities to date, get engaged, get married.

She eyed his left hand. It didn't look like he was wearing a ring, but a lot of people didn't bother with rings. Heck, a lot of people didn't bother with marriage.

An old-fashioned idea.

That's what Dan had thought. Which was

why she'd been surprised when he'd proposed. Surprised and a little appalled. She'd been happy enough to keep things the way they were, a little boring, a little mundane. Marriage meant a wedding, which meant making a big deal about something that hadn't felt all that big.

River must have noticed the direction of her gaze.

He smiled. "Don't worry. There's no one waiting for me back in Portland."

"Why would I worry?"

"Because you're the kind of person who worries about everything." He said it as if he knew it to be a fact, and she wanted to be offended, but she couldn't.

He was a straight shooter, a guy who said what was on his mind. She was the same way, so she couldn't hold it against him. "Not everything. Just people's hearts being broken."

"Because yours was?"

"Not even close."

"Then I guess it's good you dropped your ex." He fished keys out of his pocket and unlocked the front door.

"Because my heart wasn't broken?" She laughed nervously.

They were getting a little personal, touching on things she wasn't comfortable with.

Her fault, because she hadn't insisted on going home.

"Because if your heart wasn't broken, it was never invested, and if you weren't invested, why be in the relationship?" He flicked on the light in the kitchen, opened the refrigerator, and pulled out a package wrapped in white paper. "Grass-fed beef," he explained, unwrapping the package. "There are potatoes in the pantry closet. Want to grab them?"

"Where . . . ?"

"Right here." He leaned past, his arm brushing her abdomen as he opened a narrow door. Her breath caught, her mouth went dry, every single cell in her body screaming *this is what it's supposed to be like.*

He must have felt it, too.

He paused, his arm against her stomach, his eyes blazing.

"Onions too," he finally said, his voice gruff.

He turned away, busied himself with pans and knives and a bunch of things that had nothing at all to do with whatever had been between them.

Thank God!

That's what Brenna should have been thinking.

More was what her brain was shouting.

"Idiot," she whispered, grabbing a bag of potatoes and one of onions. They hadn't come from any store she'd ever been to. These were in white cloth sacks.

"What's that?" he said, and she just shook her head because what could she say?

I want you and that makes me a fool ten times over?

He eyed her for a few seconds too long, his expression unreadable; then he gestured to the sink. "Go ahead and rinse four of the potatoes. Then I'll show you how I want them cut. This is a quick meal. If we work together, we'll be eating in a half hour."

"Sounds good," she said, making sure her voice was as light and easy as his. No way did she want him to know just how much he'd affected her. No way did she ever want to be that vulnerable and weak again.

She didn't even look at the potatoes, just grabbed four from the bag and hurried to the sink, running the water hard to drown out the wild beat of her heart.

This was probably a bad idea, but River couldn't seem to care. He showed Brenna how to cut the potatoes and how to fry them, helped her sauté the onions and some mushrooms he'd found at a market outside of town. The meal was simple, the ingredients fresh, and the company . . .

Yeah, the company.

He watched as Brenna devoured her second burger and reached for another fry, her cheeks going red as she met his eyes.

"I guess I'm making a pig of myself," she mumbled, but she didn't put the fry back.

"Do you care?"

"No," she admitted. "This is the best meal I've eaten in months."

"Then you haven't been eating very well."

"Don't underestimate the power of your burgers and fries, River. I'd marry you tomorrow if it meant eating this every night for the rest of my life." Her blush deepened. "That was a stupid thing to say."

"Depends on which side of the table you're sitting on," he responded lightly, because that was the kind of response the comment deserved.

A joke. A little flirtation. A sincere thank you for a good meal. How many times had he gotten the same from other women?

She'd planted an image in his head, though. The two of them cooking meals together, cleaning up together, setting tables and cleaning them off and doing a dozen things couples did when they'd known each other for so long that the little things had

185

become much more important than the grand gestures.

"I'm sitting on this side," she muttered, "and it sounded stupid. Sorry. All that good food went to my head." She grabbed her empty plate and his and carried them to the sink.

"Leave them for now. I'll wash them after we do a tour of the house."

"Better now than when all the grease is set." She squirted soap into the sink, ran steaming water on top of it, scrubbed each plate to within an inch of its life.

Her cell phone rang as she set the last one in the drainer and she scowled. "If that's Jeff again . . ." She glanced at the screen. "Damn!"

"Want me to talk to him?" he offered, and she shook her head.

"It's not him. It's my mother. She's almost as bad, but with her, I have an obligation to answer. Excuse me for a second." She stepped into the hall, and he could hear a few mumbled words.

No.

No way in hell.

I'm sorry you feel that way.

Then nothing for so long River thought she'd finished the conversation. He waited another heartbeat, was just about ready to walk into the hall when she started talking again. "Fine. I'll be there."

She stepped back into the kitchen, shoving the phone into her pocket.

"Trouble?"

"A dinner party next month to celebrate Willow's birthday."

"Your older sister?"

"Yes, and I'm pretty sure she doesn't want a dinner party at Mom's house as a present."

"Then why have one?"

"Because Janelle loves any opportunity to show off her daughters' successes." She frowned. "Sorry. My mouth seems to be getting away from me tonight. My mother loves us, and she enjoys letting people know how successful we all are."

"There's nothing wrong with that, is there?"

"Only if you're the one who isn't successful."

"From what I hear, you've accomplished a lot."

"The problem with the things we hear is that they're not always accurate. Or timely. Or even true. Come on. Let's look around the house and see what Belinda already has. In a place this old, there's got to be some antiques lying around just waiting to be polished up and displayed."

The end of the conversation.

At least, that was what Brenna seemed to want, but River was just curious enough to hold on to the words, think about them as they walked through the hallway and into the parlor, the dining room, the living room. She searched each room like she was on a treasure hunt, peering under tables and behind furniture that had probably been standing in the same place for decades.

She found a lot more than he'd realized was there.

Old lamps that sparkled when she wiped dust from their glass shades. Framed paintings hidden on the floor behind the couch. Several photos hidden behind a clutter of knick-knacks on the fireplace mantel, all of them displayed at Freedom Ranch during its heyday.

"These are perfect," she said, her eyes gleaming with enthusiasm, her cheek smudged with dust. For some reason, Huckleberry had been cleaning like a madman, dusting every visible surface in the house, cleaning off mirrors and dry mopping floors. He hadn't thought to pull out the furniture or sweep dust bunnies out of the corners.

Neither had River, but then, he'd been

working every minute he wasn't taking Belinda to doctor appointments and therapy sessions.

"We can hang them in the parlor. Guests will love looking at them." She carried the pile through the hall and into what had probably once been a formal sitting room. This room, more than any of the others, reminded him of Dillard. The old leather armchair, the huge rolltop desk piled high with papers and bills and photos of Belinda and dozens of foster kids, the dark shelves filled with old books that only the most responsible of the ranch kids could touch.

"Wow!" Brenna breathed, her eyes widening as she took in the room. She set the photos on the chair and walked to one of the shelves. "I didn't realize you had a library in here."

"It was Dillard's office. They kept the door locked when they had parties." Another thing he'd forgotten until he'd come back: how much Dillard had loved his old desk and his old books.

"He must have hundreds of books here." She lifted one from the shelf, dusting the old spine and the cover. "I wonder where he got all of them."

"He used to go to yard sales every Saturday. When I first got to town and was get-

189

ting into all kinds of trouble, he'd drag me out of bed and make me go with him."

"That's a creative way of punishing someone," she said as she lifted another book — this one large and thick — and flipped open the leather cover.

"It's a Bible," she murmured. "Look." She pressed in close, her arm right up against his, her head blocking his view of the huge tome.

Chocolate, strawberries, and a hint of misty rain, and that soft red hair that glowed in the lamplight.

He could have taken the book from her hands, let his fingers trail up her arms and slide through her hair. He could have pulled her in for the kiss he'd been wanting from the moment he'd walked into Chocolate Haven and seen her standing in the midst of the wrecked kitchen, specks of chocolate on her hands and cheeks. He didn't think she'd complain because he was pretty damn sure she felt what he did: that zing of heat that made him think of long nights and early mornings, wild hair and wilder kisses. That spark of electricity that made him forget his life was too busy and full for someone like Brenna.

Yeah. He wanted to turn her into his arms, take the book from her hands, see just how far one simple kiss would take them, but she was looking at the Bible like she'd just found a pot of gold, the look on her face joyous and full of wonder.

He leaned over her shoulder, saw the page she was looking at and the list of names and dates written in beautiful calligraphy, the margins filled with colorful scrollwork.

"Can you believe it?" she asked, turning to face him, the huge Bible between them. "The first birth listed is 1745."

"Yes." He could believe it. What he couldn't believe was that he was looking into the face of the pretty little girl who used to carry books all over town, the one who'd been gangly and young and a little different from the other kids, and that he was thinking she was still pretty and gangly and a little different, and he liked that. He liked it a lot.

"I bet these pages are hand painted," she murmured, turning to a beautiful illustration of the Garden of Eden. "And I bet this Bible would be worth a small fortune to some collector somewhere."

"I'd never get rid of it," he said, and she looked up, met his eyes. He knew the minute she felt that thing, that little tug of attraction that seemed determined to pull them together.

She blushed. "You must think I'm nuts, getting excited about an old Bible." She closed the book, set it back on the shelf, turning her back to him just the way he'd known she would.

Once bitten, twice shy.

One of Dillard's favorite things to say when he was dealing with hardheaded kids who'd refused to trust because every adult they'd ever counted on had betrayed them.

"Not every dog bites," he said quietly, his hands settling on Brenna's waist. She turned, and they were just . . . there. The two of them, alone in a house that needed to be filled. He could smell that hint of chocolate, that subtle scent of strawberries, could feel the warmth of her skin through layers of fabric.

"What?" she murmured, not pulling away but not leaning in. She'd been through hell. He could see that. If her family didn't, if they really thought she'd just come home to help in the chocolate shop, they were blind.

"Dillard used to say that to me every time he came through for me when I didn't think he would. My first year here, it was a bike. He'd told me that if I got straight As on my report card, he'd get me one of those dirt bikes all the kids at school had. I didn't believe him."

"So, you didn't get the grades?"

"I did. Just to prove he was a liar. I flashed my report card in his face, and I probably said a few words that would have gotten my mouth washed out with soap if Dillard and Belinda were a different kind of people. I can't remember much about that, but what I do remember saying — and I've never forgotten this — is *See, Old Man? You're just like every other loser I've ever met. You make all kinds of promises you can't keep. We both know you don't have money for a bike, and we both know you were never going to get me one. So you can take these damn grades and shove them where the sun don't shine.* Once I finished my tirade, I stomped to my room and slammed the door."

"Did he go out and get you the bike?"

"He didn't have to. It was already in my room. Sitting near the window. I'll never forget that either. I slammed the door and I was so full of arrogance and pride, thinking I'd finally gotten one over on Dillard, that I didn't notice it at first. Then the sun hit the handlebars just right, and I got a flash of light right in the eye. When I realized what it was, I started shaking. Up until that point, no one had ever come through for me."

"I'm sorry," she said, her hands resting on his forearms, her fingers light and cool

193

against his skin.

"I'm not. All those people, the ones who failed me over and over again, led me to the people who never did. Not every dog bites, red. Not every person disappoints." He brushed the smudge of dust from her cheek, let his hand slide to her nape. "And just because you've been to hell doesn't mean you have to keep revisiting it."

"Who says I am?"

"Your eyes." He leaned in, did what he'd been wanting to, his lips just brushing hers, just getting a taste of chocolate and strawberries and something infinitely darker and richer.

Her hands slid around his waist, and he knew he could take more. He wanted more. God knew he did, but she'd regret what he took and what she gave, and that wasn't a game he was willing to play.

He cupped her face, his thumbs resting at the corner of her mouth. Her pulse thrummed beneath his fingers, the frantic pace of it heating his blood.

"Where do you want to go with this, red?" he asked.

And she shook her head, took a step back. "It's late. I need to get home."

"That wasn't the question."

"I don't have an answer." She smoothed

194

her hair and her hand was shaking, her fingers trembling as she touched her lips. "My life is . . . complicated."

"So's mine," he responded, moving into her space just enough to watch her pupils dilate and hear her breath catch.

God! She was beautiful, the sharp angle of her jaw and her cheekbones, the softness of her skin and hair. He ran his thumb along her lower lip and she sighed, levering up for another kiss that he knew she wanted just as much as he did.

The front door banged open and she jumped back, nearly tumbling in her haste to get away.

"I think I'd better go," she muttered, turning on her heels and running into the hallway.

He followed more slowly, not sure if he was more relieved or angry at the interruption. Rushing into things wasn't his style, but he wanted to rush into this with Brenna.

Whatever *this* was.

Cold air and rain swept through the hallway, the wide open front door letting the wind carry both in. The rain had turned into a downpour, and Huckleberry and Angel seemed to have gotten caught in it. Both stood in the foyer, dripping wet and staring Brenna down.

"What's she doing here?" Angel asked, not even bothering to look in River's direction. She wore a soaked shirt, black work pants, and sandals that exposed toes turning purple with cold, but she didn't seem in any hurry to go warm up.

"Helping with the house," he responded, grabbing one of Dillard's old coats from the coat closet and dropping it around her shoulders.

"We don't need help. Do we, Huckleberry?" Angel's teeth were chattering, her belly pressing against her nearly translucent T-shirt.

"Not from a troublemaker like her," Huckleberry spat.

Brenna frowned. "I haven't caused either of you any trouble, but if you don't want me here —"

"It's not their choice," he cut in, and Angel's scowl deepened.

"Do you know what everyone in town is saying about Mack?" she demanded, the coat falling to the floor as she took a step in Brenna's direction. "They're saying he attacked you for no reason, that he's crazy, and that he needs to be in a mental institution."

"I'm sorry about that," Brenna said, the sincerity in her voice and on her face apparently lost on Angel and Huckleberry.

"Sure you are," Huckleberry muttered. "Everyone is always sorry, but that doesn't stop them from doing the same things over and over again."

"I didn't make Mack tackle me," Brenna said. "And I didn't press charges against him. I'm sorry people in town are talking, but that's the way towns this size are. Not enough going on to keep people occupied, so they make things up."

"Like the fact that your fiancé dumped you for a woman with bigger tits and better hair?" Angel mocked. "Was that made up? Oh. Wait. It couldn't have been, because here you are, with no ring on your finger, no man by your side, and nothing but time to make messes of other people's lives."

"That's enough," River snapped.

"It's true and she knows it."

"What I know," Brenna said, her voice cool, her expression cold, "is that kindness is vastly underutilized in this world. When you find someone who gives it to you, it's best to return it with interest."

She walked through the open doorway, and Angel had the good grace to look embarrassed, her face the color of overripe tomatoes.

"I guess I forgot about that," she mumbled.

"What?" River asked as he stepped outside. No way was he going to let Brenna walk away without clearing this up.

"Every day she's stopped by the diner and left me a bag of chocolate. Just left it. Sitting on the counter in a white paper bag with my name on it. I'm an idiot," she sobbed, running up the stairs.

"Women," Huckleberry muttered, as if he knew something about them.

River didn't have time to explain that he didn't.

He jogged down the porch steps as Brenna's headlights came on and the Chrysler's engine sputtered to life. Died. Sputtered again. Died.

On the third attempt to start it, she gave up.

He could see her sitting behind the steering wheel, her hands in her lap, her eyes closed, her lips moving.

She could have been praying or counting to ten.

He knocked on the glass and she rolled down the window.

"I need to go home," she said, as if that would make the engine suddenly come to life.

"I'll take you."

"I'd rather drive myself."

"That probably won't happen until you get new spark plugs."

"Do you think that's the problem?"

"I do." He opened her door, rolled up the window, and took her hand. "It's an easy fix. I'll take care of it tomorrow. While you're working in the house."

"I don't know if that's a good idea. Angel —"

"Is a pregnant teenager. She's got no control over her tongue or her emotions."

"Still —"

"It will make Belinda happy." He helped her into the truck, touched her silky cheek, his knuckles sliding down over satiny skin. "And I know how much you care about her."

"You play to win, River," she murmured.

"You're wrong," he countered. "I don't play."

Then he shut the door and rounded the truck, the icy rain falling in sheets around him, the lone light on the porch reminding him of just how much he had to lose if his plans for the place didn't pan out.

CHAPTER EIGHT

Midnight, and Brenna couldn't sleep.

Not because of the endless rain splashing onto the tin roof of the apartment. Not because of the howling wind that rattled the window. Not because Jeff had called her three more times.

No. None of those things were keeping her awake.

It was the kiss. That one light touch of lips and her entire world had shifted. For the very first time, she understood what she'd been missing with Dan, why all his praise and ego-stroking and telling her every day how beautiful she was had done nothing but leave her cold.

That one little kiss River had given her? It had packed more punch than all the sweet caresses Dan had offered, because that kiss — that one damn kiss — had been filled with tenderness, patience, passion, and something so indefinable, so real and alive

200

and wonderful, that she still couldn't wrap her mind around it.

It had been like finding the last piece of the puzzle, the one that had fallen on the floor and gotten swept into a vent and seemed destined to be missing forever. And then, right before dismantling and tossing the incomplete puzzle, seeing a hint of color in the vent, pulling out that one last piece and fitting it into the slot.

Yeah. That's how the kiss had felt, and she'd wanted it to go on and on.

She scowled, pacing through the apartment hall and into the living room. All the lights were off and the lights from Main Street filtered in through the closed sheers. She pulled them open, looked out onto the empty road. Not a car in sight. Not a person either. The place was empty and silent, shop owners home for the night. Shoppers tucked into their beds. Benevolence was sleeping soundly and she was up, worrying about something that shouldn't matter.

One little kiss, and there didn't have to be more.

No matter how much she wanted there to be.

Her cell phone rang and she ignored it. She'd said everything she could to Jeff and she didn't have the energy to repeat herself.

When the apartment phone rang, she nearly jumped out of her skin. Phone calls at midnight were never a good thing, and she hurried to answer it.

"Hello?"

"Did I wake you, doll?" Byron's grumbly voice filled the line and she nearly sagged with relief. She'd had enough trouble and bad news in the past few months to last a lifetime.

"No. Is everything okay? Did something happen to Adeline? Or Mom? Did something happen to Mom?"

"Calm yourself down, kid. Everyone is fine. You know that old busybody who lives at the corner of Main and Howard?"

"Do I?"

"Mable Grunge. Could you ever forget a name like that?"

Obviously she could because she had no idea who Byron was talking about. "What about her?"

"She was out with that nasty dog of hers. Big brute of a thing called Otis —"

"Granddad," she cut in, "could you get to the point?"

"She thought she saw someone near the shop. Being a busybody, she decided she'd better call the cops. They called me."

"Near the shop?" She tried to walk back

to the window, but the old-fashioned phone had a cord that was too short to reach. "Where?"

"The sheriff didn't say. Just said she thought the person looked suspicious, so he was sending someone to check it out. I wanted to give you a heads-up. You've got the apartment door locked, right?"

"Yes."

"And all the windows?"

"Someone would have to scale two stories to get to them, but yes —"

Somewhere below glass shattered, the sound muted but distinct. She froze, her heart beating a slow, terrible rhythm. A broken shop window? Was someone trying to get into Chocolate Haven?

"You okay, doll?"

"When is the sheriff sending someone?" she hedged, because she didn't want Byron to show up and try to face down the perpetrator.

"What's going on over there?"

"Nothing."

"You're lying. I'm coming over."

"Granddad —"

He'd already hung up, and she was left standing with the phone in her hand, her ears straining for some other sound, some sign that whoever had broken the window was still hanging around.

She placed the phone in its cradle, crept across the kitchen and into the living room. She couldn't see anything from there. Just Main Street and the businesses across it, the twinkling of light from neighborhood houses, the trees whipping in the wind.

Maybe the person had gone around back?

She hurried into her bedroom and looked out the window that faced the back lot. At first she saw nothing but rain bouncing off the wet pavement. Then a shadow moved near the edge of the parking area, someone running toward the park that edged the property.

She couldn't make out a face, gender, height. Whoever it was seemed like part of the shadows, just a black shape against the darkness. There for just a few seconds, then disappearing behind a tree. She waited, her breath held as if somehow that would make the person appear again.

Someone rapped on the apartment door and she screamed, all her tension and fear letting loose in a high-pitched screech that probably could have shattered crystal.

"Brenna?" Another hard rap. "It's Kane Rainier. I got a call that there might be trouble over here. Everything okay?"

"Yes. No," she called, running to the door

and yanking it open. Kane was there. Not dressed in his uniform. Just a black T-shirt soaked with rain, faded jeans, and work boots.

"What's going on?" He stepped into the apartment, his hand on the gun still in its holster.

"I don't know. Byron called, and while I was on the phone with him, someone broke a window. At least, that's what I think it was. I heard glass breaking, but I didn't see what happened. I did see someone running into the park, though."

"Stay here. I'll check it out."

"I'd rather check it out with you." She grabbed one of Byron's old rain coats from the closet and pulled it on over her tank top and flannel pajama pants. She had an obligation to her grandfather and to the family to make sure everything was okay.

"I think your family would rather you waited here. There's no sense putting yourself in danger, Brenna."

"I saw the guy running away. How much danger could I be in?" She followed him onto the landing, the metal cold beneath her bare feet. She probably should have gone back for shoes, but he was moving fast, jogging down the stairs and around the side of the building while she picked her way down the slick exterior staircase. These were the same stairs Byron had fallen down. He'd gotten a broken hip and femur out of it.

Brenna didn't want to repeat his mistake.

By the time she made it to the back of the building, Kane was snapping pictures and speaking to someone on his cell phone. He put up his hand as she approached.

"Watch it," he said, pointing to a few shards that had fallen from the kitchen window. The glass had been pristine when she'd left for the night. Now it had a fist-size hole in it.

"What the he . . . ck?"

He tucked the phone in his pocket. "I've got a couple of deputies on the way. Do you have your keys? I'd like to see if there's any damage to the interior."

"I'll get them." She darted back the way she'd come, stopping short when headlights splashed at the mouth of the alley.

Suddenly, she was being yanked backward with so much force she nearly fell over.

"Get near the building," Kane growled. "Stay there."

"What — ?"

But he was already running toward the oncoming vehicle, his hand up as if the power of the gesture could stop whoever was driving toward him.

She had about three seconds of panic.

Three long seconds of thinking the person she'd seen running into the park had come back and was going to run Kane down.

Then the vehicle braked. A door opened and closed.

"What in the name of all that is holy is happening here?" Byron shouted, and Brenna was so relieved her knees nearly went out from under her.

"Broken window," Kane responded as if he hadn't nearly been run down.

"Broken by who?" Byron strode through the rain, a tiny hitch in his stride. He was probably tired from the cakewalk and his hot date. His limp was always more pronounced when he'd worn himself out.

"That's what I plan to find out," Kane said grimly. "You want to get the keys so we can go inside, Brenna?"

"I've got keys." Byron unlocked the door, flicked on the light. "Damn it! That fool took out my favorite mixing bowl."

"And your window," Kane reminded him.

"Windows can be replaced. This —" Byron bent over the shattered remains of the big yellow Pyrex bowl he always used to mix the dry ingredients for his fudge, "can't."

"I'm sure I can find one on eBay or at

some little antique shop somewhere." Brenna touched his shoulder, realized for the first time just how frail he felt, how thin. He'd always seemed larger than life. Had he shrunk or had she just grown up enough to see him for the man he was? Tall and lean, a little stooped. Strong but not superhuman.

"Nah," he said, his voice tight. "This one your grandmother bought the day I took over the shop from my dad. We'd just gotten married and we didn't have much money. She'd scrimped and saved to buy it. Said a cheerful color would brighten up the store. She was right." He lifted a large piece of yellow porcelain. "But Alice brightened it up more." He tossed the piece into the trash, kicked a brick that lay a few inches from the bowl. "I guess I'm a little tired, doll. You mind cleaning this up for me?"

"Of course not." She hugged him, and he grumbled something about foolish emotions, kissed her cheek, and left.

Kane followed him, and she stood in the kitchen alone, looking at the broken pieces of her grandfather's favorite bowl. How had she not known what it meant to him?

Had she been that self-absorbed, that determined to separate herself from the town and the people, all the traditions, that she'd forgotten how important those things could be?

She grabbed a broom and dustpan from the closet.

"Hold on a minute," Kane said as he walked back into the kitchen. "I'd like to get a look at the brick and take a few pictures before you move anything. You can wait in your apartment or in the storefront. Whichever you prefer."

She nodded, but she didn't leave.

She kept hearing her grandfather's words and seeing his face: tired and a little defeated.

Kane snapped picture after picture, then used gloved hands to lift the brick, frowning when he saw the white letters scrawled across the red-brown surface. "Interesting," he said.

"What?"

"See what it says?" He held it so she could, the words all block letters: I'M WATCHING YOU.

"That," she mumbled, her heart racing, "is about the creepiest thing I've seen in a while."

"Anyone you can think of who might have a reason to taunt you?"

She thought about Angel, the anger in her face when she'd accused Brenna of causing trouble for Mack. And then there was Jeff, calling her all day every day, trying to get information out of her that she didn't have.

"Brenna?" he prodded, a hint of impatience in his voice. "Protecting someone isn't helping them. It's just enabling them to continue down the wrong path."

"I'm not protecting anyone. I just . . . Angel seemed unhappy about what happened to Mack."

"Nothing happened to him," he pointed out.

"She says people around town are talking about him. She thinks I ruined his reputation."

He dropped the brick into a plastic bag. "I guess I'll head over to the ranch to see what she has to say for herself."

"It's past midnight."

"That doesn't mean she shouldn't have to answer for herself if she did this."

"But, Belinda —"

"Raised a lot of kids who got into a lot of trouble. She'll take the visit in stride."

"Kane, I really wish you wouldn't."

"Unless you have some other lead, this one is all we've got. I have an obligation to find the perpetrator, Brenna. I think you know that."

"There's something else," she said hurriedly as he walked to the door. She hated bringing it up. She hated admitting how stupid she'd been, but Angel wasn't the only possibility and she couldn't let Kane think she was.

"What?"

"My ex got into some trouble. He embezzled money from his business partner, then he skipped town."

"You think your ex did this?"

"No, but his business partner has been calling me several times a day every day. He thinks I know where my ex is and he's determined to get me to tell him."

"What's the guy's name?"

"Jeff Winthrop. He's a plastic surgeon in New York. A really busy one. I doubt he's hopped a plane to come to Washington to stalk me."

"He's not so busy that he hasn't had time to call you several times a day," he pointed out.

"I know, but —"

"Brenna, someone did this. More than likely it's someone you or your grandfather knows. Your grandfather has been here for decades and never had any trouble, so I'm thinking the brick was probably for you."

He paused and she nodded, because she wasn't sure if he expected a response, wasn't sure what the response would be if he did.

"If that's the case, the perpetrator is someone who has a bone to pick with you," he continued. "It's my job to find out who and why and put that person in jail. I'm sure you understand that."

"I do."

"Good, because I'm going to the ranch and I'm calling your ex's partner. I'd also like to speak with your ex. Do you have contact information for him?"

"Are you kidding? He stole me blind before he left the country. For some reason, he didn't bother leaving a forwarding address." She sounded flip. Which was better than sounding angry or bitter.

Kane didn't even blink. Maybe he'd heard it all before. Maybe he'd dealt with more than one sordid tale of betrayal. Whatever the case, he just took out a notepad, scribbled something on the top page. "What's your ex's name?"

She gave it and Jeff's, provided the phone numbers she knew, answered a couple more questions about Dan's crimes. As she finished, a marked cruiser pulled into the back lot.

Kane watched as it parked next to his vehicle. "Jax is here. He'll dust for prints and look for other evidence. I'll have him jerry-rig something in the window to keep anyone from getting in tonight."

"I appreciate it."

"We've also got a couple of deputies in the park. If the guy is still there, we'll find him. Or her," he added. "I'll call you with an update tomorrow. Go on back to your apartment for now. If Jax needs anything, he'll knock."

It wasn't a request. It was an order, and she could see Kane expected her to obey it.

"I'll need to clean up the mess," she said. The last thing she wanted was for Byron to arrive in the morning and see the smashed bowl still lying on the ground.

She hadn't expected him to get so upset.

Not the guy who'd stood at his son's funeral, holding his wife and his daughter-in-law and telling them that everything was going to be okay. Not the one who'd stepped in and helped finish raising his three grand-daughters. He'd always been larger than life, seemingly indestructible. But, that bowl — that one shattered bowl — had nearly broken him.

That pissed her off.

A lot.

Whoever had been running through the field needed to pay for what had been done. She bent to lift another yellow porcelain shard, and Kane stepped in front of her.

213

"It's going to have to wait, Brenna. I'll have Jax let you know when he's finished. You can clean up then."

"I can wait in the front of the shop," she said, and he shrugged.

"Suit yourself. Just don't touch anything in here." He tossed the order over his shoulder as he walked away.

She obeyed it because she didn't want to do anything that would hamper the investigation. She didn't even flick on the light as she walked into the hall and headed past Byron's office. The door was open and she could see the desk, the shelf of recipe books Byron had collected. Inside each one, he'd taped some of the family recipes, ones that had been perfected over generations. She'd looked at them a few times, used them to try to recreate the candy the Lamonts were known for. Aside from the chocolate roses and milk chocolate bonbons, she still hadn't developed any skills worth mentioning. She couldn't clean up the mess and she wasn't going back to her apartment, so she might as well read. The recipe books were the only thing available. Who knew? Maybe poring over them would help her accomplish what she hadn't yet: candy making proficiency.

She sat at one of the two booths that had been added to the shop sometime in the fifties, the old book falling open to the center. She'd planned to start from the beginning, but there was a recipe card attached to the page with a paper clip. Laminated and smudged from years of being held and read, it was handwritten in spidery cursive that looked nothing like Byron's. Surprised, she lifted it from the book.

Forever Kisses was scrawled at the top. Beneath that, a list of ingredients:

A dash of humor.
A pinch of patience.
A tablespoon of truth.
A cup of love.
A pint of faithfulness.
A gallon of commitment.
Mix well and dust with laughter, sprinkle with tears, bake with friendship that lasts through the years.

She smiled, turning the recipe over and looking for a name. There was nothing. Just that sweet little card with its cute little recipe. She probably should have put it back in the book, but she tucked it into her pocket instead.

She had a heck of a lot to learn about candy making, but she was beginning to think she had even more to learn about love.

She'd seen it in action with her grandparents, but she'd forgotten just how close they'd been, just how much they'd clung to each other in the good times and in the bad. Dusted with laughter and sprinkled with tears, baked with friendship that lasts through the years.

She could use a little of that.

She pushed the thought aside, the sound of Jax moving around in the kitchen filling her ears as she opened the recipe book to the beginning and began to read.

It had been a hell of a night and River was in no mood to have a hell of a day. Based on the fact that Byron Lamont was standing on the porch, banging on the door at five thirty-four in the morning, he had the feeling he was going to get one anyway.

He opened the door, tried to smile. "Good morning, Byron."

"What's so good about it?" Byron snapped, stepping into the foyer without being invited.

"If this is about last night —"

"It isn't, but if you want to explain how a brick ended up being tossed through my shop window, I'm willing to listen."

"If I had answers, I'd give them to you."

"Were those two nitwits here when I

dropped Belinda off last night?" he demanded.

"Which two nitwits?" He might not be all that keen on Huckleberry and Angel, but he wasn't going to let someone else bad-mouth them.

"Don't be dense. The pregnant girl and that red-haired boyfriend of hers."

"Huckleberry isn't Angel's boyfriend."

"Huckleberry? What kind of idiotic name is that?"

"Apparently, the one his mother gave him."

"If you believe that, I've got some swampland to sell you in Florida."

"Look, Byron, I appreciate your frustration —"

"*Frustration?* I'm damned angry. I've been running that store for over fifty years and I've never had even a hint of vandalism. Until now."

"I appreciate your frustration," River repeated. "But you don't have the right to come into Belinda's house and add stress to her already stressful life. If you want to discuss last night and the two kids who might or might not have had something to do with it, let's go outside."

Byron's mouth opened, slammed shut.

Finally, he shrugged. "You're right. And

you're a lot more polite about it than Dillard would have been. He'd have booted me out five minutes ago, and I'd have let him because I'd have known I was wrong. Sorry, son. Long night, and I'm not fit for company. Or so my granddaughter is telling me. Which is why I'm here. Brenna said Belinda has therapy this morning."

"She does, but not until nine."

"She didn't mention that part. Just told me to get my sorry behind out of the shop until I could be more pleasant company. Then she said I might as well make myself useful while I was at it and take Belinda to therapy. Next thing I knew, I was outside the shop and she'd locked the door on me."

"Don't you have extra keys?"

"Sure as hell do, but it's good for Brenna to open the shop by herself because she's going to have to do it Monday."

"She mentioned you were going on a fishing trip."

"Alaskan fishing. You ever been, son?" Byron walked down the hall and straight into Dillard's office. He took a seat in the easy chair, pulled a cigar out of his pocket, and clamped it between his teeth.

"I can't say that I have."

"That's surprising."

"Why?"

218

"I do my research. Saw some write-ups on your restaurants. Fresh and local, right?"

"Yes." He wasn't sure where Byron was going with this, but River was supposed to be at Chocolate Haven in fifteen minutes, so he'd better get there quickly.

"Seems to me, a highbrow chef like yourself would know the joy of fresh Alaskan salmon and halibut."

"I've eaten it."

"But you've never caught it and then fried it up, right there in a pan on the beach, have you?"

"No."

"Tell you what, son. You help me out and I'll bring you the next time I go."

"Fishing?" The last time River had fished, he'd been a teenager still living at the ranch.

"Just think of all the recipes you could come up with while you're out there in the Alaskan wilds. Think of how you could market that down in Portland." He was selling it hard, and River was just curious enough to ask what he wanted for the favor.

"What do you need help with?"

"I'll tell you, but you breathe a word of it and I'll swear you're lying." He took the cigar from his mouth and leaned forward, his light green eyes gleaming. "I've got a problem with Brenna."

219

"What kind of problem?"

"She's got no confidence. The girl has everything she needs to make chocolate right here." He jabbed himself in the region of the heart. "But she's so busy doubting herself that she's just about useless in Chocolate Haven's kitchen."

"I'm planning —"

"Wait." Byron held up a finger. "Give me a minute to say my piece. With Adeline laid up with morning sickness and Chase tied up with college, there's no one around to help Brenna out. If I hadn't been planning this trip for a year, I'd cancel out, but I have been."

"Brenna —" *And I already have an agreement* was what he was trying to say, but Byron was on a roll.

"She's smart. No doubt about that, and she's got the heart for it, but that bastard fiancé of hers wore her into the ground. You've seen her. Skinny as a rail, no color in her cheeks. She's lost her confidence. Her mojo. And she needs some people to come alongside her to help her find it again. I'm trying to do that, but since I'm going to be gone for two weeks, I need a stand-in. I've thought about it long and hard, and you're the only one I can think of who has the skills necessary to make the chocolate and run the business. You help me out and I'll make it more than worth your while."

"Okay."

"Now, hold on a minute," Byron said, then he frowned. "You said okay."

"Right."

"Hmm." He clamped the cigar between his teeth again. "That went a lot easier than I imagined."

"Are you complaining?"

"Just considering why that might be."

"Tell you what, Byron," he said, glancing at his watch. "How about I go check on Brenna's progress and you stay here with Belinda." He walked out of the room and Byron followed.

"Now, hold on a minute, son. I'm thinking that Belinda would not appreciate me helping her get ready for therapy."

"Angel will take care of that. She'll get her up before she goes to work and have her ready before she leaves."

As if his words had conjured her, Angel appeared at the top of the stairs, an oversized nightshirt barely covering her belly, the cuffs of her flannel pajama bottoms dragging the floor.

She saw Byron and stopped cold, her eyes wide with surprise, her hair falling lank around her pale face.

Byron looked surprised, too, the cigar nearly falling from his lips.

He grabbed it, shoved it in his pocket.

"What's going on?" Angel demanded. "Why's he here? Does he want to accuse me of causing more trouble?" If she was guilty of throwing a brick through the window at Chocolate Haven, she wasn't showing it.

"He's taking Belinda to therapy this morning."

"Like hell he is," she growled. "If you can't do it, I'll take the day off and take her."

"You better watch your mouth, young lady," Byron snapped. "In another couple of months you're going to have a kid listening to your every word. You want that kind of language coming out of your toddler's mouth?"

"No." She had the good grace to look embarrassed. "But Belinda doesn't need someone like you causing her problems."

"Someone like me? All I've done is call the police because someone threw a brick through my window. Whoever threw the brick is the problem," he countered. "Besides, me and Belinda go way back. Dillard was my best friend. You ever meet him?"

"No."

"Well, come on into the kitchen and I'll tell you how Dillard and I got to be buddies while I make some breakfast. You hungry?"

"I guess," Angel said, and to River's surprise, she walked down the stairs, stopping just a few feet from Byron. She looked softer than River had ever seen her, all the hardness that was usually in her face gone.

"You guess? Doll, you've got to eat for that kid. You want him to be healthy, right?"

"How did you know it was a boy?"

"Looks like you're carrying around a basketball. My late wife always said that meant it was a boy. Now, hurry it up. I'll teach you how to make the best scrambled eggs and French toast you've ever eaten."

"I'll eat any French toast anyone puts in front of me."

"Not after you taste mine. Best in the state, but don't tell Laura Beth I said so. Wouldn't want to offend her."

"No, I guess not." Angel looked confused.

River *felt* confused.

He'd been sure the two were about to have a rip-roaring fight. Instead, they suddenly seemed like the best of friends.

Good.

That saved River a lot of hassle. If Angel liked Byron, she'd be a lot less likely to repeat her mistake of the previous night. *If* it had been her mistake. The sheriff had seemed highly suspicious. As a matter of fact, he'd stopped just short of accusing Angel of the crime.

She was young, but she wasn't stupid. She'd known exactly why he was there and exactly why she was the one being questioned. She'd said some idiotic things to Brenna and she'd admitted them to the sheriff, but she'd insisted she hadn't been anywhere near Chocolate Haven.

River had believed her.

For what it was worth, he thought the sheriff had, too.

That didn't mean she was innocent. River had spent most of his childhood with people who made an art of deception. He'd listened and watched and learned how easy it was to convince someone of a lie. He'd even practiced it himself, telling caseworkers and teachers what they wanted to hear because it was so much easier than telling them the truth.

Yeah. Anyone could lie, and there were plenty of people who could do it well. Hopefully, Angel wasn't one of them, but River wouldn't count on it.

He watched as she and Byron walked down the hall. Old and young. Upright citizen and pregnant runaway. They shouldn't have connected, but it seemed they had. Whatever the truth about the previous night, that connection would be good enough to get them through the next few hours.

That was all River needed. Just enough time to meet with Brenna, teach her a few things about candy making, and seal the deal they'd made: his help for hers. A remodeled house. A happy business council. A smooth-running shop. Two people working together to get what neither of them could achieve alone.

It sounded good.

It probably *would* be good.

He grabbed his jacket and his keys, walked out into the cool morning. The rain had stopped, and he caught a hint of fresh-cut grass and late summer flowers in the air. It made him think of Brenna: her vibrant hair and stunning eyes, the velvety feel of her lips, the warmth of her skin.

Good was nice.

Good was comfortable.

But maybe he'd get something great out of the little town he'd once despised.

CHAPTER NINE

Six o'clock and River hadn't arrived.

That shouldn't have surprised Brenna. How many times had she waited for Dan? How many hours had she wasted in restaurants or at parties, hoping he'd show up soon?

Too many to count, but she'd admit that she'd expected better from River. He hadn't seemed like the kind of guy who'd make a deal and back out of it. He also hadn't seemed like the kind of guy who'd be late for a meeting or an appointment.

Of course, she hadn't thought Dan seemed like the kind of guy who'd lie, cheat, and steal. She'd been wrong about that. She'd been wrong about a lot of things in her life and she really needed to start being right.

River hadn't shown and she'd kicked Byron's grumpy butt out of the kitchen, so she'd have to get everything ready for the shop to open. She had exactly four hours to do it.

That wasn't a lot of time.

The way Brenna saw things, she could either curl up in a ball and cry like a baby or she could tackle chocolate making like she'd tackled everything else in her life. Because she wasn't much of a crier, she opted for the latter. Careful planning, step-by-step execution of that plan, and clear and precise steps to reach her goal.

Her goal being *not* running Chocolate Haven into the ground while Byron was on his fishing trip.

She eyed the recipes she'd printed out and taped to the backsplash. She'd been up almost all night, reading the old recipe books and learning everything she could about what it took to be a chocolatier. It took a lot. She might not have it all down, but she had brains enough to measure ingredients properly, pay careful attention to temperature, and she sure as heck could follow a recipe.

Why that had seemed so daunting before she didn't know, but she wasn't going to let it be daunting today. She'd seen Byron's face when he'd looked at the smashed bowl. It had told her everything she needed to know about how deeply he'd loved Alice, how hard they'd worked to keep Chocolate Haven going, and how much that meant to him.

To him, this wasn't just tradition. It wasn't just a family business. It was his life, and she was currently holding it in her clumsy hands.

"Fake it 'til you make it," she muttered, grabbing ingredients from the pantry. Carefully this time. Everything set out on the counter in the order she'd need it. Dark chocolate nibs. Peanuts. Miniature marshmallows Byron had made the previous day. Nut oil.

She lined a large baking sheet with foil, set that on the long butcher-block island that stood in the center of the room. She set an empty bowl near it, grabbed the double boiler, poured in water, and set it to simmer. She found the candy thermometer in a drawer and grabbed it, arming herself for the battle.

Not too hot. That was what all the recipe books had cautioned. She poured nibs into the top part of the boiler, the heat from the simmering water turning them glossy and soft.

This was the part she'd failed at previously.

She'd been impatient, heating the water

too quickly, letting it splash against the bottom of the boiler and overheating the chocolate.

Not this time.

She attached the thermometer to the side of the pan and stirred the chocolate with a spatula. Outside, the sun was rising. She could see hints of it through the plywood Jax had nailed in front of the window.

Byron had already called someone to fix it.

She had no idea who, but the person was supposed to be there before noon.

The chocolate's temperature crept up while she stirred, the nibs just gobs of deep brown chocolate stuck together in the bottom of the bowl. She watched the thermometer, pulled the chocolate when it was nearly all melted, and poured it into the clean bowl. She stirred it there until every bit of the nibs had disappeared and all that remained was rich, velvety melted chocolate. She added nut oil, just the way Byron did, then stirred in the marshmallows and peanuts.

Finally, she poured it onto the sheet pan, let the rich confection spread out whatever way it would.

Don't mess with it, she could almost hear Byron whispering in her ear. *The beauty of our candy is that it's handmade. People like to see different-sized pieces, different shapes. They want that handcrafted look, and we always give it to them.*

She resisted the urge to use the spatula to smooth chocolate to the very edges of the pan. She didn't add more nuts on the top or toss extra marshmallows where she didn't see any.

She let it be and stood back, shocked at what she'd accomplished. The chocolate bark looked beautiful.

"Good enough," she said, even though she knew it was better than that. Byron would be thrilled that she'd finally mastered something more complicated than shaping chocolate roses.

She pulled a pen from her apron pocket, put a huge check mark next to chocolate bark on the inventory sheet.

Now, for caramel clusters.

Someone knocked on the back door as she was stirring butter, brown sugar, corn syrup, and milk, creating caramel from scratch just the way Byron did, just the way his father and his grandfather and his great-grandfather had.

"It's unlocked," she called, sure it was the window repairman. "Come on in."

The door opened and chilly morning air

swept in. She didn't dare look away from the thermometer. The temperature was increasing rapidly, the caramel bubbling happily.

"Go ahead and get started. I'm sure Byron already explained what he wanted done on the window," she said, her focus on the candy. Almost there. Just a little more and she could take it off the burner, pour it into the bowl of perfectly toasted pecans. Not one of them had burned. Not one of them was even a little too brown. A coup, in Brenna's mind, and she wasn't going to ruin everything by burning the caramel.

"Actually, he didn't."

River.

And, dear God, if her heart didn't jump at the sound of his voice, the warm velvety timbre of it.

"I thought you were the window repairman," she murmured, lifting the caramel because it was beautiful and glossy, just the way it should be.

"Are you disappointed?" He leaned over her shoulder, watching as she poured the liquid candy over the pecans.

She could feel his warmth through the back of her shirt, feel his breath fanning her hair. When his hand settled on her shoulder, she didn't complain.

Maybe she should have.

She was getting a little too used to his touch, a little too comfortable having him around.

"Disappointed that you're late," she replied, stirring the caramel and nuts. It needed to cool enough for the mixture to drop onto a sheet pan but not enough for it to harden. After that, she'd melt more chocolate. Milk chocolate this time. She'd pour it over the top of the caramel and pecans and let it harden.

She'd read all about it in one of Byron's books, but nothing in the book had mentioned how to keep focused on candy when a good-looking guy was in the shop.

"Will this make you less disappointed?" He held a brown paper bag in front of her face, the scent of bacon filling her nose.

She turned around, looked him straight in his gorgeous eyes. "Are you trying to ruin my caramel clusters by distracting me?"

"I'm trying to keep you from passing out later in the day when you've got dozens of customers screaming for your attention and all you're subsisting on is coffee and a piece of toast."

"That is not what I had for breakfast." She took the bag and opened it, her stomach growling loudly enough that River heard it.

He grinned. "In other words, you had nothing?"

"Something like that."

"Eat. I'll handle this." He lifted the mixture, started scooping it out onto a pan. "How many of these do we need?"

She checked the inventory list. "Five dozen."

"You're going to be two dozen short."

"How do you —" She stopped, eyeing the pan he'd already filled with dollops of pecan and caramel. "Wow. You're fast."

"Eat," he commanded. "The shop opens at ten? We've got a lot to do before then."

She could have told him that all she needed was a few lessons on how to do things right. She certainly didn't need a man walking into her life and taking control of it, but he'd already tied an apron around his waist, grabbed milk chocolate morsels from the pantry, and was melting them in the double boiler.

And whatever was in the bag? It smelled phenomenal.

She dragged it out, opening waxed paper to reveal a breakfast sandwich filled with egg and cheese and bacon.

She couldn't resist it. She really couldn't, so she sat in one of the rickety old chairs and dug in, watching as River worked. He was a lot faster than she was. A lot faster than Byron even. In what seemed like the blink of an eye, he had the milk chocolate melted and was pouring it over the caramel and pecan.

Before she could comment on how great the candy looked, he'd put pecans in the oven to toast and had begun a new batch of caramel.

"Better watch it," she said as she finished off the sandwich and tossed the wrapper in the trash. "You keep working like you are and I might decide you don't need my help."

He smiled and pulled her to her feet. "Sorry, red. Everyone works in my kitchen. Whether I need help or not."

"*Your* kitchen? Don't let Byron hear you talking like that."

"Wash your hands and grab some strawberries. I'm melting enough chocolate to do the strawberry dips," he responded, giving her a gentle nudge toward the sink.

An hour later, she'd dipped three dozen strawberries into silky milk chocolate and decorated them with dark and white chocolate drizzle. She set them into the display case right between the caramel clusters and the chocolate bark.

River moved in next to her, a tray of cherry cordials in his hand. She didn't know how he'd done it, couldn't quite figure out how he was moving so quickly. They had nearly half of Byron's inventory of necessary candies made. Another hour and they'd be ready to open.

Almost.

There'd still be the fudge to make.

The Lamonts' top-secret recipe was locked away in a safe in Byron's office. No way could she give River a look at it. If she did, Byron would kill both of them.

"Looks good, huh?" River said, placing the cordials into the display case. He'd put each one in a small silver cupcake liner, the pretty foil paper adding charm to the domed candy.

"It does. Byron will be impressed."

"He'll be more impressed if we finish. What do you want to tackle next?" His arm brushed hers as he closed the display case door, and she caught herself leaning toward him just a little, imagining for just a second a repeat of that sweet, sweet kiss.

Forever Kisses.

The words ran through her head and she blinked, took a quick step back, the display case keeping her from actually turning and running.

No way in hell she was going down that path.

"Bonbons?" she murmured.

"Sure," he said, but he didn't head back to the kitchen. He didn't even move. Just stood right where he was, studying her face as if there was something utterly fascinating about it and her.

Had Dan ever looked at her like that?

She couldn't remember, and that was pretty sad. All those years with a guy who'd never, ever been fascinated? Not cool.

Mooning over a guy like River? One who obviously had his life all planned out, his course set? That wasn't cool either.

Sure, he'd kissed her, and sure, she'd kissed him back, but they were both in Benevolence for a season. Neither planned to stay. Eventually, their lives would pull them on different trajectories, and then where would they be? Brokenhearted? Alone?

She'd rather just stay alone to begin with.

"I saw a recipe for coconut dream bonbons," she said, the words coming out in a rush. "Granddad has never made them, but they're a play off the cocoa and cream ones he makes every Saturday. I thought I'd make half his and half the coconut. They'll look really pretty together in the case: cocoa dusted bonbons next to ones rolled in coconut." She was blabbering on like an idiot because he was still standing between her and the kitchen and she wasn't sure why it mattered. Why she didn't just step to the side and walk past him.

She could have very easily. Just like she could have told him that the kiss they'd shared had been a mistake, that she didn't ever want a repeat of it.

"You're nervous."

"And?"

"I want to know why."

"Because I've got a lot to do in a limited amount of time."

"Liar."

"Maybe, but what good would the truth do?"

"It might help me understand."

"Why do you even need to?" She tried to laugh, the sound echoing hollowly through the shop as she finally got herself moving past him and into the hallway.

"We're going to be working together a lot these next two weeks. Understanding each other will go a long way in making that easier."

"Hasn't it already been easy?" she asked, because it had been. Somehow, they'd just kind of moved into each other's rhythms, synched with each other's energy.

"So, maybe I lied, too, red," he said as he

grabbed ingredients from the pantry. "Maybe I find you interesting and maybe that interest is making me want to know more."

"Like?"

"Why you're lying to your family."

He turned to face her and she couldn't get the words out, the ones she was supposed to say: *I'm not lying. Why would you think I'm lying? Who told you I was lying?*

"They don't need more to worry about" came out instead.

"Isn't that for them to decide?"

"You've seen Byron. He's not a young man anymore. Adeline is pregnant. My mother —"

"I think your mother can handle anything you throw her way."

"Don't let her fool you, River. She puts on a good show, but she spends way too much time and energy worrying about us."

"Like I said, isn't that for her to decide?"

"You don't know my family."

"Up until I was thirteen, I didn't know any family at all," he responded. "Finally having one taught me just how valuable they are."

"I value my family." She tore open a package of coconut, dumped it into a blender, and ground it into a fine powder.

He didn't say anything, so she turned to face him again. "I *do* value them."

"I know," he said simply. "But I'm not sure you realize how much they value you."

"They value what they think I am," she said. "That's not the same as valuing me."

"You're limiting their love if you think that."

"What I think —"

Is that it's none of your business, she was going to say, but something in his expression stopped the words before she could say them.

"Go ahead," he offered. "Say what you're thinking."

She didn't have a chance. The back door flew open and Janelle rushed in. She'd pulled her hair back into a tight bun, wrapped some kind of frilly fifties apron around her waist.

"I'm here to help!" she proclaimed. "I heard you were in the weeds and I . . ." Her voice trailed off as she saw River. "I didn't realize Byron had hired a professional. How fun! We'll all work together and get this shop open!"

"Wonderful," Brenna muttered, but Janelle was too busy eyeing River like he was a piece of dark chocolate fudge to hear her.

■ ■ ■ ■

Janelle was a force to be reckoned with.

It took River about three minutes to realize that and about a half a minute longer
to realize she knew nothing about making
candy. She sure as hell thought she did,
though. She moved around the kitchen like
a whirlwind, gushing over everything he did
and criticizing Brenna's efforts.

It seemed like nothing her youngest
daughter did was right.

Not the coconut she'd turned into powder: too chunky.

Not the white chocolate she'd melted for
her coconut dream bonbons: too thick.

Not the way she'd rolled the chocolate for
the bonbons or the way she'd set them in
the display case. An hour in and River had
had about all he could take of the woman.
He also thought he'd figured out why
Brenna hadn't been honest with her family.

It would be really hard to admit to a
woman like Janelle that you'd been tricked
by your fiancé. Not just cheated on but
robbed blind and left with nothing.

That's the way River read things.

He could be wrong.

It could be that the guy hadn't taken

nearly what River thought he had. Didn't matter. He was still a bastard, and Brenna deserved better.

She also deserved better than what she was getting from her mother. He washed the last pot, eyed the inventory list. They only had one thing left to make: the Lamont fudge.

"You have a recipe for the fudge, red?" he asked, and Janelle frowned.

"Red? Is that any way to describe a beautiful woman?" She laughed, but there was a sharpness to it that set River's teeth on edge.

"It is if she has the reddest hair a person has ever seen."

"Not red, River," Janelle corrected. "It's more of a —"

"Let it go, Mother," Brenna said with a sigh.

"I'm simply saying —"

"You don't have to say anything. I like the nickname. It doesn't bother me that he calls me that." She met River's eyes and offered a tight smile. "Let it go."

"Fine, but I hope you're not planning to show him Byron's recipe. Your grandfather will have a stroke if you do."

"Only if he finds out," Brenna muttered.

"I hope you're kidding," Janelle huffed. "You know how he feels about it."

"Yes, Mother, I do. Rest assured, I'll keep the secret recipe secret. If a dozen armed men break into the shop, demanding that I either reveal the recipe or give up my life, I'll gladly sacrifice myself for the cause."

"Well!" Janelle set her hands on her slim waist. "There's no need to be sarcastic, Brenna."

"And there's no need for you to criticize someone who has done nothing wrong."

"Is that what you think I'm doing? Criticizing?"

"What would you call it?"

"Standing up for my daughter." She frowned. "But obviously, that isn't necessary or needed." She lifted her chin, her eyes flashing with irritation and something that looked a lot like hurt. "So, I'll just go to work and do what I do best: stay out of my daughters' lives."

"Mom —" Brenna began, but Janelle was already at the door.

"Don't forget your sister's birthday party. Unless you think you'll be too busy making chocolate to attend," Janelle said, as she broke into whatever apology Brenna might have offered. "I'd suggest you bring a date." Her gaze cut to River. "But you're probably too independent and accomplished to worry about such things."

"I don't —"

Janelle didn't wait for Brenna to finish. She closed the door firmly enough to rattle the bowls in the cupboards.

"Shit," Brenna muttered, squeezing the bridge of her nose and shaking her head. "How do I manage to constantly piss her off?"

It was a rhetorical question, but River was just irritated enough to respond. "I think she did a fair job of pissing you off first."

"No. She didn't."

"She was critical of you since she first walked into the shop," he pointed out. "Are you trying to tell me that didn't bother you?"

"She's my mother. She's been criticizing me my whole life."

"That doesn't mean it doesn't hurt."

"It doesn't."

"Maybe it should," he argued.

"Why? She means well, and I know it. Getting offended is a waste of time and energy."

"And yet, you're worried about offending her."

"What's your point, River? That I'm some weak-minded woman who lets everyone take advantage of her? That somehow I'm too stupid to know that my mother is putting me down? Or too wimpy to tell her to stop?"

"That's a hell of a lot of baggage you're dumping on me."

She frowned. "You're right. I apologize. Thanks for your help today. I couldn't have done this without you."

"Now go away and leave me alone? Is that what you're saying?"

She smiled, shook her head. "What I'm saying is that I appreciate all your help, but I have to make fudge and you can't be here. So, you're going to have to leave. The shop opens in half an hour, and the only fudge I've got is what's left from yesterday."

"You sure you don't want my help?"

"I want your help, but if I take it, I'll betray every Lamont who ever came before me. That'll piss off Janelle and Byron. Not something I'm in the mood to do."

"It might be fun," he said, brushing thick strands of red hair from her cheeks.

"I have this strange feeling," she responded "that anything we do together would be."

"We can test your theory out tonight," he said, his hands gliding along silky flesh, settling on her narrow shoulders.

"Tonight?"

"I'll pick you up at seven."

"That's probably not a good idea."

"Have you forgotten about our deal? I help you, you help me?"

"You don't really need my help. Admit it. You're not the kind of guy who'd let someone else design his restaurant. You're not the kind of person who doubts his taste or his abilities. You probably had your hand in every single aspect of building your brand."

"You're right," he admitted, because she deserved the truth. She'd been lied to enough, hurt enough, and he'd never add to that. Not even for Belinda and the ranch. "But I do need your help if I'm going to convince the business council to grant my permit. They want someone local —"

"You can buy local without my help. No one around here is going to turn away your money."

"So, maybe it's not your help with the business council I want. Maybe it's just you."

"Not the right time," she said, but she didn't move away.

He didn't think she could any more than he could.

They were tied together, bound in some way he couldn't even begin to understand. All he knew was that there was something between them. Something he couldn't explain away as simple attraction. He'd been in plenty of relationships. He knew heat and desire and lust.

What he felt with Brenna was different.

It was warm and true and compelling.

It made him want to do the right thing. Even if the right thing was stepping back, putting some distance between them.

He let his hands fall away.

"You choose the time, Brenna. When you're ready, let me know. Now, I guess I'd better get going. I've got spark plugs to buy if you're going to bring your car home tonight."

She didn't argue.

She didn't say another word.

Not as he removed the apron, hung it on the hook, opened the back door. Not even as he walked outside.

He could feel her standing in the doorway, knew she was watching as he walked to his truck. He opened the door, turned, and met her eyes.

They were deep violet in the sunlight, her skin flawless, her expression guarded.

"Thanks again, River," she said so quietly the words barely carried on the still morning air.

"Chocolate is easy," he replied, climbing into the car.

"It's not chocolate I'm talking about," she said. "See you tonight."

She closed the door, and he sat where he was for just long enough to convince himself not to go back, not to take what he thought she might be willing to give.

She wasn't ready and he wasn't going to push.

He had time.

Benevolence wasn't what he'd wanted. It wasn't where he'd thought his life would be headed, but there he was. He couldn't say he didn't like it. He couldn't say there wasn't something quaint and wholesome and nice about being back in the place where he'd finally learned what family meant.

He'd let that last for as long as it did, and if that meant forever, who was he to complain? He'd built his restaurants. He'd made good money doing it. Maybe it was time to put a little of the love Belinda and Dillard had given him back into the place they'd always called home.

CHAPTER TEN

Twelve hours into her fifth day on the job and Brenna still hated fudge.

She didn't just hate it. She hated it to the very depth of her soul.

She stood at the stove anyway, stirring up another batch of what had made Chocolate Haven famous: Lamont family fudge. The stuff had won awards. Its praises had been sung in magazines and on talk shows. There were celebrities who raved about the stuff, brides who ordered pounds of it for their nuptials, and moms-to-be who craved it like other women craved pickles and ice cream.

Yep. Lamont family fudge was the keystone to Chocolate Haven's success.

Brenna couldn't make it to save her life.

Which was a problem, considering she needed about fifteen pounds of it. Stat. She had orders for it coming out of her eyeballs: Internet orders, call-in orders, walk-in orders. It seemed every person who'd walked into the shop, called the shop, or gotten on the shop Web site that day desperately wanted Lamont fudge. She'd sold all that was left from the previous day and now she had to find a way to make more.

Brenna eyed the pan of melted chocolate, condensed milk, and a few other ingredients that seemed determined to float at the top of the sludgy mess that was supposed to be fudge. *This* definitely wasn't the way.

She'd read the recipe in Byron's office.

She'd reread it and reread it again.

She'd committed it to memory because Byron had made her swear not to leave it where anyone could see it.

She'd followed the recipe. *To a T!*

And this was what she had for her efforts: a pot full of crap.

She stirred it frantically, hoping to smooth it out a little more. No such luck. Even with the temperature exactly right, the ingredients precisely measured, the kitchen clean and neat and prepared for greatness, she'd still managed to make a mess of the one thing she absolutely had to get right.

She dipped a spoon into the sludge and tasted it.

It looked disgusting, but it wasn't horrible. So, maybe she wasn't making a mess of things. Maybe she was just making a mediocre facsimile of Lamont fudge. Someone would probably eat it and be satisfied, but that someone sure as hell wouldn't be anyone who'd ever tasted the real deal.

She sighed, pouring the lumpy mixture into a prepared pan and doing everything in her power to make it look glossy and luscious.

It looked like a big pile of shi—

The phone rang and she grabbed it and the yellow pad Byron took orders on. No doubt she'd be asked for another pound of fudge. Milk chocolate. Peanut butter. S'more. Or one of the six other flavors Chocolate Haven offered. She could add another pound of impossible to the list of what she needed, and then she could try the recipe again.

What was this? The sixth time today? The seventh?

"Chocolate Haven. Brenna speaking. How can I help you?"

"It's your mother," Janelle said, her voice knife-edged sharp.

"Hey, Mom. What's up?" She tried to sound pleasant. God knew she tried, but Janelle had special mother radar that detected every hint of attitude in any of her daughters' voices. Right at that moment, Brenna had a serious attitude. Twelve hours of chocolate, several pans of mediocre fudge, and she had a chip on her shoulder the size of Mount Everest. She was willing to admit it. Just not to Janelle.

"No need to get snotty before we even begin the conversation."

"I'm not snotty. I'm busy," she corrected, scowling at the pan of fudge. It looked like her life: a mucky mess of disparate parts that would not go together no matter how much she tried to make them.

"Too busy to return my texts?"

"Did you text me?" She hadn't had time to grab lunch, let alone check her phone and return texts or calls. She pulled it out of her apron pocket. Four text messages and three phone calls, probably from Jeff. She set the phone on the counter, went back to trying to smooth the fudge.

"Did I text you? I texted you *four* times."

"Like I said, I've been busy. Granddad wasn't in the shop today."

"Because you kicked him out," Janelle replied. Obviously she and Byron had been talking, and obviously the discussion hadn't made Janelle happy. The two might disagree at times, but they loved and respected each other. No way would Janelle let any of her daughters treat Byron badly.

Not that any of them would.

Not that Brenna *had.*

She'd simply stated the obvious: Byron was in a pissy mood and he needed to get out of the kitchen until he got over it.

He'd taken her suggestion seriously.

So seriously he hadn't bothered returning.

She'd managed.

With help from River.

She shoved thoughts of him away. She wasn't going to think about how nice it might be to take a chance, be a little adventurous, allow herself to explore what he was offering.

"You did kick him out, right?" Janelle pressed, that sharp edge still in her voice.

"Kick him out? That's a gross exaggeration." She poked the fudge with a fork. Hard as a rock, it now looked like brown cement. Gorgeous.

"Not according to Byron. He said you told him to leave his own store. He was very hurt by your rudeness."

"Byron can take it as easily as he can dish it out, Mom. I'm sure he wasn't heartbroken."

"You didn't see the look on his face when we met for coffee. Fortunately, I was able to smooth things over by reminding him that you just recently got out of a bad relationship."

"It's been months."

"It still must hurt. You loved Dan so much, and to have him betray you with another woman like he did . . . I just can't even imagine."

Brenna could picture Janelle shaking her head, her hair not moving an inch from whatever perfect style she'd lacquered it into. "Like I said, it's been months, and I'm trying to put the entire fiasco out of my mind."

"As well you should. There is no sense wasting another second of your passion on that asshole."

"Mother!" Brenna exclaimed, genuinely surprised by her mother's language. Janelle had always been too refined and ladylike to use crass language.

"What? It's not like you haven't referred to him that way."

"Not in front of you."

"Does that make it any less the truth?"

"I guess not."

"My point is this, Brenna: You're young and beautiful. There are dozens and dozens of men out there who'd gladly take Dan's place."

"I'm not looking for a replacement."

"You should be. Look at your sisters. Both of them are so happy."

"I know," she mumbled, hacking at the chocolate cement as if it had committed some crime against her. Bits of hardened fudge flew into the air, smacked her in the cheek, bounced off the wall.

"They are, Brenna. It shocked me more than anyone when Adeline and Sinclair got together, but they're the perfect couple. Don't you think?"

"As perfect as any couple can be," she admitted, telling herself that she wasn't at all envious of that. She loved Addie. She was excited to see her in love and married and pregnant, but — God help her — she wanted all those things, too.

"And Willow . . . she's such a lovely girl. She's always been just so . . ."

"Perfect?" Because that was how Brenna had always thought of her. Perfect student, perfect daughter, perfect sister. Unlike Brenna, she'd never caused her family a moment of worry. A prosecuting attorney with a reputation that had brought her into the national spotlight on more than one occasion, Willow made her living putting criminals behind bars. When she wasn't doing that, she was volunteering in homeless shelters, working with battered women, mentoring young women.

"No one is perfect, but Willow sure tries. Hopefully, that won't come back to haunt her the way it did . . ." She paused. "Never mind. I didn't call to talk about your sisters. And I didn't call to harass you about Byron. I know the man can be a pain in the butt. I called because I owe you an apology."

"For . . . ?"

"This morning. You girls are too sweet to complain about it, or maybe you're just too used to it to notice, but I can be a little critical sometimes. A little more negative than I should be."

"It's okay."

"No. It really isn't. I used to be like you, Brenna: a free spirit, the entire world stretching out in front of me. I had big dreams and I thought they'd all come true. Then I met your dad, and none of those things seemed to matter."

"Until he was gone?"

"No. They didn't even matter after that. I'd had what I wanted, and I wanted to make sure you girls had it, too. All the love and contentment and joy. I guess I started nitpicking to make sure none of you got on the wrong path. Noah says . . ." She stopped herself again.

"Noah?"

"Story. He was here for May's wedding. Remember?"

Of course she remembered. Janelle had blushed like a schoolgirl every time she'd looked at the guy. If Brenna hadn't been so caught up in the drama of finding out Dan had cheated, she would have asked some questions, found out a little more about the guy who'd once taught at Benevolence High.

"I remember him. Is he still in town?"

"He moved back a few months ago."

"And you talk to him often, do you?"

"Did I say that?" Janelle hedged. "I need to go. I've got a meeting with Katie Flemings at In Season Blooms. She's going to make flower arrangements for your sister's party."

"Do you really think Willow is going to want you to go to the trouble? She likes things simple."

"These will be simple and elegant. Just like your sister. I'll see you at church tomorrow, dear."

"I'm not going to —" *church.*

"Of course you are. Adeline needs her family's support while her husband is away."

"He's in Seattle, Mom. It's not like he's been deployed."

"Does it matter? Adeline has always been

there for us. Never once has she ever said no when we've needed her."

True. Every bit of it.

"So, of course you'll be there to sit beside her when her husband can't."

"What about you?"

"I always attend church. Wear a dress that covers your thighs or Millicent Montgomery will have something to say about it." Janelle hung up.

Great. Wonderful. Now Brenna was going to have to walk into the Lord's house with dozens of lies hidden in her heart.

Lies about why she'd closed her store.

Lies about what had happened between her and Dan.

Lies about her financial situation, her home, her happiness.

Lies about her ability to make the Lamont family fudge.

She scowled, snatching the pan from the counter and carrying it to the trash can. She tried to dump it out, but it stuck fast. Just like all the stupid lies she'd told.

I'm fine.

Things are good.

I've lost my passion for retail and I think it's time to try something new.

It's easier to drive to Benevolence than to fly.

Why couldn't she have been transparent? Why couldn't she have been as vulnerable and real as Adeline had been when her high school sweetheart had dumped her? Why couldn't she have just run home the minute she'd realized what Dan had done, let her family enfold her the way they'd enfolded Adeline all those years ago?

Because she wasn't Adeline, that's why.

The expectations for her were different. It was fine for Addie to stay in Benevolence. It was fine for her to buy a little house and run a business there. It was fine for her to mourn the loss of her first love.

Brenna was supposed to be above that.

Janelle thought she was.

The entire town thought she was, and she hadn't wanted to disappoint. She hadn't wanted to let them know just how human she really was.

"Idiot," she grumbled, grabbing the knife and sliding it between the fudge and the side of the pan. She tried to pry the chocolate out, but it still wouldn't budge.

"Give me a break! Okay? Just this one time, can something please just work?" The fudge suddenly flew from the pan and the knife slipped, slicing across her knuckles so quickly she didn't even realize what had happened until blood bubbled from the wound.

Wound*s*?

She eyed the gashes that ran across the pointer, middle, and ring finger on her left hand.

"Dang it!" she yelled.

She probably would have been proud of herself for the improvement in her language if she hadn't been bleeding like a stuck pig.

She grabbed a hand towel, pressed it to her knuckles, kicked the lump of fudge that had somehow missed the trash can and landed on the floor.

"This was not what I meant," she muttered, blood seeping through the towel and dripping onto the floor.

She'd need stitches. No doubt about that.

She ran into Byron's office and grabbed the first aid kit, found a roll of gauze she could use to wrap her fingers. The towel was too bulky, so she replaced it with gauze pads, wound more gauze around that.

"Good enough," she muttered as she grabbed her purse and headed for the back door.

She was out in the parking lot before she realized she didn't have a car. It was right around that time that she realized she didn't have her phone either. She did have her keys. At least she thought she had her keys. She dug through her purse, found a pack of tissue, a piece of gum, her empty wallet. Keys!

She lifted them triumphantly, was dancing her way back to the door, feeling pretty damn accomplished, when a car pulled around the corner of the building, what looked like a window hanging out of the trunk.

Not just any car.

Her car. Purring like a contented cat. She almost couldn't believe it was the same car that had sputtered its way across the country.

She waited until River parked, then ran toward him.

"Perfect timing," she exclaimed, yanking open the passenger door before she realized Mack was in the seat.

"Ma'am," he said as she backed away. "Your grandfather wants me to fix the window." His gaze dropped to her hand. "You okay?"

"Just a little cut," she responded, even though blood was already seeping through the layers of gauze.

"Looks like more than a little one to me." He strode to the back of the car, lifted the window out of the trunk. "Got the keys from Byron. You go on and get that hand looked at. I'll take care of things here."

"The kitchen is a mess. I had a fight with some fudge and —"

"Brenna," River cut in, "Mack has seen worse than whatever you left in the kitchen."

"I know, but —"

He got out of the Chrysler, walked around, and lifted her gauze-wrapped hand. "Mind if I take a look?"

"Knock yourself out."

River unwrapped the gauze.

She'd done a hell of a job on herself. Three fingers had been cut. At least one deeply enough to require stitches. He wasn't sure about the others.

"I'd ask you how you did this, but that would waste time you could be spending getting it stitched up. I'll give you a ride over."

"That's not necessary. I can drive myself."

"Why would you?"

"Because I've been doing things for myself for a long time? I drove myself to the ER when I busted my left ankle three years ago. I walked to the hospital last year when I had a reaction to an antibiotic. Six months ago, I sprained my wrist when I tripped over a curb, and I —"

"Let me guess," he muttered, rewrapping her hand and nudging her into the car. "You walked to the ER? Drove yourself to a clinic? Took the metro to the nearest medical facility?"

She laughed. "I hailed a cab and paid someone to drive me."

"Where was your fiancé during all of this?"

Must have been the wrong question to ask. The laughter died, all the amusement seeping out of her face. "Working."

"That sounds like an easy excuse for him to make." He pulled out of the parking lot, turning onto Main Street and heading toward the edge of town. There was a small medical clinic there. Serious injuries or trauma required transportation to a hospital in Spokane, but cut fingers, broken bones, colds, flus, and other everyday medical issues could be dealt with there.

"I guess it was," she responded, pulling her knees up to her chin and wrapping her arms around them. "I guess it also was an easy excuse for me to accept."

"Did it bother you?"

"It should have."

"So . . . no?"

"I realized after we broke up that the relationship had become more of a habit than anything else."

262

"I went there one time," he admitted. "Spent a lot of time with a woman who should have been perfect for me. Turns out, she wasn't. We liked each other enough, got along well enough, but we both realized enough wasn't what either of us wanted."

"You broke up?"

"More like we just sat down and discussed things and realized we weren't going to miss what we had. Then we went our separate ways. She got engaged six months later. They invited me to the wedding."

"Did you go?"

"Why wouldn't I? We were still friends, and I knew he made her happy in a way I never could have."

"That seems . . . sad."

"It isn't. The way I see it, better to let her go off and be happy with someone else than cling to something that really wasn't working for either of us."

She sighed. "Wish I'd realized that before Dan and I got engaged. Actually, I wish I'd realized it before we started dating."

"Kind of difficult to see the truth about something before you're actually doing it."

"Not really. Dan was smart and charming. He knew exactly what to say to make a person feel special. I knew that from the beginning. It should have been enough to send me running."

"There had to be a reason why it wasn't."

"Truth?" she asked, and he could feel her steady gaze, knew she was watching him intently. "I didn't want to settle. I wanted the most romantic story ever told. The kind of love that was just meant to be. No questions. No explanations. No rhyme or reason to it."

"That kind of love doesn't just happen, red," he said as he pulled into the clinic parking lot. "It takes work. It takes remembering every day that the person you're with is the person you're meant to be with."

"Maybe," she admitted, opening the door and getting out of the car. The sun had just drifted below distant mountains, the pink gold sky and dusky light shimmering behind her and turning her hair to burnished fire. She had the lean, hungry look of her trade, a body that somehow made jeans and a chocolate-flecked T-shirt look avant-garde. No earrings. No jewelry. No oversized sunglasses or huge handbag, but River could still picture her walking the runway or standing in a garden or stirring chocolate at the Chocolate Haven stove.

"You're beautiful. You know that?" he said, and she smiled.

"I've never been beautiful and I'm especially not beautiful with chocolate in my hair and all over my skin, my hand wrapped in layers of gauze, and a hole in my T-shirt." She poked at a spot near her stomach. "If Janelle were here, she'd be appalled."

"She's not," he said simply, walking around to her side of the car. "And whoever told you that you weren't beautiful lied."

"I'm interesting, River. Didn't anyone ever tell you that that's what runway models are? We're not the fashion magazine beauties, we're the odd ducks, the gangly, awkward misfits who kids laughed at in school."

"Kids laughed at you?"

"Who knows? I always had my nose so deep in a book, I didn't know what anyone else was doing."

"I remember that."

"The wagonload of books, huh?" She smiled, a tiny little curve of the lips that changed her face, made the sharp angles softer, the edges less defined. The awkward beauty she'd so quickly described became a different thing: a unique and gorgeous twist on the girl next door, the nerdy bookworm, the girl he probably would have ignored in high school but that he'd noticed when she was a kid.

"Yes."

"Did you ever imagine when you were

watching me pull that wagon that you'd be taking me to the clinic with a cut hand?"

"I never imagined I'd come back to Benevolence once I left it." He slipped his arm through hers and tugged her to the clinic door. "But here I am, and here you are, so . . . Why not be bringing you to the clinic with a cut on your hand?"

"Or helping me in the kitchen?"

"Or getting your help at the ranch." He brushed a few flecks of chocolate from her hair. "Which, by the way, is a hit with Belinda. She'd forgotten all about the photos you pulled out. Angel said she took one look at them and started gushing with happiness."

"I'm glad someone is happy with what I'm accomplishing."

"Who isn't?"

"My family."

"Not Byron. He's been singing your praises all over town." He opened the clinic door and let her walk through in front of him. Could he help it if he noticed the way her faded jeans hugged her hips, the way her fitted T rode up her back, revealing just a hint of silky skin between it and her apron strings?

Probably, but he noticed anyway. Just like he noticed the strands of burgundy in her

266

red hair, the streaks of strawberry and auburn.

"He's lying." She signed in at the receptionist's desk, dropped into a chair, her long legs stretched out in front of her. "To protect the family name."

"Why would he need to do that?"

"Because I can't make the dam—rn fudge, River. Why else? Then there's the fact that I've made a mess of his kitchen every day for the past five days."

"It looked good this morning."

"That was before this!" She raised her gauze-wrapped hand, brushed a few flecks of fudge off her jeans.

There was more of it on her shoulders, in her hair, speckled across her neck and collarbones.

Seeing her sitting there looking completely comfortable in her fudge-flecked skin made him smile. "You really did have a fight with that fudge, didn't you?"

"A knock-down, drag-out battle. Which I lost."

"You'll win the war, though. That's what counts."

"How do you know? I could spend the next two weeks trying to make that fudge and never succeeding. Byron could return from his Alaskan fishing trip to a closed shop with a FOR SALE sign on its front door."

He chuckled and she scowled. "It's a serious concern of mine, River. What if I'm the one who runs Chocolate Haven into the ground? What if everything has been going just great for over a hundred years and then I walk in and wreck it? Generations of tradition taken down by one clumsy candy maker."

"If Byron thought you couldn't handle it —"

"Don't even go there. We both know he asked you to help out."

"I knew. I didn't know you did."

"It was pretty obvious. He spent thirty minutes muttering under his breath this morning, saying he needed to find someone who could help me before he left. Chase is busy with school and Adeline is busy with morning sickness, so there weren't a whole lot of options. And he had no idea we'd already made a deal, or that you were already planning to teach me your mad skills."

He smiled at that. "Mad skills?"

"You're a wizard in the kitchen. I read it in the Portland *Times* and in the *Bay City Confidential*."

"You've been stalking me online?" he

asked, amused by the conversation and by Brenna. She might have been through hell, but she still had a sense of humor.

"Of course. It's what people do."

"People?"

"People like me." She grinned.

"That explains it," he said, lifting her uninjured hand and running his thumb along the underside of her wrist, brushing away the bits of chocolate and specks of sugar that coated the silky flesh.

"Explains what?" Her voice had gone a little husky, her eyes a little dark, and if they hadn't been sitting in a waiting area in a medical clinic, he might have leaned in and answered the question with a kiss.

Hell. He might just do it anyway.

"Why I've never been stalked before. I've never had anyone like you in my life."

"Lucky," she said with a nervous laugh, and he brushed her lips with his, just barely a touch to capture those nerves and those sweet, velvety lips.

Better than chocolate.

That's what he was thinking as he backed away.

"I'm not going to apologize," he said quietly.

"I'm not going to ask you to."

A nurse appeared, looking at a clipboard

269

as she called Brenna's name.

"That's my cue," she said, nearly jumping to her feet.

"Want me to come back with you?"

"No. Thanks. I'm fine." She nearly ran to the nurse's side, didn't look back as she disappeared into the treatment area.

He should have been satisfied with that.

He'd told her he'd wait.

He'd said she could decide what she wanted and how much.

He'd told himself he had time. *They* had time.

But he still wanted to walk back with her. He still wanted to be the one sitting beside her as the doctor examined her hand. If she needed a hand to hold, he wanted it to be his.

"You've got it bad," he muttered, and the receptionist looked up from her computer, smiled.

"Pardon me?" she asked.

"Nothing," he replied, crossing his arms over his chest and settling in for however long the waiting would take.

CHAPTER ELEVEN

By Brenna's standards, things were going pretty well. The nurse hadn't made her put on one of those god-awful hospital gowns. The doctor hadn't questioned her intelligence when she'd explained how she'd cut her hand. Two of her fingers had only needed to be cleaned and butterfly bandaged. The other one needed stitches, but she could deal with that.

So far, she hadn't gotten a call from her mother, Byron, or either of her sisters. The fact that she'd left her cell phone at the shop might have had something to do with that, but she was celebrating the little things, so she'd celebrate that.

Yep. Things were going astoundingly well.

Until she heard sirens.

Not typical in Benevolence, so she stood up and took notice. Literally. She jumped off the exam table and looked out into the deepening night. She could see emergency lights in the distance. One set. Two. Not ambulances or fire trucks. These lights were from law enforcement vehicles. It had to be something big, then. A robbery? Assault? Murder? Those things were rare in Benevolence, but they'd happened.

She leaned closer to the glass, her forehead resting against the cool pane. The evening light made it difficult to calculate distances, but she was pretty sure the emergency was between the clinic and Main Street.

Actually, from where she was standing, it looked like the emergency was *on* Main Street. She could make out the roofline of the brownstones that housed Chocolate Haven and a few other shops. Were the police cars right in front of it?

As she watched, an ambulance sped through the clinic parking lot. She followed its progress, her stomach churning. Hopefully everyone was okay. In a town the size of Benevolence, one person's heartache was everyone's. Like the time Cramer Lister beat his wife to a pulp. She'd been rushed to Spokane for surgery on her broken jaw and shattered cheek. He'd been taken off to jail. Their six-year-old twins had been left alone in the house. Brenna's father had still been alive then, and she remembered the sirens mixing with the sound of his voice as he'd answered the phone. She'd heard the rise and fall of his voice, the emotion in it. After he'd hung up, he'd talked quietly to her mom, and then he'd left the house. An hour later, he'd returned with the twins.

They'd stayed with the Lamonts until their grandmother arrived. She'd taken them somewhere. California? Oregon? Brenna didn't remember that, but she did remember the hushed morning that had followed. She remembered how quiet her classmates had been at school, how somber the teachers had been.

It had been the same when her father was diagnosed with brain cancer, and even worse when he'd died. The hush. The silences. The helpless people working tirelessly to make something that couldn't be anything but tragic better.

In small towns people felt communal joy, communal contentment, communal grief. They had the deep, unrelenting need to connect with one another, to be part of whatever the town defined them as. In Benevolence, the town was like its name: compassionate caring. No one ever went hungry there. No one was ever left alone. Memories never died either. Nothing was ever let go of or released. A reputation made was forged forever and almost impossible to change.

Brenna had learned that young. Maybe it had been one of the reasons she'd left. She hadn't wanted to cling to her father's memory the way other people had. She hadn't wanted to grow up in the shadow of his greatness or her sisters. There'd been days when she hadn't wanted to be a Lamont, when she'd thought she'd rather be a librarian, a book seller, an author; anything other than one of the Lamonts.

The ambulance lights seemed to merge with the others, coalescing into a mass of flashing strobes.

Leaving her cell phone behind hadn't been such a good thing after all.

If she had it, she could call someone, find out exactly what was going on.

"Knock, knock," the nurse called, rolling a cart into the room. "How's that finger? Numb enough for stitches?"

"I think so."

"Great! The doctor is on the way. I've got everything set for him, so it shouldn't take long."

"Any idea what's happening in town?" Brenna asked, tearing her attention away from the lights and turning to face the young woman. She looked like a teenager, her hair pulled up in a high ponytail, her makeup a little overdone for the workplace. She had Hello Kitty scrubs and enough earrings in her left ear to qualify her as a jewelry dispenser. She had a nice smile, though, and a face that made Brenna wonder if they'd known each other a decade ago.

"I wish. Dottie at reception said —" She paused, glanced out into the hall, and then moving close enough to whisper in Brenna's ear. "They found a body."

"What?"

"That's what she heard." The nurse pulled back, tugged at the end of her ponytail. Her name tag read RAYNA. Not a name Brenna found familiar. Maybe she knew her older sister?

"From who?"

"A guy named Andy. He's an EMT."

"Is he at the scene?"

"No. He's off duty, but he heard it on the police scanner."

"He actually heard them say there was a body?" she questioned, because she kept thinking about the person she'd thought she'd seen running toward the park, the brick that had gone through the window, and the emergency lights that seemed to be somewhere on Main Street. Her heart gave a sickening little thump and she swallowed down a lump of cold, hard fear.

"Who knows? Dottie likes to exaggerate. Don't we all? But she seemed pretty certain of what she was saying. There was a body, or something that made the police think there might be a body."

"Did he say where?"

"Somewhere on Main Street. If he gave the address, Dottie didn't have it. Go ahead and sit down. Dr. Wilson —"

"Is right here." The doctor stepped into the room, pulled a chair over, and got the stitch kit ready.

Seconds later, Brenna's finger was being sewn back together.

One. Two. Three. Four.

She counted each stitch impatiently.

Main Street. That's what the nurse had said. It's what Brenna had thought, and that lump of fear filled her throat again. She felt sick with it, her pulse racing frantically.

"You okay?" the doctor asked as he placed another stitch.

"Fine."

"You look pale."

"I'm a redhead."

He eyed her dispassionately, then shook his head. "Can you go get her friend, Rayna? She might need some moral support."

276

"I don't need —"

Rayna had already run from the room; Brenna didn't bother finishing. Just counted the last two stitches, the sound of sirens seeming to grow louder.

"Is that an ambulance?" she asked, and the doctor nodded.

"Sounds like it."

She wanted to ask more questions, but he seemed more interested in finishing the job than talking. She pressed her lips together, waiting impatiently while he tied off the thread.

"This looks good," he exclaimed happily, wrapping gauze around the finger and using medical tape to hold it in place. "I used small stitches, so it shouldn't scar too badly."

"I'm not worried about scars."

"With your career, I thought it might matter."

"I work in a chocolate shop," she said dryly.

"You've come full circle, huh?"

"What's that supposed to mean?"

"You were working in the shop when I was a teenager and you were about this high." He held his hand up to his waist. "Then you went off on your big adventure and now you're back."

"Thanks for the truncated version of my life story."

He smiled and stood. "I'm sure I missed a lot. I didn't know you very well. I'm Porter Wilson. I graduated with your sister Willow. She and I used to hang out."

"Porter the football player?" She did remember. He'd been a tall, loud, brash young kid who'd been absolutely nothing like Willow.

Brenna had despised him on sight.

"That was during another lifetime, Ms. Lamont," he said with a grin. "I gave that up after I graduated high school and decided that chasing after a ball or running it into an end zone wasn't my thing."

"And medicine was?" she asked, surprised, because his father had owned one of two private medical practices in the town and Porter had always been very verbal about his disdain for that. He'd had bigger dreams, wanted better things.

"As hard as it is for everyone around here to believe, yes." He washed his hands, glanced at his watch. "Strange how life works, right? I used to think I'd be some national football star making millions of dollars in the NFL. Instead, I followed in my old man's footsteps. Now I'm a small-town doctor in a tiny little clinic."

"If you don't like it, I'm sure there are plenty of other opportunities for physicians in bigger towns than this one."

"You're right. I got offers from hospitals in Seattle, Portland, and San Jose. I decided to come back home." He jotted something on her chart. "Oddly enough, sometimes the things we think we'll never miss end up being the things we long for most. Besides, it makes me happy to see my parents happy. I was a cocky little pain in the ass when I was a teen, and they probably thought I'd never amount to anything. Now we eat dinner together every Sunday night and they tell me how good it is to have me home."

"That's really nice, Porter," she said, and meant it.

"You know what would be even nicer?" he asked as he tucked a pen into the pocket of his lab coat. "Spending next Friday having dinner with you."

It was a completely inappropriate invitation. He knew it. She could see the gleam in his eyes: amusement mixed with a healthy dose of self-deprecation.

"I have a feeling," she said, "that you won't have any trouble finding someone else to have dinner with."

"Is that a no?"

"It's a hell no," River growled as he

walked into the room, the nurse scurrying along behind him.

"River Maynard," Porter responded, giving River a once-over that probably didn't make him happy. "You haven't changed a whole lot, brother."

"I'm not your brother."

"We used to call each other that," Porter said mildly.

"That was a long time and a lot of shit ago," River growled. "I'm surprised you're working here. I'd have thought they would have kept someone like you far away from a place like this."

That was an odd thing to say, and Brenna wondered if there was something between the two men, some past drama or trauma that she didn't know about.

"People change," Porter replied, shoving his hands into the pockets of his lab coat. "When they do, they deserve to be given second chances. You, more than anyone else, should know that."

"What I know is that I'd have been happier if I hadn't run into you tonight."

Porter shrugged. "Your happiness or unhappiness doesn't matter to me. I'm here to do a job. You're obviously here to make sure your girlfriend is well taken care of. Let's just agree to be pleasant to each other until we've both accomplished our goals."

"I'm not his girlfriend," she said, but the words were drowned out by a flurry of activity in the hall.

"We expecting a trauma patient?" Porter asked, frowning as the sound of a woman's sobs drifted into the room.

"Not that I know of," Rayna answered. "Want me to go see what's going on?"

"Let's just finish up here. Whatever it is, they'll come find me if they need me."

"I thought you were done." Brenna eyed the thick gauze he'd wrapped her finger in.

"I'm just writing up your after-care instructions." Porter pulled the pen from his pocket, scribbled something on her chart. "Are you allergic to —"

"She's dead," a woman wailed, the voice so familiar, Brenna froze.

Janelle?

That's who it sounded like, but it couldn't be.

Could. Not. Be.

Because if it was, the evening that had been going pretty well had suddenly taken a very sharp turn for the worse.

"Are you allergic to anything?" Porter continued, apparently determined to ignore the chaos that was happening in the hall.

"No."

"I'll write you a prescription for some pain medicine. I'm also giving you a topical antibiotic. Only use it on the cuts I didn't stitch. If you —"

"Please!" the woman in the hall cried. "Someone tell me this is a nightmare. Tell me she's not dead!"

Porter frowned. "Maybe you'd better check on that, Rayna. It might be a mental patient. If so, we'll need to call Sacred Heart in Spokane. They're the closest facility."

"It's okay, Mom," a second woman said, her voice smooth and soothing and definitely one Brenna recognized.

"It's Adeline," she said, and everything seemed to happen at once. A gurney rattled past the open door, her sister's red hair visible for about three seconds.

"Addie!" she called, but Janelle's distraught cries drowned out the word.

"Are you sure that was Adeline?" River asked as she ran out into the hall.

"Of course I'm sure, and that's my mother crying." She sprinted to the end of the hall, took a hard left, nearly barreling into Kane Rainier's back.

"Sorry," she gasped, and he turned, his eyes widening as he met her gaze.

"Brenna?" he sounded . . . dumbfounded and, maybe, a little relieved.

282

"Where's my mother?" she said, stepping past him and following the sound of Janelle's sobs. They were coming from the other side of a closed door. She didn't let it stop her, just barreled into the exam room, River and Kane right behind her.

People were everywhere.

EMTS.

A nurse.

Jax.

Adeline, bent over a gurney, murmuring something in Janelle's ear. If Janelle was listening, she gave no indication; her eyes were closed, an oxygen mask over her face, a blood pressure cuff on her arm. She had a dark bruise on her cheek, a splint on her right wrist, and tears streaming endlessly down her face.

"Mom!" Brenna said, rushing to her side. "What's going on? Who died?"

Janelle's eyes flew open, her face losing even more color.

She didn't speak, and Brenna was terrified she'd had a stroke or a heart attack.

It wasn't Janelle she should have been worried about.

She heard her sister gasp, just a quick, sharp intake of breath, and then Adeline was falling, her tiny little baby bump heading straight for the ground.

"Grab her!" someone shouted, but Brenna was already reaching for her. So were River, Kane, and Jax.

Somehow they managed not to knock one another over as they lowered her to the ground.

"Addie," Brenna cried, patting her sister's cheek, trying to get her to open her eyes. She could see the pulse beating in the hollow of Adeline's throat, could see the rise and fall of her chest, but she was still terrified.

What if she stopped breathing?

What if something happened to the baby?

What if —

"Breathe," River said quietly, his fingers on Adeline's wrist, his gaze on Brenna.

She sucked in a huge gulp of air, tried to calm her frantic thoughts.

"Addie," she managed to say again, her voice calmer, her pulse slowing. "Sweetie, wake up."

"She's just passed out." Rayna, crouching next to Brenna, waved a vial of something under Adeline's nose.

Addie's eyes flew open and she sat up, pushing away River's hand, ignoring Kane, who was telling her to stay down.

"Brenna! You're alive!" she cried, as if that had ever been in doubt.

"Of course I am." Brenna wrapped her arms around Adeline. "Why wouldn't I be?"

"The blood," Janelle said, her voice muffled by the oxygen mask. "It was all over the kitchen. Mack said you cut yourself, but there's no way a simple cut could have caused that much blood." She struggled into a sitting position, the bruise on her cheek dark purple and red.

"I did cut myself, Mom." She held up her bandaged fingers. "And you know me. When I do something I like to do it big. River brought me here to get it stitched up."

"Holy cow! Are you kidding me?" Adeline struggled to her feet, eyed their mother with a mixture of frustration and bemusement. "You do realize what you've done, right, Mom?"

"I did what any mother would," Janelle retorted.

"Got an innocent man carted off to jail?" Adeline shook her head. "Did you even ask Mack where Brenna was?"

"Of course I asked. He just stared at me like I'd grown two heads and mumbled something about a cut hand. That's when I noticed the bloody dish rag he was holding." She shuddered, shoved the oxygen mask down. "There was blood everywhere, Brenna. How did you manage it?"

"It's a long story and I'd rather not tell it here."

"You might as well," Kane cut in. "No one is leaving here until I know exactly what happened."

"What happened —" Janelle began.

She didn't get a chance to finish.

Byron appeared in the doorway, Huckleberry on one side of him, Angel on the other.

"Brenna!" he nearly shouted. "Thank God! We thought —"

"I was dead?" Brenna guessed.

"I didn't think it," Angel responded. "I thought you were just doing what you do best: causing trouble."

"Cool it," River said, and then he frowned. "Where's Belinda?"

"At the sheriff's department with Mack," Angel spat, her gaze focused on Brenna. "You did it again, you stupid —"

"Stop," River said, his voice deadly quiet. "Name-calling won't accomplish anything."

"It will accomplish making me feel better," Angel huffed, but she didn't finish her thought, just stood glaring.

"What will make me feel better," Kane commented, his voice just as quiet, just as sharp, just as filled with authority, "is an explanation."

■ ■ ■ ■

Blood. That was the first part of the explanation.

Misunderstandings and confusion were the next.

Janelle had stopped in at Chocolate Haven, hoping to speak with Brenna. Instead, she'd seen Mack, a bloody dish towel in his hands. There'd been drops of blood on the floor and on the counter, more blood near the trash can. And, of course, the abandoned cell phone had been lying in plain sight. Apparently, that had been proof positive to Janelle that her daughter had been murdered in cold blood, her body tossed in the Dumpster or hidden in the walk-in.

She'd panicked, run back toward the door, tripped over Mack's tool chest, and fallen face first into the kitchen island.

That explained the sprained wrist and the bruised cheek.

It didn't explain why she'd been so convinced Mack had murdered her daughter. It also didn't explain why Mack — who'd been openmouthed enough to call 911 and ask for an ambulance — had allowed himself to be carted off to the sheriff's office.

All he'd had to do was explain.

Clearly.

Succinctly.

Without any embellishment or drama.

That seemed right up Mack's alley, but instead of speaking up, he'd let himself be driven to the local jailhouse.

If River remembered correctly from the three times Dillard had allowed him to be locked up there overnight — and he was sure he did — it was a small cell at the back of the sheriff's office. Just a holding place for criminals to wait until the county police arrived to cart them off to prison.

Didn't matter what kind of jail it was, Mack hadn't deserved to be in it. A comedy of errors is what Adeline had called the entire fiasco. River called it a waste of everyone's time.

A little more thought on Janelle's part and none of this would have happened. A little more honesty on Mack's and it wouldn't have continued.

Instead, they'd all spent three hours sorting everything out. Three hours he couldn't get back. He was tired. He was pissed. And the last thing he wanted to do was return to the ranch with the mismatched mess of humanity that was currently filling Brenna's car.

"I guess you have a reason why you didn't

just tell the sheriff the truth," River growled as he pulled away from the sheriff's office, the smell of sweat and fear and stale perfume filling the vehicle.

Mack grunted.

"What the hell kind of answer is that?" River demanded, and Belinda touched his arm, her fingers cool through his shirt.

"Language," she scolded, and it was so much like old times, he shut his mouth.

"I told the first deputy to respond that you'd taken Brenna to the hospital," Mack said, his voice gritty and tight. "But that dang woman was screaming so loud by that time, no one heard me."

"Maybe you should have repeated yourself, or offered my phone number, or done any one of a dozen different things that might have prevented them from carting you off to jail."

"I wasn't in jail," Mack growled. "I was in a deputy's office answering questions. He should have passed the information along. It would have saved people some distress."

Distress?

Janelle had nearly had a coronary. As far as River knew, she was still at the clinic, hooked up to a heart monitor. Adeline had been taken to another triage room. The last time he'd seen *her,* she'd had an IV in her hand and a frustrated look on her face. The doctor had been discussing the possibility of having her transported to the hospital.

Brenna had told River all that in a rush of words that he'd barely been able to make sense of.

Yeah. Distress wasn't the right word to describe what Janelle and Mack had accomplished.

Panic.

Horror.

Terror.

Soul-crushing fear.

Those were more the ticket, but sometimes silence was the better part of valor.

River kept those thoughts to himself.

"The deputy was very kind, too," Belinda added. "He made me a nice cup of tea and offered me some cookies. What was his name, Mack?"

"I don't remember him introducing himself."

"Tanner, I think," Belinda continued, as if he hadn't spoken. "I taught him a few times when I worked as a substitute. Tanner Millwood; that was his name. Nice boy, and he's turned into a fine young man."

"Did the fine young man say you were going to have to return for more questioning, Mack?" River asked. He hoped not. There'd already been enough talk after the incident with Brenna and the knife. This would just add fuel to the gossip.

"Maybe."

"What kind of answer is that?"

"The kind I give people who try to make my business theirs."

"Boys," Belinda said wearily, "let's not argue. Family always sticks together. Whatever happened tonight, we need to take one another's sides, not go at one another's throats."

Family? River didn't think so.

At least it wasn't any kind of family he'd ever want to be part of.

He kept the thought to himself, speeding along the country road that led to the ranch, all his plans for the night shot to hell. He'd wanted to take Brenna to a couple of antique shops. Not the swank ones scattered along Main Street. The ones that dotted the countryside; old houses with signs stuck to their gates and their fences — ANTIQUES, PICK YOUR OWN JUNK, TREASURES UNLIMITED.

Instead, he was going back to the ranch to fix Belinda a good meal because she looked pale and seemed a little shaky. Lean protein, colorful vegetables, a piece of the rye bread he'd baked a few days ago. She'd enjoy that.

So would the rest of the motley crew of *guests.*

Speaking of guests . . .

He glanced in the rearview mirror, counting heads even though he knew damn well they were one person short. Joe had arrived the previous night. Right on schedule, he'd meandered off the little bus that always dropped him off, tripped his way along the driveway, a huge pile of books in one hand, a bouquet of wilted flowers in the other. He'd thrust those into Belinda's hands as soon as he'd seen her, then carted his books and his backpack up to his room.

The bouquet was currently sitting in a cup of water on the fireplace mantel.

River had no idea where Joe had gone.

That worried him. A lot. Joe had the mental capacity of a seven-year-old. That made him sweet and kind and sometimes capable of getting himself into trouble.

"Where's Joe?" he asked.

"Why do you care?" Angel nearly spat the words.

"Because he shouldn't be left by himself, that's why. He could get hurt or lock himself out of the house. Or —"

"We dropped him off at the neighbor's place," Huckleberry offered. "He's helping Elmer mow the back field. Elmer said he'd bring him back in a few hours."

"It's been a few hours," River pointed out.

"Elmer isn't stupid," Angel snapped. "He knows Joe can't be left alone. He'll keep him until we get home."

Which was right about then. Thank God.

River drove under the sign that had once shouted Freedom Ranch's presence to the world. Now the fading letters and tilted placard seemed more like a whisper of what used to be.

He glanced at Belinda. She'd shifted in her seat, was craning her neck to see the sign.

"I'm going to fix it," he promised, and she shook her head.

"There's no need. The ranch is gone. Now it's just a house that needs some work on a piece of land that should probably be sold."

"Don't say that, Belinda." Huckleberry leaned over the seat and patted her shoulder. "This place is way more than a house and a piece of land. It's all your memories, and all those kids you and your husband helped raise. It's a legacy. A tradition. Without it, the town wouldn't be the same."

That was a lot of insight coming from Huckleberry's mouth. It surprised River the same way the beautifully prepared and plated food had.

"Where'd you go to school, Huckleberry?" he asked as he parked the car.

"What's it to you?"

River ignored the rebuttal. He couldn't help someone if he didn't know what kind of help was needed. He'd asked these questions before and been ignored. This time, he was going to get answers. "Do you have your diploma? A GED?"

"I'm not stupid," Huckleberry muttered, opening his door and jumping out of the car. "I got my GED when I was fifteen."

"That's pretty early," he pointed out, and Huckleberry shrugged.

"I was highly motivated to finish high school."

"That was what? A year ago?"

"Almost two." The truth slipped out and he scowled. "Yeah. It's true, River. I'm seventeen. Go shout it to the mountains, call in CPS, get me carted back into foster care. I'll just leave again."

"I'm not going to call anyone," he tried to reassure the kid, but Huckleberry was already halfway to the house.

"You know what you are, River?" Angel growled. "You're an —"

"Language," Belinda said with a sigh. "I'm really tired. I think it's best if I lie down for a while. Mack, can you make sure Joe gets home and make sure he eats?"

"You need to eat, too," Mack said gently as he took her wheelchair from the trunk.

"I'll have some toast later. Right now I'm just . . ." She glanced at the sign again. "Exhausted."

Like the house.

The property.

The sign.

The porch swing River still needed to fix.

He helped Belinda into the wheelchair and rolled her around to the side of the house. Mack had installed a ramp there. In the days when things had been touch and go and the doctors wouldn't say one way or another whether Belinda would survive, Mack had worked hour after hour to craft a handicap-accessible entrance that would help Belinda return to the home she loved.

River supposed it had been an offering of hope, an act of faith.

It had paid off.

Fixing up the ranch, getting the fields and the garden going again? That was River's act of faith. He had to believe it would make a difference in Belinda's life, that it would take the sadness from her face and leave her with the kind of happiness she deserved.

He didn't tell her that, though.

Getting her hopes up and crushing them

would be worse than letting her believe the glory days of Freedom Ranch were behind her and all she had to look forward to was a slow fading of the vibrant property she and Dillard had loved.

Angel unlocked the side door, scowling as River pushed Belinda into the huge dining room. Years ago, the doors had stayed unlocked. Belinda and Dillard hadn't believed in keeping people out. Since River had returned, he'd insisted on keeping the house secure.

The world had changed. It only made sense for the ranch to change, too, but even that seemed to make Belinda sad. She shook her head. "Time just keeps marching on. Whether I want it to or not."

"Would you rather it stood still?" he asked, wheeling her through the dining room. Someone had been cleaning the old china cabinet and wiping down the picture frames, the wood gleaming, the glass smudge-free. Even the old seventies chandelier Dillard had probably installed before the first foster kid ever crossed their threshold, had been polished to a high shine.

"No, I guess I don't. There are things I miss and things I might even want to have back, but if time stood still, you wouldn't be so successful and accomplished. All the children Dillard and I helped would still be in need of helping."

"You two did a great thing. I hope you know how much of a difference you made."

"To just a few people," she said quietly. "There's a whole world filled with hurting people out there, River. And they're all just waiting for the next Dillard and Belinda Keech to come along."

"They may be waiting a long time, Belinda. You and Dillard were one in a million."

"So are you, River. I've always known it. Dillard did, too," she said quietly.

He didn't want to think about what he meant.

He refused to put her comment together with his.

No way was he the kind of person Dillard had been. No way was he the kind of person Belinda still was.

He didn't want to be.

Cleaning up messes other people made wasn't his thing.

Taking care of people who didn't want or appreciate it?

Also not his thing.

He stopped the wheelchair at the stairs, helped Belinda out of it. Up until a week ago, she'd had a hospital bed in the living room. Now, she insisted on making the long walk up the stairs and into the room she'd once shared with Dillard. It wasn't the biggest room and it wasn't fancy, but she'd refused to give it up.

She brushed his hands away as she took the first step and then the second. She'd been working hard in therapy, but stairs were still a challenge, and he couldn't imagine a time when he wasn't going to worry that she might fall.

"You need to stop hovering," Angel hissed as she followed him up the stairs. "She can do it without you. We can all do it without you."

There was a message there.

He heard it loud and clear.

Too bad he had no intention of listening.

Whether Angel liked it or not, he was there.

She could get used to it or . . .

She could leave?

He glanced at her, saw her pale face, her tired eyes. A backpack dangled from her arm. Belinda's purse hung from her wrist and her free hand clutched a library book about childbirth.

She met his eyes. "Don't you dare feel sorry for me."

"Why would I?" he asked.

But, he did, because she was a kid having a kid and she had nothing but this drafty old house and the people who lived in it to support her.

A family?

River didn't want to think so, but he supposed, in some strange way, it was.

Chapter Twelve

Family: Couldn't live with them. Couldn't kill them.

Unless you wanted to go to jail.

Brenna didn't.

What she wanted — all she wanted — was to get through church without Janelle commenting on the length of her skirt, the style of her hair, or the fact that she hadn't applied a stitch of makeup.

Not powder. Not blush. Not foundation or lipstick.

She hadn't even had time to put on Chap-Stick.

Because she was running late.

Very late.

As a matter of fact, the entire parking lot of Benevolence Baptist Church was full. She managed to find a spot on the street, parked the Chrysler, and sprinted up the hill that separated her from the building she should have been in five minutes ago.

The double-wide doors that led into the sanctuary were closed and she stopped in front of them, smoothing her hand down the simple blue dress she'd worn. The hem fell just above her knees, the sleeves hitting midforearm. Everything that could be covered had been.

Janelle should approve, but she probably wouldn't.

She took a deep breath.

It had been a long time since she'd attended church with her family. Who was she kidding? It had been a long time since she'd attended church. She and Dan had made a habit of going on Easter and Christmas. Sometimes she'd gone in between those services, hoping to find some kind of connection in the filled pews of the neighborhood church.

Of course, in New York City, the neighborhood church had contained hundreds of people. Brenna had been one of the crowd, and she'd never felt more lost and more alone than when she'd sat in an old wooden pew, squeezed in between strangers who didn't even meet her eyes.

Music drifted through the door, a somber hymn Brenna remembered from her childhood. Once, an eon ago, she'd loved going to church. She'd sat between her parents, her sisters on either side of them, her grand-parents in the pew behind. She'd studied the old paintings that decorated the walls, ran her hand along the smooth wood of the pew in front of her, and thought that the church was the most beautiful place in the world.

She'd been to a lot of places since then.

She'd seen a lot of beautiful things.

She doubted the little chapel would touch her soul the way it had when she was a kid.

She opened the door, walking into a nearly full service. People were on their feet, hymnals open in their hands, voices blended in questionable harmony.

Her sister, mother, and grandfather were up near the front with Chase and Larkin Lyons. The teen and his sister had moved in with Adeline a few months before she'd married Sinclair. They'd been there ever since. Which was something else, in Brenna's opinion. She'd liked Sinclair the first time she'd met him, but when she'd realized he was willing to provide a home to two kids who had nowhere else to go, she'd fallen in sisterly love with him.

Yeah. He was a good guy and Adeline was a great woman.

They deserved every bit of the happiness they'd found.

It was good to see her sister standing near people she loved. Adeline had pulled her hair into a pretty braid that fell halfway down her back. Her black skirt hugged curvy hips, and Brenna was certain her blue sweater emphasized the subtle swelling of her abdomen. She couldn't see past the sea of bodies blocking her view, but she was also certain Adeline had her own personal Bible. Probably a black leather one with notes written in the margins.

She was the accessible daughter. The always-there one.

The go-to gal who'd never, ever asked anyone for anything.

Seeing her unconscious, her face pale and devoid of all its normal vitality, had shaken Brenna. She'd spent years away, years not realizing people were changing and growing and aging.

She'd missed out on a lot, and she hadn't realized how much that mattered until she'd come back and seen all the things she'd left behind.

She skirted around the back pew, trying to find a place that wasn't so close to the front because she didn't want to take the walk of shame that every latecomer had to take. Up the center aisle to the only seats that were usually available: front row closest to the pulpit.

Nope. She wasn't going there. It was bad enough half the congregation had turned to watch her progress.

She scanned row after row. Not an empty seat in the place.

Fine. She'd stand in the vestibule.

She turned, nearly walked smack-dab into a hard masculine chest.

"No sense trying to run now," River whispered in her ear. "You've already been seen. May as well make the best of it."

"Where'd you come from?" she whispered back.

"The other side of the sanctuary. I figured me getting up and walking over here would distract at least half the people from watching you."

"And give everyone more to talk about tomorrow morning?"

"Do you care?" he asked.

"Maybe."

"Don't." He touched her lower spine, his fingers warm, his touch light.

She could have walked in the other direction, but somehow she found herself walking with him. They made their way to the front pew as the hymn wound to an end. By the time the last piano chord died away, they were seated. Just the two of them on a polished wood pew, Janelle, Adeline, and Byron behind them.

She thought she heard her mother whisper something, but she decided not to ask Janelle to repeat herself. As a matter of fact, she decided to do exactly what River had suggested: not care. So what if half the town's population was there? So what if she and River were going to be the topic of every conversation in town the following day? The chapel was still as lovely as she'd remembered it. The beautiful wood floors and hand-carved pews a reminder of yesterday and the yesterday before that. Generations of people had sat in the pews. Generations had been married there, baptized there, their bodies buried in the cemetery outside. The thread of belonging ran through every beam, every floorboard, every old hymnal tucked beneath a pew.

She wasn't sure anything else mattered but that.

This was what she'd been missing during her years of wandering the globe. It was what the hollow spot in her heart had been craving. Not just a place to worship but a place where everything seemed to just fall into place, where all the parts of self came together and became something more.

She'd forgotten how that felt.

Or maybe she'd never known.

Maybe she'd been so busy looking for something more that she'd failed to see what she had.

By the time the service was over, she felt more relaxed than she had in a long time, more content than she thought she could be.

"Ready?" River offered his hand and she took it, allowing herself to be pulled to her feet.

He was smiling, that easy, open smile that made her think of all kinds of things she shouldn't: hand-holding and whispered promises and kisses under the stars.

Forever Kisses.

Those words again, the old recipe card tucked in her purse. She'd been carrying it around for some reason, loath to stick it back in the cookbook and have it be forgotten again. She'd planned to ask Byron if he knew who'd written it, but things had been . . . hectic.

"You look beautiful today," River said, lifting her injured hand and eyeing the bandages. She'd removed the gauze from the stitches and covered them with a Band-Aid. She had a lot of work to do before the shop opened in the morning and she hadn't wanted to be hampered by lumpy gauze. It was bad enough that she'd be hampered by her own inability to make the fudge.

"I'm a mess," she responded, smoothing hair that hadn't wanted to be tamed. She'd tried to control it, but the short, trendy style was growing out and was becoming a shaggy, uncontrollable mop in the process.

"If you are," River responded, "you're a beautiful mess."

She wanted to say something flip and funny. She wanted to make light of the words, play them off as flirtation, but she was looking into his eyes and there was nothing flirtatious in his gaze, nothing light or humorous or simple.

He'd kissed her and everything in her had changed.

That was the truth. One she hadn't been willing to acknowledge before. Now, in the old church with all its history and connection, she couldn't deny it.

"River," she began, not sure exactly what she wanted to say, not sure what she *should* say. How much of a heart could be revealed without all of it being shown? Because being vulnerable had never gotten her anywhere with anything.

"Brenna! You made it!" Janelle exclaimed, interrupting the moment at exactly the perfect time to save Brenna from herself.

Or, maybe, to keep her from what she wanted.

She wasn't sure which, but she turned to greet her mother, wincing at the dark bruise on Janelle's cheek. She'd tried to cover it with makeup, but no amount of makeup was going to hide the vivid purple and red. She had managed to hide her splinted wrist, the sleeve of her cardigan pulled over it.

"Yes. Sorry I was late. I —"

"You don't need to explain." Janelle pulled her into a hug. "I'm just glad you're here. It feels so good to have two of my daughters in town. Who knows? Maybe Willow will move back one day."

"Not in this lifetime," Adeline said with an unladylike snort. That was one of the things Brenna had always loved about her sister: she only ever tried to be herself. She'd never worn trendy clothes when they were in school. She'd never pursued cheer-leading or dance team or sports. She'd joined the math club and been president of the debate team, and she hadn't really cared who thought she was geeky or awkward.

"Or in the next," Brenna added, and Adeline grinned, her lightweight sweater cupping her tiny little baby bump just like Brenna had known it would.

"Adeline, you are the cutest pregnant lady

I've ever seen," Brenna said, because Adeline really was. She glowed, her skin healthy, her eyes sparkling.

"Yeah?" Adeline patted her stomach. "Give me a couple of months. Once my appetite returns, I'll be the biggest one. These past couple of days, you know what I've been craving?"

"Fudge?" Byron asked hopefully.

"Ha! No way. I've been craving fried chicken, mashed potatoes. Gravy. The kind Grandmom used to make."

"She did make a mean gravy," Byron agreed.

"She did, and once I'm over this morning sickness crap, I'm going to find the recipe and make it. Then I'm going to smother potatoes and chicken in it and chow down."

"Of course you're not going to do that, Adeline," Janelle chastised. "You need to eat for the baby. Not for your tastes."

"The baby wants potatoes and gravy, Mother. And fried chicken, and maybe a nice big slice of coconut cake to go with it." The twinkle in Adeline's eyes made Brenna smile. Her sister had always loved getting a rise out of Janelle.

"You can't eat that! What if you get eclampsia or gestational diabetes?"

"One fried fatty greasy meal isn't going to

cause that," Adeline said blithely, hiking her purse onto her shoulder, a black Bible peeking out from its front pocket.

Of course.

The good girl.

The one always there.

The one who'd had to put up with their mother's nitpicking all on her own for how many years?

"Besides," Adeline continued, "Sinclair said I should eat whatever I want whenever I want, and you've always said he's the best thing that ever happened to me."

"I'll have to have a talk with him," Janelle sputtered, as if she had any influence over her one and only son-in-law. Brenna knew for a fact she didn't. Dan had always bowed to her wishes and Willow's fiancé always did the same, but Sinclair? The only one he ever seemed to listen to was Adeline.

Lucky girl.

Brenna met Adeline's eyes and smiled. Their sisterly connection, that almost psychic thread between them, still seemed strong, even after so many years and so much distance.

"He's out of town," Brenna reminded Janelle, still smiling into her sister's eyes. How had she not realized how important this was? How had she not known how much she was missing it?

"I'm well aware of that, Brenna. As soon as he returns, I'm going to explain things to him. It's possible he's just not aware of how important nutrition is to an expectant mother," Janelle huffed. "Now, how about we all head over to the house? I've prepared a wonderful roast. Lean beef for protein. Carrots. Parsnips."

"Potatoes?" Adeline asked hopefully.

"Honey, no!" Janelle said. "Starchy food isn't what you and the baby need."

"It will be after I puke up the parsnips," she muttered, and Brenna laughed.

"You won't get sick. I roasted the vegetables perfectly and added them in with the roast after that. They should be cooked just the way you've always liked them. Although, if you'd rather go home, that's fine. I understand if you and the kids want to eat without me. Maybe you don't like pot roast, Chase?"

The teen smiled. "I like everything, ma'am."

"Of course you do. You're not picky, and neither is your sister." She smiled at Larkin, who'd braided her hair in the exact same style as Adeline. "But if Adeline wants to eat at home —"

"It's fine, Mom," Adeline conceded.

"We'd love to join you."

"Wonderful! You're coming, too. Right, Brenna?"

"I have a lot of work to do at the shop," she hedged, because she loved her mother, but she didn't think she could stomach a few hours with her.

Not yet.

She had too much thinking to do about how much she wanted to reveal and about how much to hide.

The lies had to stop.

She knew that.

But how did she unsay what had already been said?

"On Sunday? It's the day of rest, Brenna."

"Leave the girl alone," Byron said. "If she wants to make chocolate, who are we to say it's work?"

"I guess we aren't, but we have important things to discuss. Willow's party for one. Her wedding for another. And I'd like Brenna to take a look at her room and give me some ideas for redecorating it. She can't stay in the apartment forever."

Like hell she couldn't!

There was no way . . . absolutely none . . . that she'd ever move back home.

"Really, Mom, I —"

"She has plans," River cut in so smoothly

Brenna almost didn't hear what he'd said.

"She does?" Janelle and Adeline said in unison.

Janelle looked suspicious.

Adeline looked . . . hopeful? She didn't know everything about what had happened with Dan, but she knew more than most about how much betrayal hurt. Maybe she wanted Brenna to find happiness again. Maybe she didn't understand that Brenna was perfectly happy on her own.

Most of the time.

"She's helping me at the ranch," River responded, glancing at his watch as if they were on some kind of crazy-tight timeline. "Speaking of which, we'd better head out. I'm sure Belinda and the gang are out front, waiting for me to drive them back. You'll have to take your car, red. Belinda's car is packed tight."

He took her hand and tugged her away from her family and she went, weaving through groups of people who eyed her with curiosity. No doubt they were wondering why she was allowing herself to be pulled away from her family. No doubt they'd be whispering about it as soon as she stepped outside.

Years ago, she would have cared.

Today, she didn't.

The sky was a vivid blue, the air crisp and cool.

A perfect day, and she wasn't going to let it be ruined by other people's opinions.

"If you want," River said, stopping at her car but not releasing her hand, "I can ask Angel to drive Belinda's car back and we can go somewhere besides the ranch."

"Chocolate Haven?" she asked, and he smiled.

"That can wait. I have a better idea."

"What kind of idea?"

"Just yes or no, red. That's all you need to give me. It's not that complicated."

"It is when I don't know what I'll be agreeing to."

"You're agreeing to me, to *us*. Just for an hour. Then we'll get back to the real world and all the work we have to do."

She should have said no.

She knew that.

Making decisions without all the necessary information wasn't something she had ever been willing to do, but she looked in his eyes and the only thing she could manage was, "Yes."

Brenna needed time away from her family and River needed time away from the house. He didn't see why they couldn't spend that time together. He had her drive toward the ranch, then turn onto a narrow dirt road that was nearly overgrown with grass and foliage. He knew where it led: up over the crest of a hill and deep into a copse of trees that he and Dillard had once spent hours wandering through.

There was a cabin there, and a view of the Spokane River that could leave a person breathless. He knew. He'd felt that way a few times. Even now, as the Chrysler crested the hill and headed down the other side, he was caught up in it — the conifers that dotted the landscape, their needles dark green against the blue sky, the river meandering lazily in the distance. Dillard's fishing cabin was just a few hundred feet from its shores, its wood gray with age, the windows boarded up.

Who'd done that?

Dillard?

Had he realized there weren't going to be any more troubled teens to take fishing? Had he decided the place would be better off sealed up than left to vandals?

Or had Belinda come sometime after his death, cleaned the place out, and closed it up? Either way, the sight of the cabin sealed off from the world hit River in the heart.

Brenna drove the Chrysler as far as the

road would let her, then parked it a few feet from the cabin's front door.

"Look at that place," she breathed. "It's like a secret hideaway, a romantic little oasis in the middle of a chaotic world. Or maybe —"

"A fishing cabin?" he suggested, and she laughed, opening her door and getting out of the car.

He did the same, the silence of the day, the stillness of the landscape filling him like no amount of success or wealth ever could.

"I like the idea of a romantic getaway better, but fishing is fun." She walked to the cabin door, her dress hugging her slim waist and skimming over her narrow hips. Her legs were long and slender, the skin smooth and more tempting than River wanted it to be.

She was gorgeous.

No doubt about that.

She was also holding back. Not just from him. From her family. From the town. From the shop she was trying so hard to run.

Because of her ex?

He could have asked, but she seemed fascinated with the cabin, taken with it in the same way he'd been the first time he'd seen it.

"Have you fished a lot?" he asked, leaning

past her to unlock the door. He caught a hint of that decadent scent — chocolate and strawberry and misty fall mornings — and he wanted to forget the cabin, the river, the beautiful scenery. He wanted to pull her into his arms, smooth his hands along her spine, kiss her until the only thing either of them knew was each other.

"It's one of Byron's favorite things to do. After my father died, he needed a buddy for his Saturday evening trips to the river. I was it."

"I wonder if he still takes those trips to the river."

"Probably not since he busted his hip and leg. I think the fishing trip to Alaska is the first one he's taken in over a year."

"You're going to miss him while he's gone." The door creaked open and he walked in, inhaling dust and mildew, mold and age. The place had been locked up for a long time, the old kerosene lamps that had once hung from the walls removed, the couch and easy chair covered with white sheets. Fishing tackle lay on the table, Dillard's tackle box beside it.

"So will the shop and the customers and, probably, the entire town." Brenna lifted an old newspaper that lay on the easy chair. "Benevolence really does love its fudge."

"It loves your grandfather, too."

"Also true. Look at this." She held up the newspaper. There wasn't much light coming through the open door, but River could see that an article had been circled in red pen.

He took the paper from Brenna's hand and took a closer look. The paper wasn't the Benevolence *Times;* it was the Portland *Herald.* The article wasn't about small-town stuff, it was about the grand opening of River's first restaurant.

"I can't believe he kept this," he said, placing it back on the chair.

"Why not?"

"Do you know how many foster kids Belinda and Dillard had? If he kept reminders of every accomplishment they'd ever made, the cabin, the house, and the barn would be full."

"Does love have some limit, River?" She walked to the fireplace, ran her hand along the polished wood mantel. A few photos sat there. One of Dillard and Belinda. One of the two of them with River. One of the land the way it had been before Dillard died: lush cornfields, apple trees heavy with fruit. "It seems to me that someone like Dillard could love every single one of his foster kids,

318

but it also seems to me that you were special."

"Yeah, special at getting into trouble."

"Dillard never said you were trouble. He said you were more creative than most kids. I can remember him talking to Byron about the sheep incident. He said only someone with a good brain and a lot of creativity could have thought up a prank like that."

"What did your grandfather say?"

"I can't repeat it. I'm trying to clean up my language before Adeline's baby is born."

He chuckled. "I'm sure your sister will appreciate that."

"She'll appreciate the fact that I quit smoking more."

"A smoker, huh?"

"Since I was eighteen. It's the kind of thing that happens when you're a kid spending most of your time with other kids who are all independent and have been for years."

"I get it. I smoked until I was thirteen."

She laughed, the sound fading away as she realized he was serious. "You're not kidding."

"That's when I moved to the ranch. The first couple of weeks, Belinda and Dillard didn't say anything about my smoking. About a month into my stay, Belinda started making pie."

"Pie?"

"Peach. Pumpkin. Apple. Every night, that's what she'd serve for dessert. One night she made chocolate cream. My favorite, and she knew it."

"What does that have to do with smoking?"

"Belinda refused to let me have any; not one slice of any of the pies she'd made. She said smoking put me at high risk for all kinds of diseases, and she wasn't going to nudge me closer to the grave by feeding me sweets. After a couple of nights watching everyone enjoy pie, I decided I just might like that more than I liked cigarettes."

"I wish someone had made me pie. It might have made the process easier," she joked, but there was a hint of longing in her voice and a softness in her eyes made him think she'd needed what he'd had: people who'd cared.

Strange, because he'd always thought the Lamonts were an impenetrable wall, a fortress built to protect everyone who bore the name.

"You don't think they would have if you'd asked?"

"Probably, but I guess I've forgotten how."

"To ask for something you want?"

"To admit there's something I need. I had it all, River. A career that people in town admire, a decade of traveling the world, a million opportunities opened up to me. That's what everyone around here thinks. Even my family. What am I supposed to say? That it's not enough? That all the wonderful things so many people would give anything to have aren't good enough for me?"

"Would it be the truth?"

"I'm not even sure I know the truth anymore." She sighed, walking to the door that led out onto the back porch and lifting the wooden bar that held it closed. He followed her out into the afternoon sunshine, stood beside her as she leaned against the porch railing and looked out at the river.

"Is it that complicated?" he finally asked, and she shrugged.

"It didn't used to be. It used to be that I just wanted to get away from all the expectations, be something other than the third Lamont sister. When the opportunity to model presented itself, I jumped at it. Not because it was something I always wanted to do. Because it would get me out of a town that was just too . . ." She shook her head, her hair brushing her nape and falling across her forehead.

"Confining?"

"Maybe." She turned to face him, her eyes violet blue, her lashes a rich, deep red. She'd worn no makeup, no jewelry, nothing but that simple blue dress, those conservative heels, that bright orange purse she'd slung over her shoulder. She still looked stylish, fashionable, ready for the runway. "Probably. Especially after my father died. I guess everything changed then. I had to always pretend like I was happy, that the family was doing okay, but really? We were all falling apart."

"That must have been tough."

"Not once it became a habit. Kind of like smoking: you do it because it's what everyone expects. For a while, it doesn't feel natural. Eventually, though, it's just part of who you are."

"So, you came back to find out who you really are?"

She smiled at that, but there was no humor in her eyes. "That would be sad, wouldn't it? To come back home to find myself?"

"Why?"

"Because I'm closing in on thirty. I should already be found. Look at Adeline: she's got it all figured out. Her life, the people she loves, what she wants to be when she's thirty, forty, fifty, and forever. Willow is the same way. She's settled down, happy with what she's accomplished so far, determined to accomplish even more."

"Why?"

She frowned. "Why what?"

"Why look at Adeline and Willow when you're the one standing here?"

"I —"

"It's a waste of time, Brenna. Just like it's a waste to stand in front of a beautiful view like this and think about the New York skyline or the Swiss Alps."

"You really need to stop, River," she said with a sigh.

"Stop what?"

"Being so . . . right. I find it completely annoying."

"Then I guess it won't hurt to annoy you more," he murmured, tugging her closer, his fingers threading through her hair, his lips finding hers as easily as the sun found the dawn.

She moaned, pressing closer, giving as much as she was taking, and he knew they could lose themselves to the moment, forget about the ranch, Chocolate Haven, the dozens of obligations they both had.

That scared him, because he'd never wanted to fall headfirst into something he might not be able to get out of.

But he *was* falling.

And there didn't seem to be a damn thing he could do about it but hold on tight and hope he'd land on his feet.

CHAPTER THIRTEEN

Someone's phone was ringing.

Brenna ignored it because right at that moment, it didn't seem like there could be anything more important than River's hands, his lips, his body pressed close to her.

It rang again, the loud trill pulling her from a haze of longing that she hadn't felt in . . .

Ever?

God! What a terrible thing to admit, and what a true one. She had never *ever* felt so completely engulfed and consumed that she didn't care what she lost, what she had to give up, what she might surrender to get what she wanted.

She broke away from River, looked into his beautiful eyes.

"What is it with you?" she whispered, and she wasn't sure whether she was talking to herself or to River.

"Hell if I know," he responded, his voice as rough and raspy as her breathing seemed to be.

She needed to stop this. Now. Before it went too far and she found herself in so deep she couldn't get out, but his hand swept down the curve of her hip, settled on her upper thigh. Skin to skin and, God help her, she wanted so much more.

The blasted phone rang again, and River's hand dropped away.

"Damn!" he muttered. "You'd better get that."

"What?"

"Your phone." He gestured to her purse, and she dragged it from her shoulder, her hands shaking as she pulled out her cell phone.

She didn't recognize the number, but with all the trouble that had happened the previous day, she figured it could have been anyone: police, clinic, doctor's office.

"Hello?" she said, her voice as shaky as her hands had been.

"Babe?" The voice sounded tinny and far away, but she knew it immediately. How could she not? She'd lived with the guy for three years.

"Dan?" She met River's eyes, mouthed *my ex.*

"Who else calls you babe?" Dan responded. "Have you missed me?"

"I miss the money you stole from me."

"Stole? That's harsh, Brenna. It was in our account. Remember? We agreed that it was best if we combined our assets."

"We didn't agree. You convinced me. We also didn't agree that you should take every cent out and spend it on yourself and some other woman."

"I thought you'd understand, Bren. I thought you'd get that a man has needs. Especially when he reaches the middle of his life. Sometimes he goes a little crazy."

"There's a difference between crazy and criminal," she growled, knowing River was listening to every word she said, knowing he'd just learned way more than anyone in her family knew.

"Taking what's mine isn't criminal, and those accounts had both of our names on them," Dan argued. Obviously, he didn't see anything wrong with what he'd done.

Or, maybe, he was hoping he could convince her that he didn't.

She glanced at River, saw that he was watching intently, not even trying to hide the fact that he was listening. Why would he? She was having the conversation half a foot away.

"I lost everything because of you." She walked down the porch stairs, the heavy scent of pine needles and wet earth filling her nose as she headed toward a path that led from the cabin to the river.

"Babe, you still have your looks, your body, that special something that made you a hot commodity in the modeling world. All you'd have to do is say the word and you'd be working again."

"You know I hated modeling." He was one of the few people she'd ever told the truth.

"And you know what I told you when you said that to me: you don't hate it. It paid a lot of dividends, and once you appreciate that, you'll appreciate the job."

Not true. Any of it, but she'd explained that over and over to him and he'd never listened. He'd wanted what she didn't: Brenna as the runway-walking, world-traveling model.

She wasn't going to explain things to him again.

"What do you want, Dan?"

"Us. Together. The way we used to be. I'm in Thailand: one of the most beautiful places on earth. Blue water. Sunny skies. But I don't have the most beautiful woman on earth with me."

"What? Your new girlfriend's left?" She'd

reached the water's edge and she stood there, heels sinking into muddy earth.

"You're not listening to me. I want *you.* I even hooked you up with a great gig. There's this cutting-edge fashion designer in Bangkok, and when I showed him your pictures, he wanted to hire you to walk in his December show. He's not the only one. I've got six other designers begging to work with you. You know how much money you could rake in working the runway here?"

"Not the amount of money you took from me."

True to form, he completely ignored the remark. "Brenna, I'm being honest. I'm speaking from my heart. Walking away from you was the biggest mistake I ever made."

"Funny, because saying yes to our first date was my biggest mistake."

"Come on, babe. Don't be that way."

"Do. Not. Call. Me. Babe." The sun was bright and high. She could feel it on the crown of her head and on her nape, but she was cold with rage.

"That's what you are to me. Remember how good we were together?"

"What I remember is what an asshole you were for cheating on me, emptying our bank account and my business account. What I remember is —"

"Let me," River growled, snatching the phone from her hand.

"Hey!" she protested, but River turned away, pressed the phone to his ear.

"Dan? Brenna's done with you, so how about you hang up and call your business partner? Jeff is a lot more interested in hearing what you have to say." He ended the call, handed the phone back.

"What the hell was that?" Brenna demanded.

"Me. Getting rid of a nuisance."

"I know how to handle myself." She shoved the phone back in her purse, every cell in her body humming with anger.

"I hope you also know you need to call the police and give them the loser's number."

"I'm not stupid."

"I don't think I said you were."

"Well, you're sure as hell acting like I am." She stalked back to the cabin, knowing she was being unreasonable, knowing the way she felt wasn't River's fault.

It was Dan's.

Hers.

She hated failing. Hated it, but she'd failed at what should have been as simple as breathing. Her parents had had a great relationship. Her grandparents, too. She'd seen what love should be and she'd known that wasn't what she'd had with Dan.

But she'd stuck things out with him because it had been comfortable and easy, and because she hadn't wanted her mother and sisters and grandfather to think the Lamont who'd traveled the farthest, seen the most, couldn't find a man who could really, truly love her.

There it was.

The crux of the issue: she'd been so busy trying to fulfill other people's expectations, she hadn't fulfilled her own.

Whatever they were.

She rounded the cabin, her feet wet and muddy, the pretty dress she'd chosen for church suddenly seeming lank and lifeless.

God, she was a mess.

Which only pissed her off more, because she'd come to Benevolence to help Byron, but she'd also come to figure things out, to find the path she needed to take so she could damn well take it.

She opened the door of the Chrysler, slid into the seat, and waited while River locked the cabin door.

A few seconds later, he climbed in beside her.

He didn't say a word.

She didn't either.

They'd planned to go to the ranch and do some work, but she wasn't sure that was in the cards anymore. It would probably be better if she just dropped him off and went to the store herself. She'd come a long way in her candy-making abilities. Eventually, she'd conquer the Lamont family fudge. In the meantime, she could just muddle through alone.

Except she didn't want to.

She was getting used to having River around. She was getting used to his smile, his voice, his hand on her back or her arm or her thigh.

She wanted more of that, more of the little nuances that were part of being a couple.

The silence between them stretched out, became its own thing, big and daunting.

She wanted to break it, but she didn't know what to say.

By the time she stopped in front of Belinda's house, she knew she'd blown it.

River climbed out and didn't even glance her way.

She thought he'd walk into the house and leave her sitting there in the car, wondering if she should drive away or stay.

He rounded the Chrysler, opened her door.

When he offered his hand, she took it, allowed herself to be pulled out of the car. Her cut fingers hurt, each slow, hard beat of her heart echoed by that throbbing pain.

She needed to call Jeff.

She needed to call the police.

She needed to do a lot of things, but none of them seemed quite as important as telling River she was sorry.

She stopped as they reached the door. "River —"

"It's okay, Brenna," he said, the words as cool as the breeze that wafted under the porch eaves. "You'll figure it out eventually."

"Figure what out?" she asked, but the front door flew open and a dark-haired man with a receding hairline peered out at them.

"River? That you, River?" the guy said, his blue eyes wide behind big round glasses.

"Yeah. It's me, Joe," River responded kindly. "How did you like church today?"

"I always like church, River. I always do. We're going to paint. Are we going to paint? Belinda said we're going to paint?" Joe said.

River patted his shoulder and smiled.

"We're going to choose paint. You can help, but we're not painting today."

"Tomorrow? I can help tomorrow."

"You'll be home tomorrow."

Joe's face fell. "I'm not home?"

"Of course you are. Sorry, buddy. I wasn't thinking. Let's go inside and look at the paint colors." He steered Joe back inside, and Brenna was left to follow.

She walked into the foyer, nearly bumping into a ladder that stood against the wall. Mack was perched on top of it, removing the chandelier that had hung there for as long as Brenna had been around. Pretty little plastic raindrops falling from swirling metal arms, that's what it looked like, but as he lifted it, she could hear a soft musical chime.

Crystal and brass?

At the end of the hall, Huckleberry was on his knees patching a hole in the floor with some kind of wood putty. Belinda, River, and Joe were a few feet away, eyeing paint that had been dabbed onto the wall. Creamy beige. Butter yellow. Pale gray. Soft blue.

"What do you think?" River asked as she approached.

What she thought was that he looked like a hero, his hand still on Joe's shoulder, his hair ruffled by the breeze.

"Gray," she said. "And all the trim crisp white. You can go darker in the living room and parlor and use that yellow for the kitchen."

"That sounds lovely, dear," Belinda said, beaming as if Brenna had just cured cancer or found the answer to world peace. "I'm so excited to have the place updated again. River is so sweet to do all this before he goes home."

"Goes home?" she repeated, meeting River's eyes.

Apparently, he still hadn't shared his plans with Belinda.

"I'll be out of this chair in no time." Belinda patted the arm of her wheelchair. "And then I'll be back to cleaning and cooking and keeping my little family happy and healthy. River will be free to head back to his restaurants. He's already been away for too long. Thanks to me."

"Belinda, I'm here because I want to be," River said gently. "The restaurants can function just fine without me in Portland."

"So you say, but if you lose everything you've worked so hard for, I'll never forgive myself."

"What does he have to lose?" Angel said, strutting into the room, an ice cream cone in one hand and a book in the other. "A couple of restaurants that will probably be six feet under in another couple of years anyway?"

"Angel!" Belinda frowned. "That's a hor-

335

rible thing to say."

"It's the truth. Most restaurants don't survive. Especially when they're run by people who don't know what they're doing."

River's jaw tightened, his gaze moving from the ice cream to the book and then to Angel's belly.

Her shirt was too small and it rode up just enough to reveal a hint of a tattoo and a few stretch marks.

Maybe the sight of them curbed River's tongue.

"Did you put that crib together?" was all he said.

"Not yet. Sunday is my only day off and I wanted to relax for a while."

"If the baby comes tomorrow, are you going to be happy that you relaxed today?"

She scowled. "The truth is, I tried to put it together. I failed. It's a lot more complicated than it looks."

"You should have asked for help," Huckleberry said, finally getting to his feet. He looked young and very tired, his thin, freckled face pale, his eyes shadowed. "I'll take care of it for you."

"You need to finish patching the floor," River said. "I've got a company coming out tomorrow to refinish it, and I want to make sure the patches are dry before then."

"I'll do it later, then," Huckleberry muttered, and Angel scowled.

"Does everyone in this house always do what the as . . ." Her voice trailed off, her gaze darting to Belinda. "Does everyone have to do what River says? Is there some reason why we've all lost our backbones?"

"Teamwork is more important than individual glory," Mack intoned as he descended the ladder, the chandelier in his hands. "Why don't you come help me clean this, Angel? And then I'll help with the crib?"

"Fine. Whatever." She stalked away.

Brenna thought River muttered something under his breath as she left, but he'd turned away, was jotting notes on a piece of paper, so she couldn't be sure.

She would have joined him, maybe said something about the paint or the project or, even, Angel, but he glanced over his shoulder, met her eyes.

There wasn't a bit of warmth in his gaze, not a hint of amusement or passion or any of the other things Brenna had gotten used to seeing.

"Belinda has a bunch of stuff in the attic," he said, his voice as cool as his gaze. "She said we could use some of it to redecorate.

Would you mind going up and taking a look? Maybe making a list of things that can be used so I have an idea of what I still need to budget for?"

She didn't mind.

Of course she didn't.

"No problem," she said, the words all hot and watery and horrible, because what she wanted to do was look deep in River's eyes and tell him that she hadn't realized how much she'd been missing until she met him.

A stupid thing to say after the way she'd acted at the cabin. Even stupider with so many people standing in the hall. The thoughts were private ones, not to be shared with a bunch of people she barely knew.

That was the excuse she gave herself, and then she took the notebook and pen River was offering and walked upstairs without saying a word.

Somehow, River managed to get through six hours without saying one more word to Brenna about her asshole of an ex. He figured he deserved some sort of prize for that, but because no one was handing him one, he settled for a couple of chocolate-covered pretzels he'd snagged from the display case at Chocolate Haven.

They were good, the pretzels crisp and

salty, the chocolate rich and sweet. What would have been better was sticking around Chocolate Haven for a while longer, helping Brenna with the rest of the prep for the next day, and saying exactly what he wanted to: *Your ex is a jackass; he was never good enough for you. Don't be sorry he's gone; be damn thankful he is.*

Discretion is the better part of valor.

Another Dillard saying, and probably a smart one to live by, but River wasn't any better at biting his tongue than he was at waiting. So, once he'd finished making a couple batches of cherry cordials, a vat of caramel corn, and a few pounds of English toffee, he'd decided it was better to say good night.

And that's exactly what he'd done.

Now he was driving through town, thinking about that kiss, the way Brenna had felt in his arms, and the phone call that had ruined it all. The way he saw things, Dan must be an idiot. He was wanted by the police, his partner was desperately trying to track him down, and if he was caught, he'd be tossed in jail.

So, why a phone call that could put him back on the radar and get his location discovered?

Not love. A guy didn't run off with everything a woman had worked for and then claim he loved her. Money seemed the more likely motivator. Dan had probably blown every bit of his cash and had decided the best way to recoup the loss was to find someone willing to work to fill his bank account.

It wasn't going to be Brenna.

That much was for damn sure.

She was too smart to fall for it.

Apparently, Dan was too stupid to know that.

River would have been more than happy to fill him in. As a matter of fact, if he ever met the guy face-to-face, he'd make sure to teach the guy a lesson he wouldn't forget.

"Asshole," he muttered as he passed the diner, the five and dime, the library.

If he let himself, he could picture Brenna as a child, walking down the sidewalk with her wagon full of books, her red hair glowing in the sunlight.

Then she'd been an oddity, a quirky-looking kid who'd caught his eye because she was different.

She was still different, but that wasn't the reason he wanted to study her face, her hands, the color of her eyes and of her hair. *She* was the reason. Just Brenna, and he didn't think there needed to be an explanation, didn't think he needed to have a reason.

He passed the sheriff's department. There were lights on in the lobby, two squad cars in the parking lot. He was tempted to stop to see if Kane was there, maybe make a few subtle hints that the sheriff should pay Brenna a visit to ask about her ex.

He didn't.

He couldn't betray Brenna's trust that way.

No matter how tempted he was.

He sped out of town, taking a back road that meandered along the river. He'd forgotten how beautiful it was there, the fading sunlight glittering on the surface of the water. If he had more time, he'd stop, find a spot to sit on the shore and just listen to what the silence would say.

Dillard had taught him that: how to be still and to wait. It had served River well in life. Every time he had difficult decisions to make, every time he was struggling to know in which direction to go, he'd find a quiet spot and wait for his answer. Sometimes he got it quickly. Sometimes he had to repeat the process over and over again. Eventually, though, he always found the answers he was looking for.

Behind him, strobe lights flashed and a

squad car moved up in back of him. He glanced at his speedometer. Twenty miles an hour over the speed limit.

"Shit," he muttered, pulling into the breakdown lane and stopping. He could see the officer in his rearview mirror, calling something in on his radio and then getting out of the car. Seconds later, Jax Gordon was peering in through the window.

"In a hurry?" he asked, his voice muffled by the glass.

River unrolled it. "Apparently."

"You do know you were going twenty miles an hour over the speed limit, right?"

"Unfortunately."

Jax laughed. "Sorry, man. I'd have let you go if you were only ten above, but twenty . . . that's pushing it. Especially when you're within the town limits. Lots of kids are still out this time of evening. I'd hate for one of them to get hit because I didn't pull over a speeding car."

"I'd hate to be the one to hit them, but I am out of the town limits," he pointed out.

"You weren't when I clocked you at sixty-five. You were passing the station and I just happened to be getting in my car when you sped by."

"I guess it's my lucky day."

"It sure is mine. This is the most excitement I've had since that brick was tossed through Chocolate Haven's window."

"Any news on that?"

"You mean suspects? No. We've spoken to a couple of people. They all have alibis. We sent the brick to the county crime lab, but they couldn't find anything. They're keeping it to do a handwriting comparison, but until they have something to compare it to, that's not doing them a whole lot of good."

"Did you call her ex?" That was it. Just the question and nothing about the fact that the guy had just called Brenna.

River deserved another award.

He had a feeling it was going to be a citation.

"We haven't tracked him down yet, but we talked to his partner. The surgeon is mad as hell and he doesn't care who knows it."

"At Brenna?"

"No. He says she's the best thing that ever happened to her fiancé, and he can't believe the guy skipped town on her. He's mad at the ex. Said the guy almost caused his business to go under."

"Almost isn't the same as it actually happening."

"In his mind it is."

"Maybe, in his mind, throwing a brick through a window to let Brenna know he's watching her is a perfectly acceptable thing to do."

"Could be, but the guy has an airtight alibi. He was in surgery the day the incident occurred."

"It's easy enough to hire someone."

"To do what? It's not like Brenna was hurt, and it's not like she was all that scared. If you want to know my opinion, it was a teenage prank." He used his pen to push his uniform hat up farther on his head.

"Who? Angel?" A couple of days ago, he would have been convinced she was the vandal. Now, he felt the urge to jump to her defense. "She's nearly nine months pregnant."

"She wouldn't be the first pregnant woman to commit a crime. But she said she was at home, sleeping in her room. No one at Freedom Ranch is willing to say differently."

"Any other suspects?"

"Mack, but he was helping a neighbor plow." Jax shrugged. "We've run into a wall. Unless the person commits another crime, we probably won't catch him."

"Do you think he will?"

"Depends on the motivation. The sheriff thinks the perp was just trying to upset Brenna. Not scare her. If that's the case, the brick might be the end of things. If the perp was trying to scare her, though, I doubt it will end with this."

"That's not very comforting."

"Maybe not, but it's the truth." A call came in over his radio and Jax listened, then frowned. "Tell you what, I'll give you a warning this time. If I catch you speeding again, it's going to cost you two hundred bucks. Drive safely, man."

He hurried back to his vehicle, and seconds later he was gone, lights on, sirens blaring.

Sirens?

They weren't common in Benevolence.

The fact that Jax was using them spoke to the seriousness of the situation.

There was some kind of emergency in town.

River could think of plenty of things it could be, but his mind kept circling back around to Brenna. The town had been quiet and uneventful until she'd arrived. Ever since then, it seemed like all hell had broken loose.

Or maybe that was an exaggeration.

Maybe it just felt . . . unsettled.

Sure, River could wait things out, read the newspaper in the morning and find out exactly what had happened. That wasn't his

style, though. He'd made his fortune by being proactive, by making split-second decisions and then having the guts to follow
through on them. He'd doubted a lot of
things in his life, but he didn't doubt his
ability to make good choices. He might have
learned the skill late, but he'd learned it
well.

At the moment, a good decision didn't
include sitting in his car, wondering what
was going on.

He pulled back onto the road and followed Jax's cruiser, keeping just far enough
back to be out of the way. He didn't want
to gum up the works or cause any more
problems than there already were, and he
didn't want to get his butt tossed in jail. He
just wanted to make sure the emergency
didn't include someone he cared about.
When he'd arrived in Benevolence, that list
had been pretty short. Now it was longer. It
included a whole group of people he'd have
kicked out of his life a month ago if he'd
had the opportunity. Now he felt responsible
for them. A pain in the ass, but the truth.
No matter how much he might tell himself
that he wanted all of them gone, he'd worry
if they were.

Which sucked, but he guessed that was
the way it had been for Belinda and Dillard

when they'd been fostering troubled teens. They'd stuck it out anyway, brought every one of the kids they'd taken in up through high school. A lot of those kids had gone on to college, and most of them had made a go of having a productive life.

Pretty impressive.

River had always thought so.

He just hadn't ever wanted to follow in their footsteps. He had no desire to sacrifice his sanity on the altar of another person's life.

He was beginning to realize that sometimes a person didn't have a choice. Sometimes they found themselves on a path and they just had to keep walking down it because there was no way to turn around, no way to step off.

That's what had happened when he'd returned to Benevolence. He'd started out thinking he had a choice about how long he'd stay and what he'd accomplish while he was there. Now, he knew the truth. The minute he'd walked into Freedom Ranch, he'd sealed his own fate. There'd been no way he could ever leave it behind again.

Up ahead, Jax raced onto Main Street, and River's pulse jumped. There were plenty of businesses there, plenty of places that could have been vandalized or broken into, but he had a feeling Jax wasn't going to any of those. He had a feeling he was heading straight for Chocolate Haven.

Chapter Fourteen

Brenna clutched a long-handled knife, her ear pressed to the office door. She didn't know what she was listening for. Maybe the sound of someone breaking the brand-new window and climbing into the shop or, maybe, the wild pounding of fists against the back door. She knew what she wanted to hear: the cavalry riding to the rescue, because someone had been in the alley. She'd seen him when she was carrying the last three batches of mediocre fudge out to the Dumpster. First, he'd been just a strange shadow, a lumpy bit of darkness mixing with the early evening shadows. Then he'd moved, shifting just enough for Brenna to realize she wasn't alone.

She hadn't stuck around to ask questions. She'd run for the back door, darting inside and slamming it closed.

She didn't think she'd ever moved so fast in her life.

The guy — whoever he was — had moved pretty fast, too. She'd seen his shadowy form outside the kitchen window seconds after she'd closed the door. She'd freaked, grabbing her cell phone and calling the police as she'd searched frantically for the knife she'd sliced her fingers with.

It was sharp, and that's what she'd wanted because there was no way anyone was going to take her down without a fight.

I'm watching you.

That's what the message on the brick had said. Brenna hadn't been too concerned. She'd figured Angel had tossed it through the window, and she'd just kind of put it out of her mind. If the police had proven the teenager had committed the crime, she'd have asked for restitution, but she wouldn't have pressed charges.

People made mistakes. They made them all the time.

Look at her. She'd gone off to pursue a career she hadn't liked for the sake of some imagined pressure from the people in her life. Then she'd compounded the matter by settling for less than what she deserved.

She'd meant every word she'd said when she'd told Dan that the first date with him was the worst mistake she'd ever made.

She was trying to make fewer mistakes.

But she was thinking that her assumption about Angel had been one. Maybe she hadn't tossed the brick, and maybe she hadn't sent the message. Maybe someone else had, someone who really had been watching her, lurking in the shadows, creeping through the alley, peering in the window while she worked.

She shuddered, dropping onto her stomach and peering under the door. She could see the light from the hallway. That was it. No shadows broke through it. No feet moved past. Still no sound of anyone entering the shop or moving through it. She thought she could hear sirens, but she didn't want to get her hopes up.

When her cell phone rang, she jumped, the knife dropping from her hand and clattering onto the floor. She flicked on the office light, saw the knife a foot away, and snatched it up, then answered her phone.

"Hello?" she gasped, fear making her voice shake.

"Brenna? Jax Gordon. I just pulled up outside your shop. I'm at the back door. You want to open the door for me?"

"Sure." She fiddled with the office lock, finally managed to get it open, raced through the kitchen she'd managed to make another god-awful mess of. She didn't know what it was about the family fudge, she really didn't, but every time she made it, chaos happened.

She yanked the door open and stepped aside so Jax could enter. His eyes widened as he took in the chocolate dripping down the front of the stove, the condensed milk spilled on the floor, the broken bottle of vanilla that had somehow slipped from her hands. The fudge recipe was lying in a pile of sugar, flecks of fudge smeared across the laminated 3 × 5 card. She grabbed it and stuffed it into her apron pocket.

"Was he in the front of the store, too?" he asked, taking out a camera and snapping a few shots.

For about a half second, she was tempted to let him believe someone else had wrecked the kitchen.

"Actually, he wasn't in the shop," she admitted. "I did this all by myself."

He lowered the camera, his lips twitching with what was probably the beginning of a smile.

"Impressive," he said, and she just shrugged because she didn't have any energy left to be amused.

"Thank you."

"Want to tell me what happened?"

She explained it all: the heavy bag of

discarded fudge, the trip outside, the shadow near the Dumpster.

"And you're sure it was a man?"

"I'm sure it was a person."

"People do walk through that alley, Brenna," he reminded her. "It isn't unusual on a beautiful Sunday evening for someone to want to stroll through the park. This is the easiest way to get to it from Main Street."

"I know, but . . ."

"What?"

"If it were someone I knew, he'd have called out and said hello. He wouldn't have been hiding near the Dumpster."

"Maybe he wasn't hiding? Maybe he was throwing something away?"

He didn't believe her. That was the impression she got. It should have been fine, but she was tired of fudge and chocolate and sugar and sweets. She was tired of drama and trauma and pretending things were okay when they weren't. She wanted to be up in the apartment, a glass of wine in one hand and a good book in the other, all the things she'd worked for still available to her.

She couldn't have any of that, so she at least wanted to be taken seriously. "I know what I saw."

"Okay," Jax conceded. "We'll say he was hiding. Did he come after you when you ran?"

"I saw him outside the window after I locked the door."

"You're sure it was him?"

"Who else would it have been? It's past seven on a Sunday night. Despite what you may think, people don't usually cut through the alley and walk past the shop's window. If they want to go to the park, it's a straight shot across the parking lot. No need at all to walk past my back door."

"You're angry," he said, looking up from the tablet he was writing notes on.

"I'm frustrated," she corrected. "I know this is small-town America, and I know the things I'm reporting are small-town incidents, but I want to feel like I'm being taken seriously."

"Am I giving you the impression you're not? Because I can tell you right now that I'm taking your complaint very seriously. I'm just trying to weed out fact from speculation. Everything you've said could mean that someone was hiding in the alley stalking the shop or watching you. It could also mean that you just happened to walk into the alley while someone was doing something stupid: sneaking a drink of alcohol where his parents couldn't see, lighting up a cigarette or popping a couple of pills. Small town doesn't mean no crime, and just because something happened at Chocolate Haven a few days ago doesn't mean this is connected."

He was right.

Of course he was. And he said it all without heat or accusation. Which only made her feel twice the fool for being frustrated.

"Sorry, I'm just —"

"There's no need to apologize, Brenna. Your feelings are well-founded. If I'd walked into the alley and seen someone, I'd be shaken too."

She doubted it.

Jax didn't look like the kind of guy who'd be shaken by anything. It wasn't just his scar; it was his whole persona. Confidence oozed out of him, but he didn't have an arrogant bone in his body, or a mean one. He never picked a fight, but he never backed down from one either. He'd been like that from the day he'd arrived in Benevolence, the wound on his face still healing, the story of how his entire family had been murdered and he'd been the only one to survive whispered in every corner of the school, every field on the playground.

He'd seemed above it all. He hadn't worked to make friends, but he'd never been unkind. As far as Brenna knew, the only one he'd really connected with was Adeline's husband. Jax and Sinclair had both had difficult childhoods, they'd both lost their parents, and they'd both wanted nothing more than to escape Benevolence.

"I know you're doing your job, Jax. I didn't mean to imply that you weren't. I just —"

"Want answers?"

"Yes. But I also just want my life to start being more . . . normal."

He laughed and shook his head. "Let me know if you figure out what that means. Kane said you got a call from your ex tonight?"

"Yes." She'd called Kane while she was digging through Belinda's attic. She'd also called the detective in charge of the New York City investigation. She'd left Dan's phone number with both of them, along with all the information she'd gleaned from the conversation. She was hoping they could track him by contacting fashion designers in Bangkok. Dan was just loud and arrogant enough not to have hidden his true identity.

"Did you contact the partner? Winthrop, right?"

"Yes. I called him after I spoke with the New York City police."

"And . . . ?"

"I gave him the number, too."

"So the likelihood that he was hanging around here, hoping your ex was going to show up is pretty slim?"

"I'd say it was nonexistent. He's got a thriving medical practice in New York. He doesn't have time to travel across a continent to lurk in an alley."

"He did hire a private investigator to help locate your ex, but he insisted he didn't send the guy this way."

"Why would he? I'm as anxious to see Dan brought to justice as anyone."

"You didn't file charges against him."

"To punish him for what? Taking money from an account that had both of our names on it?"

"Legally, half that money is yours. Whatever loss you accrued because of what he's done is half his to pay. You can't have him charged with a crime, but you can slap him with a civil suit and demand he repay your half of what was in those accounts."

She knew that. She had a friend who was a divorce lawyer. Shauna had been very clear about what Brenna's legal rights were and what legal actions she could take.

Shauna had even offered to represent her for free, but Dan was gone and Brenna had just wanted to move on, get to that sweet place where she'd crossed the river of her challenges and was prancing around on the other side of it.

So far, she'd done a piss-poor job of it, but she was working toward something better, and she'd get there eventually.

"I cut my ties, Jax. I didn't want years of legal battles and court appearances and fights over what was mine and what was his. I just wanted to move on."

He nodded, tucking the tablet under his arm and walking toward the door. "I'm going to check the alley, see if there's any evidence that could give you some closure on this."

"I appreciate it."

"It's my job." He opened the door and frowned. "Someone's in the parking lot."

"Who?" she whispered, stepping closer and peering around his shoulder. She could see his cruiser, parked right near the back door. Behind that, a truck idled in the streetlight, engine purring, paint gleaming.

Her heart jumped because she knew it was River. Knew it without seeing the color of the truck, without seeing his face, without seeing him.

Her heart thumped in acknowledgment, her pulse thrumming happily. She tried to stop it. She tried to tell herself how much trouble she was going to be in if she kept looking for River, reaching for him, hoping he'd be around.

Because it seemed he always was.

She couldn't remember the last time there'd been someone like that in her life. She couldn't remember if there ever had been.

He got out of the truck, his lean, muscular body as familiar as a sunset, as welcome as the first hint of fall in the summer air. She wanted to run to him. God, but she wanted to, but she stood rooted to the spot, watching as Jax walked outside and went to greet him.

River glanced her way, his face as cool and unreadable as it had been since the cabin and the phone call. Dan . . . ruining everything again. She could have let herself believe that, but the truth was, she was ruining it all on her own because she was afraid, because she cared too much, cared more than she ever had before.

She wanted River like she wanted her next breath, and she was terrified of what would happen if she acknowledged that. So, she took the cowardly way out. Again. She stepped back into the kitchen and let the door close.

Then she went to work scraping thick chocolate goop off the counter and the stove. She listened to the sound of voices just outside the window, but she didn't look, because if she did, she might just give in and go after what she wanted.

It would be good for a day, a week, a year. Maybe a little more, but then what?

She'd be left high and dry, clinging to the shattered bits of forever while he went on his merry way.

Not true, her heart whispered.

She was too busy cleaning up her mess to listen.

River hadn't been invited, but he followed Jax into the alley anyway. Dusky light cast dark shadows across the narrow pavement, creating alcoves and hiding places that weren't there during full light. The Dumpster was set against the wall of the building, with just enough room behind it to allow the lid to open easily. The shadows were deeper there, and he could see how Brenna might have missed a person who'd crouched low in them.

"This must be the bag she was carrying out," Jax said, nudging a black trash bag that had been abandoned near the mouth of the alley.

Fudge.

River could smell it, and he had a feeling the bag was chock-full of Brenna's discarded efforts. He'd offered to help. Again. She'd refused. Again.

The top-secret family recipe could only be entrusted to family. River could respect that, but he had a feeling she'd be willing to entrust it to someone she could actually put her trust in. Apparently, he was not that person.

A thought for another time.

A time when he wasn't still irritated by the phone call from the asshole.

Jax flashed a light toward the Dumpster. The lid was down, but there was a thick cloth grocery bag on the ground nearby.

Not empty. It looked like it was bulging with stuff.

"This might be what our guy was doing," Jax said, pulling out gloves and slipping them on, then crouching next to the bag and peering into it. "Interesting."

"What?"

"Look at this." He lifted a box from the bag. Looked like cards of some sort. Invitations? River leaned closer. Baby shower invitations.

"And these." Jax pulled out a baby-name book — well used from the look of it — a small package of cookies that looked exactly like one that had been at the ranch, a large bag of jelly beans he'd seen Huckleberry carrying into the house the previous day. For Angel, he'd said, because she was craving them.

"Shit," he muttered as Jax snapped a few pictures.

"You recognize the stuff?" Jax asked, taking what looked like a blue ribbon from the bag, something a kid would get at school. Maybe for winning a spelling bee or completing the mile run.

"Some of it looks like what we have at the ranch, but I'm sure there are dozens of houses in Benevolence that have jelly beans and cookies in them."

"And baby-name books?" Jax opened the front cover of the book. "With Angel's name written in the front of them?"

"Shit," River said again, because that was about all he could manage.

"Do you have any idea where Angel is this evening?" Jax asked as he lifted something else from the bag. A packet of crackers, a few colorful stickers stuck to its side.

"Last time I saw her, she was back at the ranch."

"I guess I'll head over there to see if she recognizes any of this stuff." He put everything back in the bag and lifted it.

"You don't seriously believe Angel was sitting in this alley, planning for her baby and spying on Brenna, do you?" River asked, following him into the parking lot.

"The evidence seems to point to that, doesn't it?" Jax opened the trunk of his squad car and placed the bag in it. Then he turned to face River. "We suspected her of tossing the brick through the window. She denied it. I'm curious to see what she has to say about this."

"She's very pregnant," River pointed out, just like he had before, because he was feeling protective again. As if he were an older brother determined to keep his kid sister out of trouble.

"So you've told me," Jax said wryly. "Even if you hadn't, it's kind of difficult to miss. That being said, Angel works eight- and nine-hour shifts at the diner five or six days a week. She's young and healthy, and I don't think the pregnancy is slowing her down. She could easily toss a brick through a window or crouch near a Dumpster."

"The brick maybe," River conceded. Angel had always been at the top of his personal list of suspects for that. "But crouching near a Dumpster? Why would she do it? And how fast could she have moved if she'd wanted to get away from the shop before you arrived?"

"Why leave a bag of her stuff around?" Jax added. "They're all good questions. I'm going to see if I can get some answers."

"And do what once you have them?"

"Not toss her into jail, if that's what you're thinking. If she was here, I'd like to know why."

"She's not easy to talk to."

"Yeah, I know. We questioned her before, remember? Look, River, I'm sure you're feeling responsible for the people who are living out there with Belinda, but you don't have to. They've all made their choices about how they want to live. Everyone in town knows it, and there's not one person who'd blame Belinda for any trouble that was caused by Angel or Mack or anyone else at Freedom Ranch."

Good. Great.

River should probably be jumping for joy and celebrating, but this wasn't just about Belinda. It wasn't about her reputation, her sanity, or, even, her health. It was about Angel. If she'd committed a crime, she needed to be punished, but River hated to see it happen.

He'd been where she was.

He'd balanced for a while between the street kid from Seattle — the one who'd spent most of his early years fending for himself and doing everything he could to survive — and the teen from Freedom Ranch. He'd bucked the system plenty, trying to maintain the independence he was used to, but mostly just trying not to be hurt again.

He could see that in Angel.

Maybe that was why he was learning to have a little more patience with her.

"I'm going to tell Brenna what I found and where I'm heading. Then I'm going to talk to Angel. Feel free to go on ahead and prepare Belinda for my visit. I wouldn't want to upset her."

"What isn't upsetting about the police showing up on her doorstep?" he responded, and Jax frowned.

"Would you rather bring Angel to the station to discuss it?"

No way in hell was he going to do that. If he did, everyone in Benevolence would know about it before morning. What the town knew, Belinda would find out. Better just to have Jax go to the ranch. "Come on out and ask your questions. Belinda should be fine."

"I guess so. The way I hear it, she had the police out at her place all the time when you were a teenager." Jax tossed the words over his shoulder as he headed back to the shop.

River couldn't deny them.

His first year or two at the ranch, he'd probably caused more trouble than every other foster kid Belinda and Dillard had ever had. And that was saying a lot, considering the kinds of kids they took in.

He'd grown out of it.

With their help.

Hopefully the same would be true of Angel.

He glanced at the alley as he walked back to his truck. It didn't make sense, Angel sitting near a Dumpster. If she wanted to watch Brenna, if she had some kind of score to settle with her, why hide in an alley? Why not knock on the door and leave some new message? Slash a tire? Spray-paint the apartment?

That was more Angel's style.

The *brick* was more Angel's style.

But hiding in alleys? He couldn't picture it.

He'd ask her, though, before Jax showed up at the house, because she was part of the little family Belinda had created and that mattered. A lot.

He pulled out of his parking space, the truck headlights splashing across the back façade of the shop. He caught a glimpse of Brenna in the window, her bright hair untamed, her face pale. He thought she waved, but by the time he waved back, she was gone.

They needed to talk.

There was no doubt about that.

Timing was everything, though, and the timing wasn't right. Not for either of them.

She had the shop to run.

He had the new project at Freedom Ranch and all the people who came with it.

The way he saw it, things would play out the way they would. His thoughts drifted back to the cabin, to the kiss, to Brenna's soft skin and softer lips, to the way it had felt to hold her in his arms.

He hadn't wanted it to end.

He didn't think Brenna had either. He could go back to Chocolate Haven later, and he was pretty sure he could make her admit it.

What good would it do, though?

He'd heard her on the phone with her ex, and he knew damn well the guy was a consummate manipulator, and Brenna? She was a romantic at heart. She covered it with her sharp tongue and dry humor, but she wanted the flowers, the chocolates, the kisses in the moonlight. Backing her into a corner and forcing her to admit how she felt? That was about as romantic as proclaiming undying love at a landfill.

No. He wouldn't do it, but he wasn't going to let her go either. He wasn't going to pretend he hadn't tasted the sweetness of her lips or rested his hand on the velvety flesh of her thigh. He wasn't going to try to convince himself that what he felt when he was with her was just a trick of the light, a fluke, a product of stress, fatigue, or, even, loneliness.

He'd been looking for something for years.

He'd tried to find it in success. He'd built his restaurants from the ground up. He'd built his brand. He'd made a name for himself, but he'd never been able to fill the void. Even his relationships hadn't done that, because they'd never touched that empty spot.

He'd figured he'd just go on the way he was because he was happy enough and content enough. He had most of what he wanted and everything he needed, and life was so good that he'd almost forgotten there could be more.

Then he'd stood on the porch with

Brenna, looking at the river and the trees, and he'd felt the contentment that came from being in the right place at the right time with the right person, and he'd realized that everything he'd had before had been a lie, and this? It was the truth.

Strange how quickly things had changed.

He'd come to Benevolence with one thought: getting back out of it. Now? It was starting to feel like home.

CHAPTER FIFTEEN

So, this was what happened when Chocolate Haven ran out of fudge.

Brenna had always wondered.

Now she knew.

People got pissy.

Especially people like Millicent.

"What do you mean, you don't have fudge?" the older woman crowed, her voice ringing so loudly through the shop every person in it shut up and listened.

Awesome. That was just what Brenna wanted: a very public announcement about the sorry state of Lamont family fudge. That way she wouldn't have to explain the situation a dozen times.

"I mean," Brenna said, making sure her voice was just as loud as Millicent's, "that we don't have any fudge."

"You just opened. How could you possibly have sold out already?"

"I didn't say we sold out. I said we didn't

have any. We do have some delicious peanut butter truffles. Would you like a few?"

"I came for a pound of fudge," Millicent huffed, but she'd obviously been distracted by the other chocolates. There were plenty of them to choose from. Which just might save Brenna's hide.

"I'll have some for you tomorrow," Brenna lied, because there was no way she'd ever have fudge for anyone by that time. She'd made her fifteenth batch that morning and it had tasted as crappy as the first one. "Today, I've got almond nougat bars, cherry cordials, mint patties . . ."

"I can see what you have," Millicent huffed, eyeing the display case, her jowls nearly vibrating with excitement.

She'd buy a pound of something. No doubt about it. And none of the other customers had gone running out the door when they'd realized there was no fudge, so the day's profits might not be totally shot to heck.

"If you want a minute to think about it," Brenna said, smiling at the gentleman who stood behind Millicent, "I could help the person behind you, and then —"

"Are you implying that I'm taking too much of your time?" Millicent set her hands on her ample hips and scowled. "Byron would never do such a thing."

"Byron is fishing. In Alaska. If you'd like to wait for him to return, I'm sure he'll give you the same wonderful service he always has. That'll happen in about 336 hours." The words just kind of slipped out, and someone at the back of the line stifled a laugh.

"Young lady," Millicent snapped, "if I wanted to wait 336 hours, I'd have stayed home. Because you're obviously struggling to keep the shop afloat while Byron is out of town, I'll do my part to help. I'll take a pound of the peanut butter truffles, six cherry cordials, and six mint patties. Do you need me to write that down so you don't forget?"

"I think I can manage." She smiled through gritted teeth, filled two pretty little boxes with Millicent's choices, wrapped both with gold ribbons, and handed them across the counter. "There you are."

Millicent slammed her money onto the glass display case and stalked off without her change.

"She's a feisty little thing," the next customer said, his gaze following Millicent as she pushed her way through the crowd.

"Little?" Brenna murmured, and then wished she hadn't. The guy looked confused. Obviously he wasn't local and had no idea just how big Millicent was. Big boobs. Big hair. Big lips and smile and teeth. Big personality and big attitude, but if the guy wanted to chase after *that,* more power to him.

"Just a turn of phrase." He smiled, ordered four chocolate-covered pretzels, and handed her a twenty. "Keep the change on that."

"Thanks." She'd add it to the coffers and hope she'd make up in tips what she was losing in fudge sales. She didn't want Byron to come home to a shop that was in the red after being in the black for a hundred years.

"So, you're one of the Lamont sisters," he said, taking the box of pretzels she offered him.

"Yes."

"All of you live in town?"

"Why do you want to know?"

"Just curious," he said. "I heard one of you is a lawyer. She live in town?"

Okay. That was a little too nosy for Brenna's liking.

"I don't answer personal questions about family," she responded, studying him a little more carefully than she had before. He had dark hair, green eyes, and a sharp, intense stare that made her feel uncomfortable.

"Too bad. It would have saved me a little

effort. Tell you what." He reached into his jacket pocket and she tensed, not sure what she was afraid of but suddenly very, very afraid. He pulled an envelope out, passed it across the counter. "When you see Willow, give her this."

He smiled, but there wasn't a bit of warmth in it, and then he walked out of the shop.

When you see Willow?

He'd already known which sister was the lawyer, so why had he been fishing for information?

It didn't sit well and she was worried, but she had a line of people twelve deep and she had to keep working.

She shoved the envelope in her apron pocket, tried to tell herself that there was nothing sinister about the guy and nothing worrisome about the envelope, but she could feel it like a lead weight in her pocket as she filled orders, rang customers up, took money, and offered change.

Two hours straight of nothing but front-of-the-house work. Constant customers. Constant questions about Lamont family fudge. Constant excuses for why she didn't have any. Constant talking people into different products. She sold so much, she had to run to the back when the line abated and whip up another batch of chocolate bark and two batches of peanut butter truffles.

She was able to do it quickly and with a minimum of mess. She was feeling pretty damn proud of herself when the bell above the shop door announced the next round of customers. She hurried out front, a sheet pan of candy in her hands. She'd fill the display case and then take orders.

"I'll be right with you," she called as she hurriedly filled the case.

"It's okay. I'm not in a hurry."

Brenna knew the voice and looked up, surprised to see Angel standing near the door. This was the first time she'd actually come into the shop since Brenna had been there, and she looked nervous, her dark eyeliner and dark red lipstick adding to her natural pallor.

"Angel, this is a . . . pleasant surprise."

"I hate liars," Angel responded and then lowered her gaze, brushed imaginary crumbs from her oversized black T-shirt. It looked like she'd either been at work or was on her way to it, her hair scraped back from her face, an apron tied under her belly. "Sorry. Bad habit."

"Being rude?"

"Striking before I'm struck."

It was an honest answer, and a more

mature one than Brenna had expected.

"I get it," she said, and Angel sighed.

"I doubt it. Sure, you've got an ass of an ex and your own problems, but you've had an easy life, Brenna. A really easy one by my standards."

"Should I apologize?" she asked as she placed the chocolates in the case.

"No, I just thought I should say it. Look, I came for two reasons. One, I have to apologize."

"You broke the window?"

"Yes." Her cheeks went bright red, her eyes filling with tears. "It was stupid. I was mad because you caused trouble for Mack and that caused trouble for Belinda."

"I didn't —"

"I know. It wasn't your fault. River already read me the riot act about it, and he told me I had to come to apologize, and that I was going to have to pay for the window. And I will." She touched her belly, frowned. "I already asked Laurie for extra hours. I'll pay fifty dollars a week until it's paid for."

"I don't want you to do that, Angel."

"Tough shi . . . tough. I owe you and I'm going to pay. The thing is, Belinda is more of a mother than I've ever had. I'd do anything for her. Seeing her hurt or upset or in pain, it just kills me." She sniffed, wiped her nose with the back of her hand, and grimaced. "I'm such a baby sometimes. I don't even know how I'm going to raise this kid."

"I don't know," Brenna said, taking a small box from the shelf and putting several different chocolates in it. "You've got a job. You're working hard. You're correcting your mistakes. That's a lot more than a lot of adults do."

"Yeah. Well, I feel like an idiot, and if River and Jax hadn't threatened to go to Belinda about the window, I wouldn't be here. That's the honest-to-God truth. But I don't want to upset Belinda more than she's already going to be."

"If she's not going to be told about what you've done, why would she be upset?" She pushed the chocolate across the service counter and Angel eyed the box.

"I can't take that."

"Why not?"

"Because I'm a horrible person, okay? Because I don't deserve it."

"Stop feeling sorry for yourself," Brenna said, keeping her tone mild and her expression neutral.

Truth?

She felt pretty damn bad for Angel.

She'd had a tough life. She obviously

hadn't had anyone care about her until she'd arrived at Belinda's. She wanted to protect the one person who'd cared about her, and Brenna really couldn't fault her for it.

"I'm not," Angel snapped. Then she smiled sheepishly. "Okay. I am."

"So take the chocolates and drown your sorrows in them."

"If only it were that simple." She sighed, took the box, and met Brenna's eyes. "Joe is missing," she said, the words flat and tight and so surprising it took Brenna a minute to process them.

"Joe?" she repeated.

"Yes. *Joe.* I was supposed to walk him down to the end of the driveway and wait for the bus with him, but I was tired. My back hurt and the baby had been kicking me all night the night before. So . . ." She swallowed hard. "I didn't. I mean, he's a thirty-one-year-old man, and I've walked him to the end of the driveway a million times. He knew where to wait. There's never any traffic on the road, and he's smart enough not to go off with strangers."

"How do you know he's missing?"

"His housemother called this morning. Thank God I was the one who picked up the phone. Belinda would freak."

"What did his housemother say?" Brenna asked, biting back impatience. She wasn't sure why Angel had come to her with the problem, but she had to get as much information as possible if she were going to help.

"He wasn't on the bus last night. I guess he told the driver he was staying another night."

"And the driver decided not to check to see if that was okay?"

"That's what I asked!" she replied, her voice breaking. "The housemother said that isn't the driver's responsibility. Joe knows what he's supposed to do. She almost didn't call to check on him, but it's so unusual for him not to return, she thought she'd better."

"Too bad she waited all night," Brenna muttered.

"I said that, too," Angel said, and then she burst into tears.

River was back at the cabin.

Just sitting on the porch and staring at the river, because Huckleberry had somehow managed to dump an entire gallon of paint on the floor that was supposed to be refinished that day. Now it wasn't being refinished. It was being cleaned. Every speck of dove gray paint wiped up. The floor guys had agreed to come the following day, but River's carefully planned schedule had been wrecked by a kid with a thing for finding trouble.

Just like you, he thought he heard Dillard laugh from somewhere inside the cabin.

Yeah.

Probably.

And at least Belinda had already been at therapy when it happened. She hadn't heard Huckleberry's loud cursing, Mack's muttered response, or River's . . .

Well, he hadn't blown a gasket. He could at least say that. He *had* asked the teen what the hell he'd been thinking, opening a gallon of paint they weren't ready to use.

To his credit, Huckleberry had a reason. He'd wanted to paint the hall foyer and hall before the floor was refinished. That way if he dripped paint or scraped the ladder on the floor, it wouldn't matter so much.

Yeah.

Well, he'd dripped the entire gallon of paint, but River had done worse in his life, so he'd told Huckleberry to clean it up and get started on the walls, and then he'd left the house.

He needed some air and a little bit of time to clear his head.

By the time he'd reached the cabin, he'd

calmed down enough to be reasonable.

So what if the floors wouldn't be done until the next day? By the time Belinda returned from therapy, the walls and foyer would be soft dove gray, the trim bright white. She'd love it, and what she loved, everyone else loved.

That was one of the things River was learning.

Everyone at the ranch wanted the best for Belinda. Even Angel, who'd stomped out of the house that morning with a muttered promise to make her apology and offer of restitution to Brenna. She loved Belinda. It had taken River a while to see that, but now that he did, he couldn't *un*see it.

It changed things for him. Made him want to be better at . . . what? Being a mentor? A friend? A father figure?

He was almost old enough to be Huckleberry's father.

Not that the kid was looking for that.

A breeze rustled the pine boughs and sent leaves skittering across the path that led to the river. Something skittered along with them. A piece of paper? A 3 × 5 card?

He watched it for a moment, tracking its course as it skipped across rocky earth.

An old recipe card?

That's what it looked like.

Maybe one that had fallen out of Brenna's purse when she'd grabbed her phone the previous day? She always seemed to be reading recipes, hanging them on the wall of the shop, tucking them into her pocket or into her purse.

He hadn't noticed one falling to the ground, but then, he'd been too busy watching Brenna's face to notice anything else.

He walked down the porch steps and grabbed the card before it could be blown farther away.

Yep. Definitely a recipe for . . .

Forever Kisses?

He almost laughed.

Then he read the ingredients. Read them again. Thought about the things Brenna had said about love and romance. He'd heard longing in her voice, and he'd known she'd never be the kind of woman who'd be satisfied with less than everything a man had to give. She'd never be satisfied giving less than everything of herself either. She wanted all of it: the commitment, the passion, the good, the bad. She'd be the kind of partner who stuck it out. No matter what.

Yeah. She'd want forever. And then some.

He flipped the card, looking for a date or a name. Nothing. The recipe looked old, handwritten in beautiful calligraphy, and laminated so the words didn't smudge. He could imagine Brenna finding it in one of the old recipe books he'd seen in the shop. She'd have been smitten by it, that romantic soul of hers longing to have exactly what the recipe offered.

His phone rang as he tucked the card into his pocket, and he glanced at the number on the screen. It wasn't familiar, but he figured it had to be something to do with Angel or Huckleberry or even Mack.

"Hello?"

"River? It's Brenna."

"Need some help at the shop?" he asked, because he hadn't gone that morning. He'd wanted to give her what she seemed to need: time and space.

Besides, he couldn't guarantee he'd stay away from her if he helped out in the shop. He couldn't promise himself that he wouldn't taste her lips, touch her soft skin again. Until she decided exactly what she wanted from their relationship, he had no intention of doing either of those things.

"No, but I need you to come down here. Angel stopped by. She says Joe is missing."

"Joe?" He headed around the side of the cabin, jogged toward the road. "He went back to the group home last night."

"He was supposed to. He didn't. His

housemother called the ranch this morning. Just to make sure he was still there."

"And Angel is just now informing someone of this?" He eyed the river, the country road, the thick forest that edged the property. A guy like Joe could find himself in all kinds of trouble out in the elements.

Did he know how to swim?

How to stay warm?

How to use a phone if he needed to?

"She didn't want to upset Belinda so she took the morning off work, and she's been looking for him."

"She should have called the police."

"I just did. The sheriff is on his way over."

"She should have called as soon as she realized he was missing."

"Should have doesn't change anything, River. Maybe you can get Huckleberry and Mack to look around the ranch? Talk to the neighbors. Angel said she checked the barn and went to a couple of Joe's favorite places."

"Shit," he breathed. "This isn't good, red. Joe has the mental capacity of a seven-year-old. And that's on a good day."

"He can't have gone far," she tried to reassure him, but River kept seeing the flowing water, the slick rocks, the trees that looked exactly like one another. If Joe had decided to wander through them, he'd never find his way out.

Summer was nearly over, the nights were getting cold, and Joe . . .

Had he brought his clothes?

Did he have a blanket?

"River?" she prodded, and he could hear an edge of panic in her voice, hear what sounded like someone sobbing in the background.

Angel?

Probably. If she went into labor because of the stress . . .

He wasn't going there.

One thing at a time.

And the first thing he needed to do was find Joe.

"I'll be there in ten." He shoved the phone back in his pocket and sprinted back to the house.

Huckleberry and Mack were both in the foyer, every wall already coated with gray.

"Hey, man!" Huckleberry said sheepishly. "I just want to apologize again for the mess I made. I should have asked before I opened the paint, and-"

"Joe is missing." He cut him off, his voice gruff with worry. "Go check his room. See if he brought his backpack and books with him."

"How can he be missing?" Huckleberry asked, but he was already running up the stairs. Seconds later, he called from the landing, "The backpack is gone. The books are here."

"What did he have in the pack?" Mack asked, closing a can of paint and grabbing a jacket from the closet. He pulled it on over his T-shirt, zipped it, and pulled the collar up so it covered the burn scars on his neck. He grabbed a baseball cap, slammed that over his hair.

"I have no idea." Huckleberry panted as he sprinted down the stairs. "What I want to know is how in the hell he can be missing. He's supposed to be home."

This isn't home?

That's what Joe had asked, and River hadn't realized just how badly he must have wanted it to be.

"He didn't get on the bus last night," River explained, checking in Dillard's office and in the dining and living rooms. No sign of Joe, but he hadn't expected there to be.

"Yes. He did. I saw him with Angel last night. She walked outside with him. She always walks him to the bus stop."

"She didn't last night."

"But . . ." He shook his head. "It doesn't

386

matter. We have to find Joe. I'll check the barn."

"Angel already checked it."

"Then I'll go over to Elmer's. Joe loves hanging around with him. Maybe he's there."

"I'll go down by the river," Mack said quietly, the concern in his face echoing River's. "Joe is fascinated by it. I told him I'd take him fishing next weekend. Maybe he didn't want to wait."

And maybe he'd gotten too close. Maybe he'd fallen in.

Maybe a dozen things had happened that River didn't want to imagine.

Mack ran outside, Huckleberry on his heels. They split at the driveway, each heading in a different direction.

River grabbed his keys and hopped into his truck.

He didn't speed toward town, and not because he was worried about getting a ticket. He rolled along the road, looking for any sign of Joe. His backpack, a piece of clothing, a footprint in the earth.

By the time he hit Main Street, his shoulders were tense, his neck tight. He'd seen nothing, and that scared him. People disappeared all the time. They walked out of houses and off buses and out of stores and were never seen again.

Someone like Joe? He was the perfect victim. Naïve, trusting, eager to please. Anyone could have talked him into anything. The more he thought about that, the angrier he got. It would have taken five minutes of Angel's day to walk the guy to the bus and watch him get on.

Five minutes in comparison to someone's life?

Yeah. It wasn't much.

He pulled up in front of Chocolate Haven, parking the car in a no-parking zone and sprinting into the store. Several customers were there, being served by an ancient woman who looked vaguely familiar.

"Thank God you're here!" she cried, the high-pitched voice familiar, too.

May Reynolds? His old home economics teacher?

It had to be.

She had the same bulging blue eyes, the same nervous tics.

"Thanks, Ms. Reynolds."

"Mrs. Welch now. I married Jim Welch a few months ago," she corrected. "But that's not for us to worry about now. That poor boy. Lost and alone somewhere." She nearly sobbed the words, and he patted her on the shoulder.

"It's okay. We'll find him."

"I certainly hope so. I've called the pastor, of course, and he's getting a group together at the church. They're going to spread out and search."

"Did you mention that to the sheriff?"

"He's been busy talking to Brenna and Angel. That poor girl is just beside herself. That's why Brenna called me. I had my own shop for years, you know, so I can be counted on to run the place for a few hours."

"That's great, Mrs. Welch. I know Brenna appreciates it." He walked past her, following the sound of voices and sobs into the kitchen.

Kane was on the phone, speaking so quietly River couldn't hear the words.

Brenna crouched next to Angel, holding the young girl's hand as she sobbed.

And Angel? She was sitting in a chair, her belly pressing against her T-shirt, black eye makeup smeared down her cheeks. She looked pale as paper, her legs and arms so skinny he wondered how she could be nurturing the baby she was carrying.

He'd been mad as a hornet in the truck, thinking about how lazy and selfish she'd been, but seeing her there, crying her eyes out, stole the wind from his sails.

"I'm so sorry!" she sobbed, as if he were the one she had to apologize to.

"We all make mistakes," he responded.

"Not mistakes that kill people," she wailed, and Kane hung up the phone, crossed the room.

"I've got the doctor on the way, Angel," he said gently. "Being this upset isn't good for you or the baby. You need to calm down."

"How can I calm down when I killed poor Joe?"

"You're assuming he's dead, and that is a pretty weighty assumption."

"He's like a little kid. He doesn't even know how to tie his own shoes or make a piece of toast." She hiccupped, her belly moving beneath the shirt.

"He's lived in a group home for a while," Brenna said. "He probably knows a lot more than you think he does."

"He doesn't know how to survive. Not like me or Huckleberry." She pressed her fingers to her eyes, but the tears were still slipping out.

"How about you stop worrying about what can't be undone?" River said, crouching in front of her, his knees brushing Brenna's. She had chocolate on her face again, bits of it in her hair and on her shirt.

She met his eyes and he could see her concern, her fear, but her voice was calm as she patted Angel's shoulder and said, "River is right. You have to stop worrying about what has already happened. Just concentrate on taking care of yourself and the baby right now. We'll take care of the rest."

She stood, untied her apron, and hung it on the hook.

"I've been thinking about last night," she continued, "and the things Jax found in the alley. They all came from the ranch, right?"

"Yes," River agreed, his mind connecting the dots, putting things together the same way she was. "The candy. The crackers with the stickers. The jelly beans. If I were seven, they'd be the kinds of things I'd pack to run away."

"What about the baby-name book and the invitations?"

"Joe was so excited about the baby," Angel said, jumping up, her eyes alive with hope. "He heard me talking about having a baby shower and he asked me all about it. I showed him the invitations and . . ."

"What?" Kane prodded.

"I said I wanted to have a party to cele-brate the baby, but I was embarrassed to invite people because . . . Well, I'm not your typical mother. And Joe, he said he'd give them to everyone because he loved me and he loved my baby and we both deserved to have a party. He also wanted to help name the baby. I guess he might have taken the book, too."

"So we can assume Joe came into town yesterday evening and stopped in the alley," Kane said, opening the back door and looking out into the parking lot. "Five miles is a long way to walk. He was probably tired, so maybe he made it to Main Street, but all the shops were closed, so he found a quiet place to rest."

"And I probably scared him."

"Or maybe the sirens did," Kane suggested. "Doesn't matter. He ran off somewhere. We just need to figure out where a guy like him might go."

"We were at the church yesterday," River said. Joe loved church. He loved the people and they all seemed to love him.

If he'd been scared, he might have found his way there.

"Looks like the doctor is here. How about we let him take care of Angel and the baby and we go to the church. See if there's any sign of him there."

It sounded like a good plan to River.

"Ready?" he asked Brenna, offering her a hand and pulling her to her feet.

"I was ready twenty minutes ago," she responded, and then she dragged him outside into the morning sunshine.

CHAPTER SIXTEEN

There were twenty people at the church when they arrived and probably seventeen dogs. Small dogs. Big dogs. Hound dogs and fluffy poodlelike dogs. Every owner of every dog insisted that Fluffy or Brutus or Hunter would be able to track Joe easily.

Brenna doubted it, but she kept her mouth shut as the sheriff organized the search and sent people out in pairs to look for the missing man.

Finally, it was just the pastor, River, Kane, and Brenna, all of them moving through the cemetery, checking behind giant tombstones and beneath memorial benches and drooping willow trees.

If Joe had been there, they didn't find any sign of him.

"This isn't working," River said, running his hand over his hair and surveying the churchyard. "If he was here, we'd have found him by now."

"Are there other places in town that he likes to go?" she asked, worry making her stomach churn. Joe had been outside all night and now it was getting later in the day and he still hadn't shown up.

That couldn't be a good thing.

No matter how much she'd tried to re-assure Angel, no matter how many times she'd said they'd find Joe, she wasn't sure they would.

"No." He shook his head, then frowned. "Actually, yes. The library. I've been taking him there on Saturdays, but I didn't have time this weekend. Maybe he was angry that he didn't get a chance to go and decided to get there himself."

"I can't picture Joe angry about anything," she said, turning away from the church and heading down the hill that led to town.

"You're right. He probably wasn't, but I think I hurt his feelings."

"I can't imagine that either, River." She meant it. She couldn't imagine River ever hurting someone like Joe. She couldn't imagine him knowingly hurting anyone. At least not anyone who was younger or weaker or less capable than he was. She'd seen his face when he'd walked into Chocolate Haven. He'd been furious. Once he'd seen Angel, that had faded away.

"Yeah. Well, I'm the guy who sheared sheep, released a bull, and got myself into so much trouble while I lived here, I didn't want to ever come back. Trust me when I say I have a way of opening my mouth and putting my foot in it. Remember when I told him he was going to be going home?"

"Yes."

"Remember what he said?"

She did. " 'I'm not home?' "

"He was probably thinking about it, trying to work things out in his head. Maybe it scared him, made him think we were going to send him away and not let him return. With someone like Joe, it's hard to tell."

"You can't blame yourself for that."

"No? Then why do you blame yourself for what happened with your ex?"

"Who says I do?"

"It's obvious from the way you act."

"How, exactly, do I act?" she asked, knowing she was going to regret it, because River might not be into hurting people, but he was sure as heck into telling the truth.

"You haven't shared the truth with your family. They have no idea Dan was way more than a cheater."

"What does that have to do with anything?"

"You're embarrassed. You think Dan's ac-

396

tions are some reflection of you as a person."

"Bull," she said, but there was no heat in the word because he was right. She knew it.

As much as she tried to pretend otherwise, she did see what happened with Dan as a reflection of her and of her failures.

"I see."

"You see what?" she snapped, angry with herself and with him.

They were out there looking for Joe.

It wasn't the time or place for deep discussions about her psychological shortcomings.

"That you haven't moved on. That's too bad, red." He stepped onto the sidewalk, turned to the east, heading toward the library. "Because I really thought we might be able to have something together, but I'm not into threesomes."

"Who said I was?"

"You are if every time we're together you're thinking about the past, about what went wrong and what should have gone right and what you could have changed and didn't."

"I'm not —"

"Sure you are."

They reached the library, the sun glinting off the glass doors. She could see her reflection and River's, could see the distance between them. A foot. Maybe less, but it seemed like miles because she couldn't make herself say what she should, couldn't get the words out of her mouth: *I've already let it go.*

They'd be a lie if she did say them because she hadn't. She was holding on tight to her mistakes, remembering every bit of her stupidity, her naïveté, her blind devotion to the cause of love.

A cause that had been useless and empty because she hadn't really loved Dan. Not in any way that mattered. She'd cared about him. She'd wanted to make things work, but she'd wanted it because she'd wanted that childhood dream, the one where she fell in love with a nice guy who fell in love with her.

Dan had never been nice.

He'd been interesting. He'd been determined. He'd pursued her with every bit of his attention, and she'd enjoyed that. She could admit it. From the New Year's Eve party to the day he'd given her a gaudy engagement ring, he'd showered her with compliments and flowers and gifts.

She hadn't wanted any of those things, but she'd wanted the dream, and so she'd accepted them and pretended what she had with Dan was good enough.

River didn't say another word, just opened

the door and walked inside. She followed more slowly, the cool, dry air of the library filled with dozens of memories of summers spent curled up in the reading corner, a good book in her hands.

For some reason, that made her teary-eyed. Or maybe it was River that made her that, his cold expression and hard gaze daring her to pick up the conversation where they'd left off.

"Brenna!" someone cried, and the moment for saying what needed to be said was over.

She turned, pasting on a smile as a short, dark-haired woman ran over and threw herself into Brenna's arms.

"I can't believe you're really here. Everyone has been talking about you working at Chocolate Haven, but I've been so busy, I haven't had time to stop in." She pulled back, smiling in River's direction. "And is this who I think it is?"

"River Maynard," Brenna offered, and the woman squealed with delight.

"I knew it! If you'd known what a crush I had on you when I was a kid, River? You'd surely have taken advantage of me." She laughed, the pealing sound of it bringing back the memory Brenna had been looking for.

Amanda Dillinger.

The shy, awkward girl she'd made friends with in kindergarten. They'd been buddies all through elementary school, but middle school had changed Amanda. She'd gotten a little wild, started hanging out with kids who liked to push the envelope. That hadn't been Brenna's kind of thing. She'd been content with her books and her daydreams and her studies.

"Sorry, I'm not sure I remember you," River said as he scanned the library.

"Amanda. Used to be Dillinger. Now it's Waters. Do you remember Jack? He was the star football player your senior year."

"Not really."

Amanda blushed, but she was undaunted. "Well, most people do. He was quite the star. Anyway, we got married right after high school, had a couple of kids. They're both in middle school now and Jack does estate planning. I work here." She smiled, waving toward the library's shelves. "Are you two looking for anything in particular today? Some special book I can help you find?"

"We're looking for some*one* actually," River responded. "A guy named Joe. He —"

"Joe? He was out back this morning, sleeping next to the Dumpster. He asked me if it was Saturday. I guess that's when he usually comes? I'm never here, so I wouldn't know."

"Did he leave?"

"No. I felt so sorry for him, I let him come in and help me stack books. Then I gave him some hot chocolate and a doughnut. Next thing I knew, he was sound asleep in the back office."

"He's still there?" River asked, and Amanda nodded.

"I didn't have the heart to wake him up. I planned to call my supervisor later to ask what she thought I should do with him, but . . . I guess I won't have to do that now. He's this way." She walked through the main room of the library, then through a dimly lit hallway. She opened the door at the end of it. "I thought he was homeless or something. Not that it's common here in Benevolence, but every once in a while people find their way here from a city."

She flicked on a light, stepped aside.

At first, Brenna didn't see anyone. Then she noticed the lump on the floor under a desk. Joe was curled up on his side, his head resting on his backpack.

"Thank God," River said quietly.

He stepped into the room, knelt down near the desk.

"Joe?" he said.

Joe didn't move.

"Joe!" he said more insistently, touching Joe's shoulder and giving it a little shake.

Joe swiped at his hand, mumbled something incoherent.

"Come on, buddy," River insisted, all the patience in the world in his voice. "We need to go home."

Joe mumbled again, but he turned over, his face breaking into a huge smile as he saw River.

"I've been looking for you, buddy," he said, sitting up and nearly bumping his head on the bottom of the desk. "Where you been, River? Huh? Where you been?"

"I've been looking for you," River replied, taking Joe's hand and tugging him to his feet. "You didn't get on the bus. We were worried about you."

"I had to run away," Joe said, waving at Brenna. "Hi," he said, and she smiled, relief making her knees weak and her muscles limp.

"Why in the world would you do something like that?" River grabbed Joe's backpack and hefted it onto his own shoulders.

"You said I was home."

"You were."

"They wanted me to get on the bus and leave, but I was at home. Right? I was already at home. And now I'm at the library. I'm at the library, right?"

"Yes." River sighed, dark shadows under his eyes and a hint of a beard on his jaw. He looked tired, and Brenna wanted to reach out and take his hand, ask what she could do to make his burden lighter. She'd waited too long.

Just like she always seemed to.

Before she could act, he was moving, leading Joe toward the door. "Come on. I need to bring you back to the house, and then I need to go get Belinda." He glanced at his watch and frowned. "Scratch that. We're both going to have to go get Belinda. Then we'll go home."

"What should we scratch? Huh, River?" Joe bounced enthusiastically. Obviously, his night outside had left him none the worse for wear.

"I'll take you home, Joe," she offered, and River frowned.

"You've got enough going on at the shop," he said, his expression still cool, none of the warmth she was used to seeing in his eyes.

"The chocolate is made. The fudge . . . well, that's going to take way longer than I'll ever have. May will be fine for another half hour. You go get Belinda. I'll call the sheriff and tell him that we have Joe. You ready, buddy?" she asked, and she walked out of the library, Joe bouncing along beside her.

She should have felt good about what she was doing.

She should have felt happy.

They'd found Joe.

She was taking him back to the ranch.

All was right with the world.

Except that it wasn't.

She grabbed her purse from the shop, let May know she'd be back soon, and then got in the Chrysler. It started up like a charm, the new spark plugs River had put in doing their thing.

She was a fool and she knew it.

Worse, she'd missed every single opportunity River had given her. And he'd given her plenty; he'd offered her plenty. He'd demanded nothing except that she be brave enough to take a chance, honest enough to admit her failures, and confident enough to move toward what she wanted.

When had she stopped being those things?

Before Dan?

After him?

Did it even matter?

"Idiot," she whispered, and Joe gasped, his eyes and mouth wide open.

"That's a bad word," he said. "I know it's

a bad word."

"I'm sorry, Joe," she said, pulling up in front of Belinda's house, her heart heavy and aching and sore.

She'd thought she'd come to Benevolence to start again, but maybe River was right. Maybe she just wasn't willing enough to let go of the past to do that.

Mack and Huckleberry were waiting on the front porch. They converged on the car, helped Joe out of it, grabbed his backpack, and ushered him into the house.

Brenna thought Mack might have muttered a thank you, but she wasn't sure.

She pulled out of the driveway, headed back toward town, but that little road, the one that led to the cabin? It was right there, and she found herself turning onto it, driving down it, parking the car.

Yes. She needed to be at Chocolate Haven.

Yes. She needed to learn how to make the dang family fudge.

But she thought that more than that, she needed just a few minutes to be alone.

All's well that ends well.

Dillard again, his voice speaking out of the past and straight into River's mind. The sun had set hours ago, the freshly painted walls glowing softly in the chandelier light

405

as River moved through the downstairs, checking windows and doors, making sure everything was locked up for the night.

Somewhere above him, a floorboard creaked. Probably Angel, checking on Joe again. She'd made one mistake and she'd vowed never to make another one. She was young. She had plenty of time to make plenty more, but River hadn't told her that.

Let her try. Let her fail. Let her pick herself up and go on again.

"All's well that ends well," he muttered, stepping into Dillard's office. The window was closed and locked, the room dark except for the muted glow of the hallway light. He thought he could smell the cigars Dillard had always loved, thought he could hear his laughter drifting on the breeze outside the window.

And why wouldn't he be laughing?

River had spent half his teenage years telling Dillard there was no way he'd ever be the guy who took care of other people's problems, that he'd never sacrifice his time, his money, his dreams to take care of a bunch of losers.

At the time, he hadn't realized Dillard had never seen his foster kids as losers. He'd never looked at their limitations. He'd never counted their pasts or their problems against them.

Now, River understood.

He looked at Huckleberry and he could see the potential. He looked at Angel and all he felt was pity. He looked at Joe and he knew he couldn't send him back to a place where he didn't feel like he belonged.

He sighed, walking into the kitchen and checking the back door. It was unlocked and open, and he could see Mack standing on the porch beyond it.

Strange, because Mack was usually in the barn by this time of night, bedded down on the hay and thick blankets he'd brought with him when he'd arrived.

"Hey, man," River said, stepping outside. Fall was there, the cold air spearing through his jacket and T-shirt and seeping into his bones, the wind carrying hints of wood-burning fires and icy rains. "Everything okay?"

"Just thinking," Mack said, his back to River.

"About?"

"This place."

"Yeah?"

"I didn't plan to stay." He turned, the light falling on the thick scars that mottled the side of his face. "When I came, it was

407

because I'd met Belinda at a food bank, and she'd told me she needed a little help around her place. I thought I could get a couple of free meals out of it, a warmer place to sleep in the winter." He shrugged. "I didn't plan to stay for very long."

"Are you thinking of leaving?"

"Depends on if I'll be stepping on your toes by sticking around."

"Why would you think that?"

"Freedom Ranch was yours before it was any of ours. Angel, Huckleberry, Joe, they're followers. They get a good leader and they can do just fine. Me and you? We're both leaders, and sometimes more than one is too much in a place this size."

"This place needs more than one leader. The kids are nuts, and Joe needs constant supervision. I'll be away a couple of times a month because I've still got restaurants to run in Portland."

"I guess I forgot about that."

"I didn't. I'm going to need a manager here. You know the property better than anyone but me, so I think that job should be yours. I'll pay you a good working wage. We can work out the details once you agree to it."

Mack snorted and crossed his arms over his chest. "I don't need your pity, River. I don't want it either."

"What pity? I'm offering you a job. Take it or leave it, but if you leave it, this whole damn place will probably fall apart while I'm gone."

"Hire someone else. There's people all over the place that can do a job like this."

"They aren't people who Belinda loves, and they aren't people who love her in return," he said bluntly, and Mack sighed, ran his hand over his scars, and shook his head.

"Do you always have to bring her into it?"

"Would anything else work?"

"No."

"Then, yeah, I do. So what's it going to be? Yes to the job? Or no?"

"You know it's going to be yes."

"Good. I'll write up an offer and present you with it later this week. You can negotiate the terms, but I'm not saying I'll change anything."

"Fine."

"One more thing, Mack."

"What?"

"How about you consider sleeping in the house? It will make me feel better about leaving Belinda when I go back to Portland."

Mack grunted a reply that might have been a yes or a no.

Then he walked down the porch stairs and disappeared into the darkness.

So much for that.

River had given it a shot. Maybe in another month or two or twenty, Mack might decide to take one of the bedrooms in the house. If not, River would offer him the cabin. It would stay warm enough in the winter with a fire going, and it was set far enough away from the house and the road to make Mack feel comfortable.

At least that was what River was hoping. He had plans for the barn, for the land, for the house, but he wanted to make sure the people who were already there didn't feel displaced.

He stood on the porch, waiting for the barn light to go on. It took a few minutes, but when it did, he felt satisfied, content that everyone was where they needed to be. He wouldn't wake up in the morning and discover Mack had taken off or Huckleberry had run away or Joe had taken another hike to town.

Five miles was a long way for a guy like Joe.

He'd been so exhausted, he'd been asleep at the dinner table, his face slack, his mouth open. River had woken him up and sent him to bed, and it had felt a little like stepping into the shoes Dillard had left behind.

Funny how time changed things.

Or maybe not so funny, because now River was in the same mess Dillard had always been in: caring a little too much for people who might not care very much back.

He shoved his hands in his pockets, felt something under his hand and pulled it out.

The recipe card.

He'd forgotten about that, about Forever Kisses and cups full of love.

He reread it, smiling as he imagined the person who'd written it. Probably some romantic Victorian lady with bright red hair and violet-blue eyes.

An old-world version of Brenna.

Brenna.

She was probably in the kitchen at Chocolate Haven, still working on perfecting the family fudge. He'd told himself he should let her be. He'd tried to convince himself that keeping his distance until she was ready to move on was the best thing for both of them.

He'd thought he'd succeeded, but now, standing there with the recipe for Forever Kisses in his hand, he wasn't so sure.

It was a little past ten, the house sleeping soundly, the silence a relief after the chaos of moving Joe in. He was sharing a room with Huckleberry while the group home contacted a lawyer to find out if he could stay at the ranch permanently. River had been surprised at how eager they'd been to work things out to benefit Joe. Apparently, his housemother really cared and wanted what was best for him. It was up to the courts to make the final decision. In the meantime, Huckleberry had thought it was safer for the two of them to share a room. A better way to keep Joe from wandering was what he'd said.

River had agreed, but he wasn't sure how long it would last.

In some ways, Joe was like a toddler, wandering around asking the same question over and over again. That would get old after a while, but for tonight the guys were quiet, Angel was locked in her room, and Belinda was sleeping soundly.

River would have been smart to go to bed, too.

He had a lot of long days ahead of him, a lot of big plans to see to fruition.

Yeah, River was pretty damn sure his best option was sleep.

But he'd never been one to take the easy road, and he'd never been one to turn away from something he wanted.

He walked inside, locked the back door,

and turned off the kitchen light. He grabbed his keys from the hook near the front door, the recipe card still in his hand, the list of ingredients kind of dancing through his head:

A dash of humor.
A pinch of patience.
A tablespoon of truth.
A cup of love.
A pint of faithfulness.
A gallon of commitment.
Mix well and dust with laughter, sprinkle with tears, bake with friendship that lasts through the years.

He'd learned a lot of recipes in his years as a chef. He'd created a lot of them, but he thought the one he was holding, the one he needed to return to Brenna, might just be the most delicious one of all.

CHAPTER SEVENTEEN

Brenna remembered the envelope, and the guy who'd given it to her, right around the time she'd messed up her twenty-fifth batch of fudge. She eyed the pan and the lumpy concoction she'd filled it with and wanted to cry. She seriously did.

She also wanted to cart the entire mess out to the Dumpster and toss it in, pan and all. She lifted the pan and headed to the back door, digging in her apron pocket to be sure she had her keys. With the way the day had gone, she'd probably end up locking herself out.

That's when she felt the envelope. The one she'd been handed by the way-too-nosy guy. She pulled it out of her pocket, looked at the stark white paper, and felt that same little shiver of fear she'd felt when the guy had pulled it out of his pocket.

When you see Willow, give her this.

For some reason, those simple words had

sounded like a threat. If Brenna hadn't gotten so caught up in helping Angel and finding Joe and . . .

River.

Yeah. She'd been caught up in him, too.

As a matter of fact, she'd wasted way too much time thinking about him, wondering if he'd made it back to the ranch, if he'd been able to keep Joe there a few more nights, if he was as tired as he'd looked when he'd walked away from her.

She should have just called and asked.

That's what she *should* have done.

But, of course, she hadn't.

She'd come back to the shop and sent May home, she'd filled dozens of orders, she'd made more candy, sold it, and repeated the process. The entire time, she'd been thinking about River.

Now, though?

Now, she was thinking about Willow.

About the creepy guy.

About the envelope and what it might contain.

She grabbed the phone and dialed her sister's number. At this time of night, Willow was bound to answer. Most other times of the day, she was in court or preparing for court, or building a case. If she wasn't doing any of those things, she was spending time with her fiancé, Ken.

But at night she was at home and usually not in bed.

Not this time of night anyway. Willow was a night owl and a morning person. Which was kind of sickening if Brenna let herself think about it.

She didn't.

Comparing herself to Willow was like comparing the moon's tired glow to the sun's blazing glory.

"Great analogy," she muttered as Willow picked up.

"What's that?" she said, her voice softer and gentler than either Brenna's or Adeline's.

"Just talking to myself, Sis."

"Which means you're stressed out." As always, Willow cut straight to the point.

"Why would I be stressed out?"

"Because you're in Benevolence working in Chocolate Haven, listening to Mom harp on your love life?"

"Good guess," Brenna said with a laugh, her gaze dropping to the envelope. "But I'm actually doing okay. Chocolate making isn't as difficult as I thought."

"So you've got the magic, huh?"

"What I've got is the burning desire not to fail again."

"When have you ever failed before?"

"Plenty of times. Dan is a prime example."

"Dan's the failure. Not you."

"That's pretty much what River said." The words slipped out before she realized she was saying them, and Willow was quick to pick up on them.

"River?"

"Maynard? You probably remember him from school."

"Of course I remember him. I just didn't realize he was back in town."

"He's helping Belinda Keech."

"I did hear she'd had a stroke. How is she?"

"Getting better, but River is here to make sure she gets back on her feet."

"And you and River have been discussing Dan, huh?"

"Not discussing exactly."

"Then what have you been doing?"

"He's been explaining his opinions."

Willow laughed, the sound light and easy. "Right. I'm sure that's all that's been happening."

"It is," she lied, because she didn't have the time or the energy to tell Willow everything.

"Well, maybe it shouldn't be. You're young. You've got a lot of dreams left in you.

You need to pursue them."

"Dreams? Since when am I the dreamer in the family?"

"Since forever. It's one of my favorite things about you. Me? All my dreams died a long time ago. Now I'm just trying to be content." There was a hint of something in her voice: sadness, maybe. Or resignation.

It hit Brenna in the heart because it had never occurred to her that Willow hadn't pursued her dreams and hadn't made them come true. "You're not happy, Willow?"

"Happiness is a relative term."

"That's not an answer."

"It's the only one I have." She sighed. "Listen, I may as well tell you now because you're going to find out when I come home for my birthday. I broke up with Ken."

"No way!"

"Yes way."

"Why? I thought you guys were . . ." *Happy* was on the tip of her tongue, but then she remembered what Willow had said and the word died away.

"We were good together. He's a good guy. Everything was just . . . good, but I'm in my thirties, Bren, and good just doesn't seem like enough anymore."

"Mom is going to have a cow."

"She's going to have two because I don't

418

want a party, and I plan on telling her that tomorrow."

"I already tried, Willow. She's determined."

"I'm more determined. I hate parties. I've hated parties for a long, long time. I want to spend my birthday just being with people I really love, relaxing for a few days, maybe getting some of my energy back."

That *really* worried Brenna.

Willow always had boundless energy.

Now she was tired?

"Are you okay? There's nothing wrong is there?" She lifted the envelope, her heart thudding painfully.

"I've just been burning the candle at both ends lately and I need a break. Anyway, enough about me. There must be a reason for your phone call."

"Someone came into the shop today. A man."

"Men come into the shop all the time, Brenna."

"This guy was different. He was asking questions about the family. Specifically, about you."

Willow was silent for a moment. When she finally spoke, her words were clear and precise and absolutely devoid of any emotion. "What kind of questions?"

"He wanted to know if you lived in town. I told him it was none of his business. Then he handed me an envelope and told me to give it to you when I saw you next."

"That's . . . odd. Did he give his name?"

"No."

"What did he look like?"

"Tall. Dark hair. Maybe in his midfifties."

"That could be a dozen different people I know."

"You want me to open the envelope?" Brenna asked, her heart still thudding against her ribs, her stomach churning. There was something very, very wrong here and she had no idea what it was.

Willow hesitated again and then sighed. "Sure. Go ahead."

"You're sure?"

"I won't be in town for another month. By that time, whatever is in the envelope might be old news."

"Okay." Her hand shook as she broke the seal.

There wasn't much in the envelope. Just a folded piece of paper. She pulled it out, unfolded it, a check falling to the ground.

Surprised, she stooped to pick it up.

"Well?" Willow demanded. "What is it?"

"A letter and a check." She looked at the number on the check, the dollar amount with so many zeroes she wasn't sure she was reading it correctly.

"Good God," she whispered, and she thought she heard Willow's breath catch.

"What?" she said. "What is it?"

"Twenty thousand dollars." She read the letter, just a few stark words that made no sense. "The letter says, 'Silence is golden. Happy birthday.' No signature. The check was printed by a company. It says —"

"Burn it," Willow barked, the words so sharp, Brenna wasn't even sure it was her sister speaking them.

"What?"

"Burn the damn thing."

"Willow!" Brenna protested, shocked by her sister's attitude. Willow never lost her cool, she never swore, she never made rash decisions or said things she might regret.

"Brenna, I mean it. If I find out that check and letter are still around when I get there, or if I find out you said one word to anyone about this, I swear I will never forgive you."

"Will —"

"I mean it. Promise me you'll burn it. Promise me you won't say a word to Mom or Adeline or Granddad."

"I promise," she said, because she couldn't not say it.

"Okay. Good. Thanks. I'll see you in a few

weeks." Her voice broke and Brenna stomach's lurched, her body icy cold with fear for her sister. Willow never cried, but she was crying now.

"Willow, what's going on?" she tried to say, but Willow hung up.

Brenna dialed her number, the check in her hand, the letter somehow on the floor.

Willow didn't answer.

Not the first time. Not the second. Not the third.

Brenna slammed the phone into the cradle, tore through drawer after drawer until she found a candle and a book of matches.

Her hands were shaking, but she still managed to strike the match and light the wick.

She burned the check first, smoke filling the kitchen and setting off the alarm. She dragged a chair across the room, climbed on it, yanked the alarm from the ceiling, and tossed it into the hall.

Then she returned to the candle, making sure every last piece of the check had been turned to ash.

She didn't realize she was crying until a tear dropped onto the flame. It sputtered, relit itself, and she grabbed the letter and tore it into three pieces, still crying. She wasn't sure why.

This was Willow's thing, but it felt like hers.

It felt like she was failing again. Her sister this time, because she couldn't get her to pick up the phone, and she couldn't call anyone in the family for advice because she'd damn well promised she wouldn't. She'd tied her own hands and now she couldn't help someone she loved more than she'd ever loved Dan, her modeling job, the money she'd earned walking runways all over Europe.

She held the first torn piece of paper over the flame, the fire licking her finger as it devoured the letter.

She yanked her hand back, the tears coming even harder, the disconnected alarm beeping, the air hazy from smoke and filled with the scent of chocolate and marshmallow and dead dreams.

Someone knocked on the back door.

She ignored it, grabbing the second piece of paper and holding it over the candle.

Next thing she knew, the person was rapping on the window.

"Damn it, red," River shouted through the glass. "Open the door or I'm going to break the window and climb in."

He meant it.

She knew it just like she knew that whatever she was burning was a secret her sister had to bear, a burden only Willow could carry, one that all the burning in the world couldn't rid her of.

She unlocked the door and opened it, cold air sweeping in. And then River was there, looking at the paper she was holding, the candle and ashes on the counter, the fudge everywhere, and her face, which she knew was smeared with chocolate and smoke and tears.

He touched her cheek, her chin, looked into her eyes for a heartbeat, and then he pulled her into his arms, so gently, so sweetly, she cried even harder.

River stood there for a long time, cold air sweeping across his back, Brenna's hot tears soaking his shirt.

He didn't speak because he didn't think Brenna could.

Sometimes there were no words for pain. Sometimes the hurt was so deep, the wound so raw, no amount of talking could mend it.

He smoothed his hand up her back, kissed her temple, and waited. There was nothing else he could do, nothing else he wanted to do but be there for her.

A candle flickered on the counter, the flame sputtering and dying. Next to it, a torn piece of paper fluttered into the sink. Brenna had been burning something, a small singed scrap of it still in her injured hand, her other hand clutching his shirt.

She took a deep, shuddering breath, tried to step away, but he held her in place, his hands on her slim waist.

"There's no rush," he said quietly.

"I need to finish," she said, her voice hoarse, her eyes red-rimmed.

"Tell me what needs to be done. I'll do it for you."

"No. I promised." She stepped around him, closed the door against the wind.

"Promised who?"

"Willow." She relit the candle, held the singed paper over the flame. It blackened and curled, but she didn't release it until it was nothing but ash.

"You're going to get burned," he cautioned, but she'd grabbed the scrap out of the sink and was repeating the process.

He watched as the last bit of white turned to dust; then he blew out the flame, pressed Brenna into a chair.

"Sit."

"I don't have time. The kitchen is a wreck and I can't make the fudge, and tomorrow will be here before I know it."

"Tomorrow will be here whether the

kitchen is a mess or the fudge is made. When it comes, it will be good if you're well enough to be here for it." He grabbed a glass from a cupboard and filled it with water, then handed it to her.

"Thanks." She took a sip, set it on the counter next to the candle. "I'm sorry about your shirt."

He shrugged. "Tears wash out."

"It's the soot I'm worried about." She stood, her gaze sweeping the room. "Who'd have thought a check and a piece of paper could cause so much smoke?"

Her voice was shaky, but the tears had stopped.

"What happened, Brenna?" he asked, and she shook her head.

"I promised Willow."

"Promised what? That you'd burn the shop down?"

She laughed shakily. "Wouldn't that have been something?"

"Not if you'd been in it." He tilted her chin, looked into her eyes. "What did you promise, Brenna? Whatever it is, you can trust me with it."

"Trust isn't an easy thing when you've been betrayed a few million times."

"You think I don't know that?" he asked, and he saw the moment she understood,

426

saw it in her eyes — that quick connection, the realization that their stories weren't all that different.

"A man came into the shop. He asked me to give something to Willow." She paced to the candle and then into the hall, where a smoke alarm was beeping. She was nervous. He could see that, but he was willing to wait her out.

He watched while she took the battery out of the fire detector.

"I'm probably going to have to get a new one. I tossed it pretty hard."

"I'll get one for you in the morning," he said, and she met his eyes, smiled.

"You shouldn't be so perfect, River."

"I'm not even close," he said.

"And yet here you are, standing in my wreck of a kitchen, your shirt stained with soot because I cried all over it. It seems like every time I need you, you're there."

"Isn't that the way it's supposed to be?"

"I . . . don't know. I never had anything like this before." She used a dish rag to brush soot off the counters, ran water into the sink to wash it out, and then turned to face him again. "The thing the man gave me? It was an envelope with a note and a check in it. Twenty thousand dollars, River. That's a heck of a lot of money."

It was, but he stayed silent, just watching her face as she cleaned soot off the cupboards, swept it off the floor. Finally, she finished, the counters and cupboards gleaming, her hand stained black.

"There was a note. It said, 'Silence is golden. Happy birthday.' When I told Willow that, she freaked. I've never heard her so upset. Ever."

"She made you promise to burn it?"

"And to never mention it to my family."

"Sounds like she's got a big secret."

"We all have them and she's welcome to keep hers, but . . ."

"What?"

"It feels bigger than a secret. It feels like it's something she's carrying around, something that's haunting her."

"A person can only be haunted by things if they let themselves be. Willow is an adult. She's made her choice. Until she wants to share the burden, there's not a whole lot you can do but be there for her."

"I know." She sighed and lifted a pan of fudge she'd left on the counter. "I've got to dump this. Want to come?"

What he wanted was to take her in his arms again, but he followed her outside, walking to the Dumpster and helping her scrape the fudge from the pan.

"I'm never going to get this right," she said as they walked away, but she was smiling, her face pale and pretty in the moonlight.

God, she was gorgeous.

And he couldn't help himself. He kissed her, because the air was cold with the beginning of fall and she was the most beautiful woman he'd ever seen.

When he pulled back, she was clutching his arm with one hand, the pan dangling from the other, holding on as if she were afraid letting go would mean giving up what they were creating together.

He could have told her not to worry.

He could have told her that what they had was going to last.

"You didn't tell me why you stopped by," she said, her voice husky, her breath hitched.

"You made me forget," he said, and she laughed.

"I guess my hysterics were a little distracting."

"*You* were distracting, Brenna. Just you." He reached into his pocket, pulled out the card. "Here's the reason I came. I found it near the cabin."

She took it from his hand.

"Forever Kisses," she said, running her fingers over the letters. "I must have dropped it when I grabbed my phone."

"That's what I figured."

"I'm glad you found it, but you could have brought it tomorrow," she said, tucking it into her apron pocket and walking back into the shop.

"I could have," he responded. "Except for one thing."

"What?" she asked, dragging a bowl from the cupboard and measuring sugar into it.

"I didn't think there was any better time than the present to start creating them."

"Creating what?"

"Forever Kisses," he said, taking the card from her apron and taping it to the back-splash.

She met his eyes, smiled the sweetest smile he'd ever seen.

"You know what, River?" she said, levering up on her toes so they were face-to-face, eye-to-eye, lip-to-lip. "I couldn't agree more."

CHAPTER EIGHTEEN

It was two in the morning before they finished setting up for the next day. They'd worked together for hours, talking and laughing and creating, the recipe card still taped to the backsplash, the ingredients so simple and pure: Humor. Patience. Truth. Love. Laughter. Tears.

Friendship.

Faithfulness.

Commitment.

How had Brenna never realized just how easy forever could be?

The display case was filled with beautiful chocolates.

The kitchen was spotless.

And Brenna?

She was happier than she could ever remember being.

She stirred her twenty-sixth batch of fudge as River poured vanilla into it, the smooth mixture everything the Lamont family fudge should be. She didn't have to taste it to know it was right. She could see it: the glossy sheen, the silky consistency. She'd watched Byron make it a million times over, and this was exactly the way it had looked.

"It's perfect," she said, lifting the pot off the burner. "Of course if Byron finds out you helped, he'll kill me."

"Will he?"

"No. The recipe is for family, and you're more than that to me," she said, the honest words coming from that place in her heart where dreams lived and romance blossomed, that place where second chances always happened, and where sweet surprises waited around every corner.

"I'm glad you think so," River said, pouring the fudge into a pan and smoothing the top of it. "Because I've been thinking."

He dipped a spoon into the pot, scraped out a little of the fudge that was stuck to the sides. He held it out to her and she tasted the rich chocolate, felt the smooth, creamy perfection of it fill her mouth and her senses.

This was what people paid money for.

This was the fudge people ordered from all over the country.

This, right here? It was magic.

"God, that's good," she said, scooping up

another taste, with River's gaze burning through her. She could feel it like she could feel the heady richness of fudge on her tongue.

"You didn't ask me," he murmured, leaning in, his lips brushing hers.

And God! She wanted so much more than that.

"Ask you what?"

"What I've been thinking."

"What have you been thinking?" she said, the fudge forgotten, the shop forgotten, everything just fading away as she looked into his eyes.

"The cabin is beautiful at dawn, and I was thinking how nice it would be to sit on the porch with you, wrapped in a blanket and watching the sun rise. What do you think about that?"

What did she think?

She thought that it seemed big. It seemed huge. It seemed like the most important thing she could ever decide to do.

She should have been scared.

She knew she should.

She'd made so many mistakes before.

She'd failed so miserably at knowing what she was looking for, but River was there, the scent of chocolate on his skin, a million promises in his eyes, and all she felt was joy.

"I think," she responded, hands trailing up his arms and resting on his shoulders, "there is nowhere in the world I'd rather be than on that porch with you."

He smiled, that slow, easy smile she loved so much, and then he lifted her into his arms, left that perfect pan of fudge exactly where it was, and carried her into their future.

The employees of Thorndike Press hope you have enjoyed this Large Print book. All our Thorndike, Wheeler, and Kennebec Large Print titles are designed for easy reading, and all our books are made to last. Other Thorndike Press Large Print books are available at your library, through selected bookstores, or directly from us.

For information about titles, please call:
  (800) 223-1244

or visit our Web site at:
  http://gale.cengage.com/thorndike

To share your comments, please write:
Publisher
Thorndike Press
10 Water St., Suite 310
Waterville, ME 04901